"I'm talking about Isaac. About you finding him."

I tensed up. Anytime I thought about the morning two months earlier when I'd found Isaac's body, I wanted to puke. Which is exactly why I tried to *never* think about it.

Kendall touched the mini Magic 8 Ball dangling from the key ring on my belt loop. She knew it was Isaac's. Everyone knew. It had been his good-luck charm for years and he never went anywhere without it—until the night he'd given it to me, saying I needed its advice more than he did. It was all a joke, really, and I would have given the stupid thing back to him the next day. If only he'd woken up.

FREEFALL

MINDI SCOTT

Simon Pulse

NEW YORK LONDON TORONTO SYDNEY

SIMON PULSE

An imprint of Simon & Schuster Children's Publishing Division

1230 Avenue of the Americas, New York, NY 10020

First Simon Pulse paperback edition October 2010

Copyright © 2010 by Mindi Scott

All rights reserved, including the right of reproduction in whole or in part in any form.

SIMON PULSE and colophon are registered trademarks of Simon & Schuster, Inc.

For information about special discounts for bulk purchases, please contact Simon & Schuster Special Sales at 1-866-506-1949 or business@simonandschuster.com.

The Simon & Schuster Speakers Bureau can bring authors to your live event. For more information or to book an event contact the Simon & Schuster Speakers Bureau at 1-866-248-3049 or visit our website at www.simonspeakers.com.

Designed by Mike Rosamilia

The text of this book was set in Zapf Elliptical 711 BT.

Manufactured in the United States of America

2 4 6 8 10 9 7 5 3 1

Library of Congress Control Number 2010012663

ISBN 978-1-4424-0278-2

ISBN 978-1-4424-0279-9 (eBook)

For Dwayne,

BECAUSE YOU USED YOUR BIRTHDAY WISH ON ME

ACKNOWLEDGMENTS

Thank you, thank you, thank you to Liesa Abrams, my amazing editor, teacher, and friend for your guidance and trust. You were the first industry professional to connect with this story, and I am ecstatic to have had this opportunity to work on it with you. Somehow you always know what I'm trying to say, even when I don't.

Many thanks as well to my agent, Jim McCarthy. The day you offered representation was one of the best I've ever had. You changed my life even before you sold this book just because you believed in it. Thank you for everything you do for me.

I would also like to offer my deepest gratitude to:

- my mommy, Leeann Ward, for being my mommy and for always believing that I have talent. This is even better than being an english teacher, right?

- Lindsey Schoenberger, Nikki Thompson, Matthew Persons, and Joyce Huttula for listening to me ramble about life and the characters in my head, and for always helping me make sense of it all.

- my family and friends who have supported me through the years. I'm lucky because there are far too many of you to name. Please know that I appreciate you all!

- the WDers, for convincing me that the things I want to write are worth reading.

- Dr. Jacob Mathew, for giving speeches just for me, and not laughing when I said that I wanted to become a published author in ten years. (And yay! I did it in seven!)

- everyone at Simon Pulse and Aladdin, who have worked hard to make this book the best it can be. I'm grateful and, quite honestly, *awed*, that such dedicated and talented people are making it possible for my long-time wish to become a reality.

- Mandy Hubbard, for coming to my rescue time and time again regarding queries and bios, and for commiserating with and guiding me in all the stages of this crazy journey.

- Phoebe Kitanidis, for being fun, smart, and easy to talk to. And, of course, for loving my book enough to make the Big Introduction for me.

- my instructors Pam Binder, Waverly Fitzgerald, Kristen Kemp, and Ila Zbaraschuk, for helping me grow as a writer.

- the many, many brilliant peeps I've encountered through LiveJournal, the Tenners, the Blue Board, Twitter, MB YA classes, and UW PopFic program (Pam's Kids).

Special thanks to Michelle Andreani, Memory Arnold, John C. Ford, Phoebe Heyman, Samantha Horswill, Ryan Hughes, Diana Jeong, Annika Barranti Klein, J. E. MacLeod, Liz Martinez, Gina Montefusco, Mandy Morgan, Andrea Perrin (Seth's #1 fan), Bradi Roberts, Kim Steffen, Jesse Stewart, and Jen VonDrak for the insightful critiques and helpful information you've supplied for me.

And above all, thank you to my husband, Dwayne Scott, for having to two tickets to Iron Maiden (baby), and for making it possible for me to become a penniless sitar player. I couldn't have done it without you, and wouldn't have wanted to. I love you the most, Lover.

FREEFALL

SATURDAY, **SEPTEMBER 4**

8:19 P.M.

This was Daniel's deal. He'd taken the order, contacted a supplier, and set it all up. I was just the sucker he'd roped into driving him for the actual delivery. Which meant, technically, I was also the guy who had the police cruiser riding his ass through town.

Just like always.

"You know, Dick," Daniel said, "I'm pretty sure you bring this cop bullshit on yourself."

"Oh yeah?" I kept the steering wheel as steady as I could and stole another glance in the rearview. All I could make out in the dusky darkness were bright headlights and the outline of the light bar on the cruiser's roof, which—so far— wasn't flashing. "How do I bring it on myself? By hauling you around everywhere in my brother's unlucky car?"

"No," Daniel said. "By driving like a paranoid old lady. You've got to blend in better on the road. And go faster. You might not realize this, but cops pay close attention when people are under the speed limit too."

"I *know* that."

What I didn't know was why Daniel thought he was some kind of speed-estimating expert; the Mustang's speedometer was always stuck at zero whether I was at a dead stop or cruising the highway.

I looked in my side-view mirror. From what I could tell, the cop had no plans to stop tailgating me anytime soon. The experience was *not* doing wonders for my hangover headache or crazy-nervous heartbeat.

"You've got to quit looking at him," Daniel said between swigs of his Jack and Coke. "And take some deep breaths or something. The street you want is coming up next left."

The moment of truth. I flipped on my blinker, and then eased into a pretty smooth turn, even with all the weight Daniel had piled in the back. I peeked in the rearview again, trying to be casual about it.

To my relief the cruiser hadn't followed. We were in the clear for now.

A minute later we hit the crest of Ray Fitch Hill— "Rich Bitch Hill" to those of us unlucky enough to live by the river—where huge houses sat on square, perfect lawns with clipped hedges and lit-up flower beds. Amazing, really, the ritziness of this part of town. Most of the cars alone were worth three, maybe even four, times as much as the single-wide mobile homes Daniel and I called home.

Daniel directed me to the place, and as I backed into the driveway, Pete Zimmer, the Kenburn High football god himself, was waiting on the sidewalk with two other jocks. They all looked alike with their buzz-cut hair and T-shirts that said, I AM COLLEGE, I'D DO ME, and SEXY NEVER LEFT.

"Just let me handle this," Daniel said to me.

"I always do."

We climbed out of the car. I fidgeted with Isaac's miniature Magic 8 Ball while Daniel clasped I-Am-College Pete's hand all secret-handshake-style. This crap had been going on for over a year, so I should have been used to it, but Daniel acting buddy-buddy with guys we'd always hated still weirded me out.

Pete nodded toward me. "Hey, Seth." Then he got down to business. "Danny, I have all these people showing up. Last big party of the summer and you're late with the beer. What's up with that?"

"Hey, these things take time," Daniel said.

The fact that he didn't correct Pete over the Danny thing bugged me too. Everyone got a nickname from Daniel—he'd been calling me Dick instead of Seth for years—but he usually didn't let people get away with calling him anything but Daniel.

I popped the trunk, which was packed tight with cases of beer and a whole mess of Jack Daniel's and vodka. Then I went around, leaned into the car, and pulled out the blankets from the backseat that had been covering up more stacks of the same.

Pete stood at the back of the car, staring down. "What's all this single-serving shit? I ordered a keg."

"That didn't work out," Daniel said, playing it cool. "But I got you a good price and threw in a bunch of hard stuff, too. You and your pals can stay sloppy drunk all night with this."

Pete frowned. "What are you trying to pull, Jackson?"

If I hadn't known better, the expression on Daniel's face would have made me believe he was actually sorry. He clamped his hand on Pete's shoulder and hunched down so they were at eye level. "Look, Zimm. I have it on good authority that the police are looking for some under-age parties in your neighborhood to raid this weekend. If you have a keg, there'll be no way to hide it. You'll be screwed, I'll be screwed, we'll all be screwed. It's safer this way."

I'd-Do-Me Eric raised his eyebrows and looked down the street like he expected to spot police cars staking out the place.

"Where'd you hear that?" Pete asked. "About the cops?"

"I have people everywhere," Daniel said, waving toward the Valley.

Pete looked like he wanted to ask more questions or possibly kick Daniel's ass, but Sexy-Never-Left Garrison cut in. "Dude, beer's beer. Let's do this."

"Yes, let's," Daniel said. "Dick and I will haul everything in for you, no extra charge. Sound cool?"

Pete shrugged. "Go for it." Then he headed back to his mansion with his friends trailing behind.

When they were gone, I couldn't help laughing. "You have people? *Every*where?"

"Hell yeah, I do," Daniel said, grinning. "And these people of mine predicted that beer will be served in huge quantities right here tonight. Which is exactly why you and me are going to stick around."

I shook my head. "No way."

It was more of a reflex than anything. Saying no to Rich Bitch Hill parties was as automatic to me as saying yes had become to Daniel.

"Come *on*, Dick," he argued. "It isn't like you have anyplace better to be."

He was right. And, well, the truth was, I actually did need to do something to get my mind off all the crap from the night before.

Daniel could always pick up on it if I was wavering, so he told me his usual lie to seal the deal: "Just give me twenty minutes here and we can take off, okay?"

"Fine," I said, pretending to believe him. "Twenty minutes."

10:44 P.M.

I'd been to enough house parties to know when everything was about to fall apart. After two hours, this one was definitely on the way to disintegration. Forty or fifty rowdy drunk kids were there, all laughing and yelling their heads off while the suck-ass dance music vibrated children out of their beds the next block over.

I was ready to leave—I'd been ready since we'd walked in, to be honest—but Daniel had disappeared with some chick, so I headed back to the kitchen on my own, even though the booze was in there and I kind of wanted to steer clear. Being around these rich assholes was messing up my head worse than ever. The room I was trying not to go into was exactly where I kept ending up; the stuff I was trying not to drink was exactly what I'd been chugging all night.

Vicki Lancaster and Carr Goodwin were standing in front of the marble-y counter with a few of their friends, sipping from cans. Carr watched my every move like salespeople always did when Daniel and I walked into a store. The rest ignored me.

"This is the nastiest beer," Vicki said, making an even bitchier face than usual. "Pete was going to get a keg, but then he got some inside scoop that the police are monitoring keg rentals. I wish he'd gone for it anyway."

Daniel's cover story had spread through the party like some big conspiracy. I was the only one who knew why he really hadn't been able to get the keg: the girl who always hooked him up was still holding a grudge after finding out he'd hooked up with her best friend.

Carr laughed his big, booming laugh and said to Vicki, "Maybe it's better this way. The last thing I need is for my position as vice president to be put in jeopardy."

Everyone started busting up at that. I never hung out with Carr, but every time I heard him talk, he was going on about school politics like he was some important man. *In jeopardy*. Who says that?

I couldn't take it anymore. I popped open a beer and gulped the whole thing down in about ten seconds. "You're right, Vicki," I said, crushing the can in my hand. "That's the worst stuff I've ever tasted."

She stared at me. It struck me that her skinny eyebrows and open mouth made her look like she'd just walked into a surprise party. I tried to keep a straight face, but burst out laughing.

"Oh, Jeez," Vicki said. "Who let the trailer trash in?"

She was always giving me shit; holding some grudge over God knows what. "Trailer trash," I said, helping myself to yet another beer. "That's a good one. Did you come up with it all by yourself?"

She tossed her blond hair over her shoulder. "I did. I also came up with 'You. Are. A. Loser.' Don't you have some meth to go smoke?"

I was bored of them already, so I gave Vicki a wink and

started for the dining room. But then I heard her say, "Maybe if we're all lucky, Seth will end up like Isaac. Such a non-tragedy *that* was."

I spun around, gripping the doorway to steady myself. If some guy had said it, I might have decked him. But since I wasn't going to hit a girl—not even an evil one like Vicki—I settled for "You. Are. A. Bitch."

It wasn't enough. Nowhere *near* enough.

I had to get away from these people.

Two seconds later I was staggering away again and Carr was after me, grabbing my arm. "Watch it, McCoy," he said in a low voice that was probably supposed to make me shake with terror. "I've got my eye on you."

"Go to hell," I said, jerking free.

I made my way back to the dance party revival in the living room and leaned against the wall. Daniel had five minutes to finish getting off, or I'd be leaving his ass behind.

Xander Yates—another kid I'd gone to school with forever but never hung out with—chose that moment to push his shaggy hair out of his eyes and stand next to me. "Hey, Seth. Great show!" he yelled over the music.

A bunch of hot girls in tiny tops and skirts were dancing in front of us. One of them was Felicia, a girl I'd been pretty into last year. I hadn't seen her since the start of summer. By now I wasn't sure if it was because of her or me. It didn't matter anyway; she was all over I'd-Do-Me Eric's older brother, and I couldn't bring myself to care.

"Yes," I said to Xander. "*Really* great show."

He laughed. "I'm not talking about any of them. I meant your gig with the Real McCoys last night. You were awesome on that upright bass."

"Yeah right." I'm usually cool about accepting compliments, even when I suck—only a real asshole insults someone else's taste—but I couldn't be this time. "That must be why everyone was saying it was the worst they'd ever seen me play."

Xander wasn't fazed. "You were better at the gig you played in June, I'll give you that. But I think your worst is a cut above most people's best. Even when you're falling off the stage you still put on a good show."

He had one part of it right: I *was* better in June. Everything was better then.

Xander leaned against the wall like he was settling in for a long talk. "What did you think of those guys who played after you? I felt like the music was all right, but it was hard to get past the rough vocals. That's a challenge, I think, when the front man . . ."

As I'd expected, he kept talking. And talking. Xander seemed halfway decent for a Rich Bitch Hill kid, but I wasn't in the mood for conversation. Especially since I'd been too busy puking in the parking lot to have seen the set he was asking about, anyway.

I zoned out and scanned for somewhere else to go.

And that's when I caught sight of the crazy red hair I'd woken up next to.

11:02 P.M.

Across the room from me, Kendall Eckman was running her fingers through her stop-sign red hair and laughing at whatever bullshit I-Am-College Pete was saying. She was all smiles in a black halter top and a denim skirt that barely covered her ass. No one would have guessed that less than twelve hours before, she'd been in her underwear, screaming and throwing things at me.

Kendall was the last chick in this town, in this country, on this planet, I would have wanted to lose my virginity to. And yet, at some point *after* I got wasted at the gig, fell off the stage, was chewed out by my brother, and puked in the parking lot, it happened. At some point *before* I'd woken up in my bed with a pounding head, stale beer/sour puke breath, and no clue how I'd gotten there or why Kendall was with me, it happened.

Turning back to Xander and his yammering, I considered my next move.

". . . play a show in Seattle," he was saying. "I told him we'd have a better chance . . ."

Kendall didn't seem to have noticed me yet. I needed to keep it that way. I could sneak away. Or pretend not to see her. If she went along with it, we could ignore each other for hours.

Not that I'd be staying for any more hours. No way.

But then it was too late for pretending. I was looking at her and she was looking at me. Her huge, dark eyes narrowed and her pouty lips turned down.

Busted.

"... wondering," Xander said, "do you ever play electric bass or any other styles of music besides rockabilly?"

"Nope." I looked around for a hiding place. "I haven't for a long time."

Dining room, kitchen, bathroom, garage. Backyard!

"Well, if you ever want to try something different, my band—"

"I'm going out. There," I said, pointing at the sliding glass door. "See you around."

I pushed past two dudes, slid the door open, tripped outside, and pulled the door shut again.

The yard was like an ad for some yuppie resort, with all the matching chairs lined up and a couple of round tables with huge umbrellas poking out of them. I went around to the far side of the pool and fell onto a cushioned lounge chair, where I had a good view of everyone through the huge living room window.

What the hell was Kendall doing here?

Or, the better question: What was *I* doing? This was Kendall's neighborhood now. These were Kendall's fancy friends. Of course she'd be here. I hadn't been thinking when I'd let Daniel talk me into this.

I finished my beer and tossed the can under my chair. I wanted another but I didn't feel like going in to get it, so I leaned back and stared at the sky instead. Aside from the people who lived here, everything was better on the Hill than in the Valley; even the fucking stars were brighter.

There was sound all around me: the conversation of the guys smoking weed by the fence, the whispering of the couple making out on the air mattress, the music coming from inside Pete's house. But I wasn't part of any of it. It was all just background, swirling over and around, bouncing off me. Maybe Vicki's wish would come true and I *would* end up like Isaac. Maybe I didn't even care.

The back door slid across its track.

Open: loud music/laughing/talking.

Closed: muffled music/laughing/talking.

The unmistakable sound of flip-flops slapping the bottoms of feet echoed from across the pool and started coming close. Closer. Closest. The shoes stopped and the chair next to me scraped on the concrete. The cushion made a deflating sound.

I turned my head, expecting to see that dreaded red hair and Kendall raring to go for round two—of arguing, I mean—but the flip-flops wearer on the lounger was this hot girl with long, black hair. We'd never had a real conversation and I didn't know her name, but I'd seen her around at school some during second semester.

"I've noticed that in movies about parties, everyone always ends up falling, jumping, or pushing each other into the pool," she said, waving toward the water. "And yet here we are and no one's in there. Not *one* single person!"

Lying down felt nicer, but I sat up anyway. This chick was too cute to ignore. "That's easy enough to fix. You stand by the edge. I'll give you a shove."

She laughed, and if there's any such thing as a pretty laugh, she had one. Just hearing her was enough to snap me out of my funk for the moment. "Actually," she said, "I think I'm good for now. Thanks, though."

To make her laugh again, I said, "All right. Fine. Be that way."

It didn't work at all; I sounded like a dickhead.

We sat there for a few painful seconds with neither of us saying anything. I glanced toward the window for Kendall or Daniel while Flip-Flops stared at me.

"I am *so* glad to be out here and away from everyone right now," she said. "I hate coming to these parties."

"Why's that?"

She bit her lip in this sexy, nervous way. "I don't know. I guess because I don't really drink or any of that kind of stuff, so being around people who do is just kind of . . . surreal."

"Surreal?"

"Everyone seems fake and weird in there," she said with a shrug.

"Oh. Like being surrounded by pod people?"

I had no idea where I came up with that. I didn't even know what I was talking about.

"Kind of the opposite, maybe," she said. "See, *these* pod people are normal humans until they get loaded and suddenly start thinking whatever they say and do is super-great. But in *Body Snatchers*, they're emotionless, freaky alien creatures. So it's a little different."

Huh. So pod people were from a movie, then?

"I know exactly what you mean," I said.

It was another lame attempt at humor because, obviously, I was partway loaded—just like probably everyone except her—but I still knew full well that I wasn't funny or interesting or deep.

For some reason, though, she missed my meaning.

"Really?" she asked, smiling. "So you're saying I'm not the only non–pod person here for once?"

I didn't want to have to tell her she'd pegged me all wrong, that she was looking happy and beautiful for nothing, so I nodded. It wasn't exactly a lie, I figured. Somewhere in that huge house was someone else who was sober. Maybe.

Another silence.

Flip-Flops looked toward the door. Was she thinking of going in because I wasn't talking? Should I say something to make her stay?

"My car has at least enough gas to get to the ocean," I blurted out.

She leaned toward me and I could see right down her strappy top. *Nice.*

"That's good," she said. "Are you taking a trip?"

"Um, well, I wasn't for sure planning to," I tried my hardest to sound serious and sober. "But I'll take you if you want. Since you hate this party so much, I mean."

She laughed again. *Such* an awesome laugh. If I had a

recording of it, I'd play it on repeat for hours. "That's a very sweet offer. Unfortunately, I'm going to have to pass."

"Let me guess." I sounded ridiculously jokey to my own ears. It was like I couldn't *stop*. "A girl like you doesn't take rides from a guy like me?"

Before she got a chance to answer, the back door was opening again and a big group came out. Carr and Daniel were with them. Almost everyone started toward the pool, laughing and making a bunch of noise, but Daniel hung back and lit up a cigarette.

I watched Carr, hoping he'd take the opportunity to drown himself. Instead, he dragged a chair over and sat down next to Flip-Flops and me. "You okay out here?" he asked, putting his hand on her shoulder.

She smiled. "I'm fine."

"Good." Carr stuck his lips by her ear and used a whisper voice that was so loud the people inside the house could almost have heard him. "This guy's pretty hammered," he said, gesturing toward me. "I just wanted to make sure he wasn't harassing you like he was Vicki a few minutes ago."

Her smile faded. She eased away from Carr and studied my face like she was making sure she could identify me in a lineup. Carr was watching me too, and I wished I'd knocked the bastard out in the dining room when I'd had the chance.

Then the wailing of sirens cut into the night. You'd think they'd have come quietly so they could catch us offguard, but here in Kenburn, Washington, the boys in blue were all about the scare tactics. "Cops," Daniel said, rushing over. "Time to bail."

No shit.

I tried to jump up but caught my foot on the cushion. The lounge chair and I crashed side by side inches from the edge of the pool. The beer can I'd stashed came rolling out and hit Flip-Flops on her foot. She glanced down at it for one long second, and then headed for the gate without looking back. I pushed myself up to get going too, but Carr gave me a hard shove, and I fell again.

Right into the pool.

The chlorinated water stung my nose and plugged my ears as I hit the shallow, tiled bottom. Being tossed in cold water while wearing all my clothes felt wrong and somehow more intense than anything I'd experienced for weeks. But thanks to the air pockets that had formed in my shirt, I surfaced easily. Carr was gone, and Daniel was poolside looking panicked. "Dick, this isn't what I'd call a good time for a swim."

The sirens sounded close now. And from what I could see through the sliding glass door, everyone inside was freaking out. Such amateurs.

I paddled to the steps and pulled myself out.

"Hurry up! Unless you *want* to get busted?" Daniel yelled over his shoulder as he went for the gate.

I bolted after him. My socks and shoes were sloshing, my T-shirt and jeans were heavy and suctioned against my skin, and my coordination was for shit. But I didn't stop running until I'd caught up with Daniel at the edge of the woods. "What about the car?" I asked.

"I hate to break it to you, but you're in no shape to drive and neither am I," Daniel said. "We'll get it tomorrow."

I followed him into the woods to go the back way home. It was a forty-minute walk, and by the time it was over, I was covered with dirt after tripping my way down the hill, through bushes, over fallen trees and branches, and across the river in soaked clothes and shoes that wouldn't stay tied.

What was it Flip-Flops had been saying about movies, pools, and getting pushed in? Because as far as I could tell, it sucked balls in real life.

TUESDAY, **SEPTEMBER 7**

6:34 A.M.

Three days later. It was the first morning of eleventh grade, and I was up at a sickeningly early hour. I had to make it to my meeting with Ms. Naylor in the guidance office at the start of zero period—and not a minute later—or else. Or else what, I didn't know, but she'd sounded threatening when she'd called, like she just might kill me if I ditched one more appointment.

Still at home, I was that miserable kind of tired where my eyes ached when I tried to open them wider than slits. My head was like a roll of wet toilet paper, and I was running ragged. After more than two months straight of partying, I was getting sick of being sick, burned out on being burned out.

My shower didn't do the job of waking me up, so I threw on jeans and a T-shirt and headed to the kitchen, where I grabbed a Mountain Dew. Then I ripped open the last pack of strawberry Pop-Tarts and set them side by side in the toaster oven.

The front door screeched open and banged shut. Jared must have been out all night. Or Mom? But ten seconds later, it wasn't my brother or my mother who came busting into the kitchen. It was Kendall.

Her bright red hair dye must have mostly washed out, because she was now sporting orangey blond, messy pigtails along with glittery makeup, huge hoop earrings, and a short red skirt.

"Good morning, lover!"

She said it in a cheery, offhand way, as if this was how we always started our days. I had no clue what she was up to or how she could pretend like everything was fine. Well, maybe for her everything *was* fine. It wasn't like this was the first time she'd hooked up with one of Isaac's friends.

Guilt hit me full force once again. Most definitely I'd kissed this girl. *Isaac's* girl. I'd touched her. And everything else too. Everything.

"I already told you," I said, "don't call me lover."

The corners of her lips turned up. She walked right over to me by the counter, grabbed the pop can from my hand, and took a sip. Standing this close, I could smell her lotion or perfume or whatever. It reminded me of how a bag of gummy bears has cherry, pineapple, and citrus flavors all mixed together. Not a sexy scent, but still kind of nice.

"This is quite a nutritious breakfast you're having," she said.

"Why are you here?"

She flipped one pigtail behind her shoulder. "Because I need to talk to you."

She needed to talk to me. Not wanted. *Needed.* Never a good sign. My heart started knocking a little harder as I braced myself for whatever bad news she was bringing. "Is everything cool?"

Instead of answering, she kept on smirking and drinking up my soda. I hated it when she looked at me like that. It made me paranoid.

I tried again. "I mean, you don't think you're knocked up or anything, right?"

That sounded pathetic, but I still couldn't remember what went on with us that night. Not one single detail. And knowing more than I liked about my brother's close calls with a few chicks over the years, I wanted nothing more than to keep from getting into a situation like that. Jared's miserable drama had a lot to do with why I hadn't tried taking any postgig or party hookups all the way.

Kendall reached over to run her fingers through my damp hair. We were about the same height—five-feet-nine—which made her tall for a girl and me short for a guy, I guess. I ducked back so she'd quit touching me.

"I thought we had an agreement," she said. "You're not allowed to talk about my menstrual cycle and I'm not allowed to sleep in your bed after passionate love-making."

Passionate lovemaking. She actually said those words.

This was entirely too fucked-up. Kendall and I were tight when she still lived next door, but I never thought we'd be hooking up. In fact, I'd kind of made it a point over the years to be sure we *didn't*. And that it happened like this only made it worse. We were both there that night, but she was the only one with memories of my first time. I mean, how sick is that?

"When did we make the agreement?" I asked. "Because all I remember is waking up, feeling like shit, and you calling me lover. And while I was trying to figure things out, you were telling me I'm an asshole and stomping—"

"How exactly do you expect a person to react when you say they're an STD-ridden whore who wants to have your baby?" she interrupted.

"I never said that!"

"You implied it." She crossed her arms over her chest, smiling like she was enjoying this. "Seth, you were a complete dick. Just admit you didn't handle it well, beg for my forgiveness, and maybe we can move on."

I shook my head. She was unbelievable. Sure, I'd freaked out a little, asked a bunch of questions about how the hell we could have done this, and stressed about whether we'd used protection. None of it seemed out of line to me, and now Kendall was twisting everything around. Like she always did.

"*I* didn't handle it well?" I asked. "Hey, at least I wasn't screaming and throwing things—"

"What *things*? I threw your shirt only because you acted like it was oh-so-offensive that I was wearing it in the first place!"

I rubbed my temples. I had a Kendall-induced headache coming on.

"Look, I didn't come here to talk about this," she said, leaning against the counter. "I just need a favor from you."

Of course she did. "Does the agreement we supposedly made include you not asking me for favors? If not, it should."

"My car's on the side of the road. I want you to take a look."

The brand-new MINI Cooper her stepdad bought had crapped out already? "I can't help you."

"Don't be a prick," she said, sighing. "Seriously."

"Sorry, but I *seriously* have to get to school in a few minutes."

"Uh-huh. You really expect me to believe you're taking a class during zero?"

Zero period at the start of the day—just like seventh period at the end of it—was set up for those overachievers who couldn't get enough of learning during the regular hours we were trapped in school. As Kendall and everyone else knew, I'd sell my left nut before signing up for extra classes.

I didn't get a chance to explain—not that I owed her an explanation anyway—because right then three of my senses were hit at once: I smelled smoke, I heard the smoke alarm, and I saw orange flames all over my breakfast.

"Shit!" I said, yanking the toaster oven door open as the alarm practically blew out my eardrums.

I grabbed one of Mom's cow-print dish towels and tried smacking at the fire, but it didn't help. The flames got higher, and then the towel started burning too. While I was stamping *that* out against the linoleum, Kendall pulled something from the cupboard above the stove and pushed me out of the way to throw a handful of white powder. The flames in the toaster oven went out instantly. Magic.

She held up an orange box of baking soda and gave me a pointed look as she yelled over the alarm, "You realize that to keep that from happening you're supposed to clean out the crumbs and melted cheese that fall under the rack, right?"

I stuck my fingers in my ears to block out the beeping and Kendall's voice.

During the commotion, Mom had come out of her room in a satiny green robe. She stood in her doorway with her auburn-from-a-bottle hair a tangled mess, managing to look dead tired, confused, and annoyed all at once. "What's going on?" she shouted over the racket while Kendall picked up the singed dish towel and started waving it toward the ceiling to redirect the smoke.

After about twenty torturous seconds, the noise stopped, but the smell lingered on.

"Sorry, Mom. It's nothing," I said.

"Right, nothing at all." Kendall shook her head. "Your son is just setting everything on fire out here."

Mom had been pulled from sleep after probably only a few hours, but she still managed a small smile. Kendall was like the daughter or little sister she never had, and they were always doing girly things together like painting their nails and watching *Gilmore Girls* reruns. They just clicked for some reason, and even after Kendall's mom got married and moved with Kendall and her sister from the trailer next door to some fancy place on the Hill two years ago, Kendall still kept coming around.

The two of them started gabbing about how much I suck at cooking while I pulled my blackened and white-powder-coated Pop-Tarts out and dumped them in the trash. The cow-shaped clock on the wall said zero period was starting soon. Which meant I needed to be out the door. So much for having breakfast.

I went over to Mom and bent to kiss her cheek. "I'm off to fix my schedule with guidance."

"Oh, thank *God*," she said, yawning. "Does this mean that woman will quit bothering me now?"

Mom's always been kind of weird about school, and I'd had the feeling for a while that she wouldn't care if I never went back. I wanted to keep going with it, though. I guess I didn't want *this* to be the smartest I was ever going to get.

"Seth, do you mind if I carpool with you today?" Kendall asked.

I *did* mind, but I didn't want to say so and get Mom all over my case. "I'm out the door, so if you want a ride, it's now or never."

"I'm *so* ready, lover."

"Then get in the car, enemy."

Mom laughed. "Aren't you two the cutest?"

6:42 A.M.

As I walked down our front steps, Kendall followed closely behind. "Would you believe I sometimes wish I still lived here?" she asked.

"Not for a minute."

Riverside Trailer Park was the roughest part of Kenburn, and the cops were constantly busting our neighbors for drug deals and drunken brawls. The mobile homes were all rusty and at least thirty years old, and the carports were crooked and loaded up with old tires, soggy cardboard, and long-abandoned sinks. I wish I could've said our place looked better, but we had our own mess of broken TVs and other crap that no one ever dealt with. The longer it sat, the more it blended in, to the point where I hardly noticed.

"It's true. Most of my best times were here," Kendall said. "And anyway, I feel like an imposter on the Hill."

"I wish I had your problems." I scooted past the out-of-control rosebush. Naturally, that's when a breeze kicked in and gave a thorny branch the push it needed to hook itself into my skin. I pulled free. Blood ran down my arm. "God-damnit," I said.

I yanked open the driver's-side door and tossed my bag in the backseat. But before I could get in, Kendall was standing next to me, making a face that looked like real concern. "I know how painful this is for you," she said.

"It barely stings."

"I'm talking about Isaac. About you finding him."

I tensed up. Anytime I thought about the morning two months earlier when I'd found Isaac's body, I wanted to puke. Which is exactly why I tried to *never* think about it.

Kendall touched the mini Magic 8 Ball dangling from the key ring on my belt loop. She knew it was Isaac's. Everyone knew. It had been his good-luck charm for years and he never went anywhere without it—until the night he'd given it to me, saying I needed its advice more than he did. It was all a joke, really, and I would have given the stupid thing back to him the next day. If only he'd woken up.

Kendall went on. "I'm dealing with stuff too, but I'm really worried about *you*. I know you're not okay. Everyone says you've been hiding and drinking all summer. I've wanted to talk to you since it happened, but during the few times that I've even seen you, I haven't been able to figure out how."

It was surprising how quickly she'd gone from obnoxious to caring. My annoyance melted a little. "I probably wouldn't have wanted to talk, anyway."

"Believe me, I know how you are." She started rubbing my arm—the one that wasn't bleeding—like it was a cat. "I just don't want to see you blaming yourself forever. You need to remember that Isaac made his own choices. It isn't your fault he died."

"I know," I said.

But I was lying.

During the weeks since it happened, I'd filled my time with working at the car wash, playing bass, and getting wasted to keep from thinking, thinking, thinking about the last time I'd seen Isaac alive. The one thing I knew without a doubt was that I'd made a huge mistake that night, and I could never undo it.

"Isaac was a lot of things," Kendall said. "Some good, some not so good. But more than anything, I think he was impulsive and reckless."

I waited, figuring she'd take back her harsh words and offer up some funny story, like some people did when they mentioned Isaac these days. But she didn't. She just kept petting and staring at me. And that's when I realized she was going to leave it like that.

Isaac was impulsive and reckless.

Kendall and Isaac's relationship hadn't been what anyone would call perfect or even decent, really. But what kind of girlfriend talks trash like *that* after a guy dies?

I jerked away from her. "Why are you saying this to me?"

"I'm trying to *help* you," she said.

Typical, unbelievable Kendall.

Telling her what I thought of her so-called help would take a while, and I'd let her waste too much of my time already. So I jumped in and started up the Mustang, slammed it in reverse, and peeled the hell out of there, not giving two shits about the gravel spraying behind me or how pissed Kendall was going to be about being ditched.

6:45 A.M.

Alone in the car with my foot heavy on the gas pedal, I blazed through the first stop sign—no one's ever coming from the other direction, anyway—and squealed the tires around the corner. Then I really gunned it. As usual, the speedometer wasn't budging, but I figured I was probably going around fifty. The speed limit was only thirty miles per hour, but slowing down was not on my agenda. Fast helped take the edge off and gave me something to focus on. Also, I needed fast if I was going to get to the guidance office on time.

A few blocks from school, I was screeching around another turn when I caught sight of some chick in the crosswalk in front of me. The same second I realized I was about to get a human hood ornament, she saw me coming and ran out of the way. I hit the brakes, jerked the steering wheel, and found myself skidding into the wrong lane. Another swerve and I was back where I should have been.

Adrenaline was still coursing through me after what had

gone down at home with Kendall, and now my hands and legs were shaking too. I pulled to the side of the road and stuck my head out the window to give the girl a piece of my mind. I couldn't stand it when pedestrians acted like they owned the road.

As she jogged toward my car with her backpack bouncing, I recognized her right off as the cute girl wearing flip-flops at Pete's party. Her hotness factor was seriously lessened at that moment, though; her face was bright red, her eyes were almost bugging out of her head, and she was dressed in some boring, preppy white shirt/gray skirt combo.

If she was in any way glad to see me, she didn't let on. "Oh my God!" she shouted. "Why don't you watch where you're going?"

"Why don't *you*?" I countered. "I had a green light!"

She gestured wildly at the intersection. "Hel*lo*! Me too!"

I looked over my shoulder, but I didn't have a clear view of the traffic signal from that angle. "How does that work?"

"It works *best* when the person in the car doesn't break the law. When the person in the car yields to the *pedestrian*, who happens to have the right-of-way!"

Now that she mentioned it, I realized she was probably right. "Sorry. I didn't know."

"You didn't know? I was almost killed because you don't know how to drive?"

This conversation, this whole miserable morning, was exhausting me.

"You wouldn't have been killed," I said, hoping to chill her out. "I'd have given you mouth-to-mouth if it came down to it."

She fixed me with a good hard glare. "You're disgusting."

The girl was still hot, but she obviously had it out for me now. Disappointing, but I'd never been stupid enough to think I had a chance with her. Not really.

I looked at the clock on my stereo. Five minutes and counting.

"I have to go, so we need to wrap up this talk," I said. "You want a ride the rest of the way to school, or what?"

It seemed like the least I could do.

She looked at me like I'd asked her to run away to Africa.

"Are you kidding? I'm not going anywhere with you."

"Suit yourself."

When I got to Kenburn High School, I parked the car, raced inside the building, ran though the hallway, and threw open the door to the main office right as the bell rang. I sat across from Ms. Naylor one minute later, panting like an old dog that had chased too many sticks. But at least I'd been able to get one thing right that morning.

7:09 A.M.

Ms. Naylor was gazing at her computer monitor and clicking her mouse all over the place while I sat there waiting for her to say something and wondering why she'd made me rush to meet her. She was supposed to be pulling up my records, but she sure was taking her sweet time about it. I started thinking she was playing a game of Minesweeper instead.

She sipped from her Starbucks cup and tucked a few strands of highlighted hair behind her ears. "This system takes a long time to load first thing in the morning."

"It's okay," I said.

And it was. I mean, I wasn't looking forward to this talk, anyway, and Ms. Naylor—or Ms. I Wanna Nail Her, as Daniel liked to say—was at least decent to look at.

When the computer system was finally ready a minute later, Ms. Naylor folded her hands on top of her desk and looked at me all serious, like she was about to tell me my mother flatlined on the operating table. "As you know, I am very concerned that you've failed basic-level algebra twice. And I'm disappointed that you wouldn't let me help you. We could have fixed this sooner. But you never showed up for the tutoring I arranged, and then you skipped out on summer school. Again. This is very serious now."

The woman made it sound like the end of the world instead of just *math*. Back when she'd called to harass me about this appointment, she'd even gone so far as to throw around words like "severe consequences."

I didn't have anything to say for myself, so I studied the big freckle near the edge of her bottom lip instead. Such a weird—and weirdly *hot*—place for a freckle.

She went on. "We're to the point now where you don't have the option of flaking out on me. If you want to graduate, you're going to have to get passing grades in two full-year math classes. We're running out of time." She flashed her perfect teeth in a way that she probably meant to be encouraging, but was mostly annoying. "What are your thoughts on how to accomplish this?"

"Three strikes, I'm out?" I suggested.

Her smile vanished, like I'd known it would. If there's one thing I've figured out during our times together, it's that Ms. Naylor gets pissy about "self-defeating attitudes."

But then I decided to cut her a break; it was only the first day back, after all. "What I meant to say is that the third time's the charm."

"I think so too," she said, nodding. "I worked on your schedule and figured out a plan to keep you on track for finishing high school with the rest of your class. You'll need to follow it. To the *letter*. It's the only way this can work."

I sat up a little straighter. For once she didn't sound like she was being all guidance-counselor dramatic. Maybe this *was* urgent, which I hadn't seen coming. The thing is, yeah, I've been kicked out of a few classes for attendance problems, and my report card has more D's than a Victoria's Secret model's lingerie drawer, but Algebra for Idiots is the only one I'd ever actually *flunked*.

Ms. Naylor took another drink of her coffee or latte or whatever. "Before we go over your revised schedule and I send you on your way, is there anything you'd like to talk about with me?"

She always did this. Set up a meeting over some school thing, tried to get me as stressed as she was, and then slipped in the "how are things at home?" crap when she thought I wasn't paying attention.

I shook my head.

"Nothing at all?" she asked.

I knew what she was getting at, but I said, "Should there be?"

"I'm not just here to help with your academic planning, you know," she said. "I'm more than willing to listen if you want to discuss Isaac Thomas's death."

Sure she was. She'd probably love hearing all the gritty details.

I was sort of curious about which version of the story she'd been told: the one where Isaac drank himself to death, OD'd on smack, or—my personal *least* favorite—had a heart attack after huffing ten cans of whipped cream. I wasn't curious enough to ask her, though.

"No, thanks. I'm good," I said, giving the 8 Ball a quick pat to make sure it hadn't disappeared or anything.

"Just know the offer stands, okay?" Ms. Naylor said. Then she cleared her throat, handed me a sheet of paper, and got back to business. "Here's your schedule."

I held up the page to take a closer look. The list of classes was like the one I'd turned in, but there were two very screwed-up additions. "No way," I said, letting the page drop onto the desk. "You stuck me in zero period *and* seventh?"

"It isn't as bad as you think," she said in a soothing voice. She pointed. "See, the first one is tutoring lab, which isn't even a graded class. I think working on your algebra for two full periods every day is really going to help you get it this time."

I hated to admit it, but she was probably right. Numbers were a foreign language to me—a difficult-as-hell foreign language—and I needed all the help I could get. But that didn't explain seventh period. "What's this Interpersonal Communications crap?"

"You need more electives," Ms. Naylor said. "Interpersonal Communications is a class we're offering from a new teacher who comes highly recommended. It's supposed to be a fun course with very little homework and no tests, which seems great for you. I think you'll agree that your grade point average could really use a boost."

I leaned forward and put my face in my hands. Of *course* my GPA needed a boost. But did I really have to rot away at school for eight straight hours, five days a week, to make it happen? "There's no way I can do this."

"I think you can, Seth. And if you put your mind to it, you *will*."

It was hard to keep from rolling my eyes. Once again Ms. Naylor had trampled right over that fine line between encouraging and annoying.

By seventh period I was dragging more than ever. The only person I'd spoken to all day since leaving Ms. Naylor's office was the lunch lady who'd given me corn dogs and curly fries. What a switch from last year when I'd spent my lunches getting stoned with my brother and our friends. Now Jared had dropped out to get his GED, Mikey had graduated, Isaac had been cremated, and Daniel—who had no excuses—seemed to be missing. It sucked being alone at school.

But what sucked even more was that nobody seemed to care that Isaac was dead. When a girl drowned during the summer before our sophomore year, there had been a tree-planting ceremony on the first day back where some kids and teachers stood in a big circle and said nice stuff about her. No one did anything like that for Isaac. In fact, if it weren't for the occasional stares and whispers as I walked past—and that shitty thing Vicki had said at Pete's party—I might have thought Kendall, Ms. Naylor, and I were the only people at school who remembered Isaac had ever existed.

When I finally got to the room listed for my so-called easy elective, the door was closed and blocked by a stocky woman with gray-streaked brown hair and huge glasses. Something about that combo and the slump of her shoulders made me think of an owl. "Are you here for IC class?" she asked in a high-pitched, chipper-sounding voice.

"Um, Interpersonal Communications."

"Exactly." Her nose kind of crinkled up as she smiled.

"But isn't that a mouthful? Ten syllables between those two words, if you can believe it. We'll call it IC, okay?"

"Sure," I said, shrugging.

"I'm teaching this class." She held a clipboard out for me. "Welcome! Before you go in, I need you to find your name on the roster and mark off that you're here."

I did as she'd asked.

"Perfect," she said. "Go on in now. Sit anywhere. Talk with whomever you'd like about anything you'd like. Just make sure not to introduce yourself by name, okay?"

These had to be some of the strangest instructions a teacher had ever given me.

She opened the door only far enough for me to fit through. It was dark inside, with a few lit candles scattered around. I turned back to her, wondering what was going on.

"It's perfectly safe," she said, nodding. "I'll be in after a minute or two."

As soon as I was inside, she pulled the door shut again. When my eyes adjusted, I saw that I wasn't alone. About ten other students were sitting on beanbags in a large circle, but they weren't following the "talk to whomever about anything" directions. They just plain weren't talking.

What the hell had Ms. Naylor gotten me into?

I set my bag down and dropped onto the first empty beanbag. Too late, I realized that Flip-Flops—of all people— was right next to me. Just my luck.

I decided to give peace another chance. "Long time no see."

She didn't reply, and her frown and forehead lines didn't seem to be about charity and goodwill toward Seth.

The door opened again and that Xander guy came in and took a seat. His shaggy hair fell over his eyes, but I could tell from the bottom half of his face that he was as confused as I was. The teacher was right behind him. After shuffling over and lowering herself onto a beanbag, she cleared her throat. "Good afternoon, class. All thirteen of us are here, so let's get started. I think thirteen is going to be our lucky number, don't you?"

No one answered, so she plowed on, smiling in that crinkly nosed way. "I want to remind you again not to tell *anyone* your name. You're each going to be choosing your own identities for this class, so start thinking of what you'd like to be called. I'm going to use Mrs. Dalloway from my favorite Virginia Woolf novel. But you don't have to choose something from fiction just because I did. Make up something you like!"

Xander raised his hand. "What if people already know our real names?"

"Then they'll have to forget those so-called real names while they're here," she said, using quick air quotes at the words "forget" and "real." "Don't worry. I'll supply name tags starting tomorrow so you won't get too confused."

Then she gave this honest-to-God, Wicked Witch of the West cackle that would have given a five-year-old nightmares. Hell, it could have given *me* nightmares. I couldn't guess why she was laughing so hard; what she'd said wasn't funny.

Everyone looked worried, and I could understand why. The candles and beanbags were a little much, and it didn't feel like school in here at all. It was more like we were around an invisible campfire or getting ready to do satanic rituals, maybe. And it didn't help that only one minute into class, Mrs. Owl-Lady Dalloway had us trapped in the dark while she laughed in an unhinged kind of way.

With her mouth curved into this freaky smile like she knew secrets about every kid in the room, she looked at us one by one. I glanced away when her hard-blinking eyes zeroed in on me.

"None of you realize it yet, but this is going to be the most important course you'll ever take. I attended one like it in college, and it changed my life." She pumped her fist in the air, and Tara—the girl closest to her—jumped. "Communication is the key ingredient for *life*! I'm excited to teach you something this important!"

I had a hard time believing that *talking* was going to make my life better, or that Mrs. Dalloway was the right person to teach me about it. By the weirded-out look on Flip-Flops's face, I thought she felt the same.

"The majority of your grade will be based on class participation," Mrs. Dalloway said. "We'll have group discussions every day in which you will role-play the communication methods. Sometimes I'll put you in pairs or small groups;

sometimes we'll all work together. Also, several minutes of class will be spent writing about your experiences in a journal. Don't worry, I won't read your journals. But you *are* required to use them."

Then she let loose with that scary laugh again.

Just great. What could be worse than being forced to write my thoughts in some stupid book?

Mrs. Dalloway went on. "All of you are here for different reasons. Some were directed by the guidance office. Some need to fill elective credits. Others have a particular interest in this subject. But whatever it was that got you here, we're *all* going to have a great time and learn a lot about who we are and who we want to become. Any questions so far?"

Xander raised his hand. "I'm just wondering, what's with the candles?"

She nodded like she was excited that someone had noticed. As if there was any way we could have missed it. "We'll be getting into this a great deal as time goes on. But for now I'll just say that it has to do with the importance of *where* communication takes place. You'll be seeing a lot of different things in this room." She looked around. "Any other questions?"

No one else had any, it seemed. Or maybe, like me, they were so confused about what was going on, they didn't know where to start.

Mrs. Dalloway clapped her hands together. "Okay, then. One of the things I want to make clear from the beginning is that we won't be labeling or judging or even *thinking* of anyone as the person they are outside this classroom. This is everyone's chance to start over and be whomever they'd like to be. Experiment! Be free! Everyone gets a clean slate. Understood?"

Then she grabbed a pile of journals from behind her and had us pass them around as she rambled on.

The weirdness was wearing off a little, so I started having a hard time paying attention. The beanbag and darkness were making my body feel like it was nap time. I closed my eyes for a few minutes, hoping I looked like I was trying to soak it all in instead of block it all out.

As I was kind of dozing, it struck me as stupid that this wacko teacher kept talking about how we were going to be communicating or whatever, but all we were doing was listening to her. I couldn't say I actually wanted to talk to these people. Still, the whole thing reminded me of bass lessons where the dudes bored me to death making me work on scales instead of having me play real songs.

Five minutes before class let out, Mrs. Dalloway was winding down. "Now, I want you to get to know one another. This is a good time to try out your in-class identities with the people next to you. Introduce yourselves with your new name if you've chosen one. For fun, maybe write your guesses of what everyone's *legal* names are in your journal. You'll find out at the end of the quarter if you're right!"

Xander raised his hand one more time. "But what if you already *know* you're right?"

Mrs. Dalloway smiled. "I can tell you're going to be a very eager student."

That was one way to look at it.

I turned to Flip-Flops first. She seemed to hate me, but if she was buying into this whole clean slate thing, maybe it would go better than our conversation at the intersection.

"Hi, I'm Dick," I said.

"Yeah, I've heard that about you."

WEDNESDAY, **SEPTEMBER 8**

6:37 A.M.

The next morning. Hungover again.

I managed to drag myself out of bed and was getting ready to leave for my ass-crack-of-dawn tutoring session, but I wanted to wake Daniel first. After I'd come home from my shift at the car wash the night before, we'd gotten wasted out by the river. He told me he'd overslept and that when he'd finally gotten up, it had been too late to bother coming in for the first day. I'd never been anyone's attendance police, but if I had to be there—for *eight* class periods—it seemed only fair that Daniel should have to come too.

I headed to the trailer next door, where he lived with his dad, and let myself in. My place looked like a dump from the outside, but Daniel and Hank's was thrashed all around. They left their McDonald's wrappers and frozen dinner boxes out for weeks and only vacuumed the ratty brown carpet about twice a year. Mom went crazy about them living in that mess and straightened up for them sometimes.

I'd made it about four feet into the living room when I spotted Daniel on the floor, sprawled on his back next to the coffee table. There was an empty bottle of Jack tipped on its side and beer cans scattered all around.

Daniel: Face pale. Eyes shut. Jaw slack. Mouth open.

I took a step forward. "Daniel?"

No response.

"Daniel!"

Still nothing.

I ran to him, fell to my knees, grabbed his wrist. Was that a pulse? Or . . . no pulse? Shit. I pressed my fingers to his neck. My own heart was beating so hard, so fast, I couldn't tell what I was feeling. Were those quick beats from him or me?

There was some sitcom on the TV. The laugh track was doing its laughing thing. I forced myself to breathe.

"Don't be dead," I said. "Don't be dead don't be dead don't be dead."

He still didn't move.

"Daniel!" I yelled, shaking his shoulders. "Open your eyes, you motherfucker!"

And then . . . he did.

"What the *hell*?" he asked, bolting upright.

"Jesus Christ." I put my hands to my chest, fell back

on my heels, and let out a bunch of loud breaths. "You just scared the shit out of me."

He leaned against the couch and glared. "*I* scared *you*? What is this, Dick? A guy can't even sleep in peace in his own house without you coming in and freaking out about it?"

If he'd been in his bed or at least on the couch like a normal, nondead person, I wouldn't have *had* to freak out. "You looked dead. I thought you were dead."

He rubbed his shoulder and stared at the mess around him on the floor. I could tell that he understood exactly what I'd thought I'd been seeing, why I'd panicked. What I didn't know was if he cared.

I stood. My eyes were tearing up and I had to get out of there before he noticed and changed his nickname for me to Pussy. "I'm about to leave for school," I said. "Are you going to be there today?"

He yawned. "Maybe. If you're lucky."

"Don't do me any favors," I said, walking out the door.

6:45 A.M.

Back home, I tried to brush my teeth, but I was losing it.

Since the bathroom shares a wall with Mom's room and the insulation is about as thin as cardboard, I turned on the sink full blast and flipped up the switch of our rattling exhaust fan to keep her from hearing me. I kept reminding myself that what I'd seen next door had been Daniel asleep.

But calming down was hard because, for those few seconds, he had seemed to me very . . . dead.

It was too much. Way too much.

Cupping my hands under the faucet, I threw cold water at my face until I was gasping and coughing and choking on it.

Fucking hell.

I held on to the edge of the counter and lowered myself onto the purple rug. Then I cried so hard my stomach hurt. So hard I had to crawl to the toilet because I thought I was going to puke. So hard I slapped my own face to try to snap myself out of it.

I'd never cried like this, not even when I found Isaac.

I *hated* crying like this.

In a way I wanted to run back to Daniel's. To throw him at a wall. To punch his face. Or maybe—*maybe*—to thank him for having enough decency not to die on me today.

2:27 P.M.

When I got to Interpersonal Communications class—IC, I mean—I had a killer headache and my eyes were still kind of red. Not that that was anything unusual; everyone probably just thought I was stoned.

The classroom looked normal today: lights on, blinds open, beanbags thrown in piles against the wall. There were three big tables pushed together to form a U shape so we could all sit there and stare at each other, I guessed. I took a seat as far from Flip-Flops as possible. No need to repeat *that* mistake. Anyway, I'd been seeing her around in the hall with Vicki Lancaster, which gave me the idea that our friendly talk by Pete's pool must have been a fluke.

Mrs. Dalloway stood behind the podium up front with a plastic name tag hanging from a string around her neck. She clapped her hands. "Okay, class, I've put together name tags just like mine for each of you. Write the name you want to use on your tag and on this sheet of paper I'm about to pass around. From now forward, these names will be how you'll address one another while you're in this room. We'll wear name tags every day until we memorize them."

I wrote DICK on my tag and used my books to prop it up in front of me. I really didn't want to wear the thing.

"Come on, everyone!" Mrs. Dalloway said, looking right at me. "Name tags *on* so we can see them."

I slipped the string over my head, feeling like a complete dork. This Mrs. Dalloway was too much.

She gave me a crinkly nosed grin. "Excellent. Before I begin the lecture part of class today, I want to hear a one-word description of how you each felt when you came to this room yesterday."

Naturally, Xander raised his hand. Mrs. Dalloway squinted at his tag. "Go ahead, Alex."

"Confused," Alex/Xander said.

Mrs. Dalloway cackled and wrote it on the white board. She had the messiest handwriting I'd ever seen from a person over the age of seven.

"Who's next?" she asked.

After sitting quietly the day before, just about everyone wanted to get in on Alex/Xander's kissing-up action, it seemed. Soon there was a list going: Confused. Nervous. Confused. Curious. Surprised. Interested. Confused.

"What about you, Dick?" Mrs. Dalloway asked.

I didn't want to be another "confused" loser, so I said, "Tired."

A few people laughed, but Mrs. Dalloway nodded and wrote it down.

For the next twenty minutes or so, she went over part of the first chapter in our textbook. In that time, I learned that listening to her talk about how and why people communicate with each other was *still* boring as hell. But then things got more interesting.

"Please pull out your journals," Mrs. Dalloway said. "I want you to examine an interpersonal exchange you've had recently that didn't go well. Write down the words you used and whether they had your desired effect on the other person."

I'd had so many shitty conversations I didn't know which to choose. I finally started in with what had happened at Daniel's that morning. It didn't take long to write because I hadn't actually said much of anything to him. And it was hard to know if it had the right effect because he hadn't shown up again.

Then Mrs. Dalloway said, "Now I'm going to put you in pairs for the rest of the class period. Please share the interpersonal exchange you just wrote down and brainstorm together about why the exchange might not have had your desired outcome. See if you can come up with ideas that could have made it more effective."

Wonderful. Just what I *didn't* want was to talk about my issues with someone in class for the next fifteen minutes.

"Wait a second," Clover/Lorraine said, waving her hand. "I thought you said the journals are private. What if we don't want to talk about what we wrote? I mean, this could be really personal stuff and maybe we don't want the whole world knowing about it?"

Mrs. Dalloway tilted her head, staring in the direction of the wall behind me. "That's a worthy point. Can we all make an agreement not to share any private things we might learn about one another here? Everything we say needs to be confidential."

Some chick I didn't know, whose name tag I couldn't see, said, "Like, what happens in IC class *stays* in IC class?"

Mrs. Dalloway nodded. "Exactly!"

"The first rule of Interpersonal Communications," Alex/Xander said in a mock-stern voice, "is that you do not *talk* about Interpersonal Communications."

That cracked all our asses up.

What a loudmouth that Xander guy was turning out to be. I vaguely remembered him saying something at Pete's party about being in a band, and I was getting a good idea that he must be the drummer. Drummers can never just shut the hell up. Still, I had to admit, he was kind of funny.

"Or!" Mrs. Dalloway said, clapping her hands together again. "How about this? We all agree to keep things confidential. But at the same time, if ever you *don't* feel like telling something private, you can fabricate a scenario to share instead. I really want this class to be an experiment for you to challenge yourselves and help you start seeing yourselves differently. If it makes you feel more comfortable to use a persona and role-play, do it. If you find yourself enjoying that persona, consider what it is you like and what you can learn from it to make changes in your life."

She'd lost me somewhere in that persona garbage, but all the girls were nodding and looking like they weren't worried about their super-duper secrets being blabbed around anymore, so that seemed like a good sign.

Then Mrs. Dalloway picked up the sheet of paper we'd written our fake names on and read us off in pairs. My partner was "Riley," whichever one he was. In our class of twelve, only four of us were guys, so I just stayed where I was, figuring he would come to me.

But it was Flip-Flops who made her way over and plopped down in the chair next to mine. "You should go first because I don't want to talk about this with you," she said, tapping the front of her journal. "I'm trying to think of a fake conversation to tell you about, but it's kind of hard to come up with one."

She was Riley? Of course. Because Mrs. Dalloway would just *have* to pair me up with someone who hated me.

Discussing Daniel was not going to be happening here. I was sure Riley had some charmed life where her friends didn't lie around on their living room floors and look dead. There was no way she could understand.

"I don't have anything ready to talk about either," I said.

"Great."

Then she started writing. I sat there staring at the clock on the wall, wishing the hands would move faster. After two minutes and seventeen seconds, Riley poked my arm. "She's watching us," she said.

I looked at Mrs. Dalloway, and, sure enough, she kept glancing over at Riley and me while jotting notes behind her podium. Everyone else was talking to their partners while *we* were failing to communicate.

I needed this easy good grade, and I wasn't going to let this Riley chick screw it up for me. "Then we should probably wing it so we don't lose points for not participating or whatever," I said.

Riley put her pen down and crossed her arms over her chest. "Fine."

I wouldn't have minded if she'd chosen something to talk about, but she was clearly expecting me to start.

I pointed at her name tag. "Why did you name yourself Riley? Isn't that a guy's name? Or a last name?"

"It's both. And it's a girl's name. I wanted something unisex because the name I'm stuck with in real life came from a romance novel."

"You mean, like, Lusty Lucy?"

She rolled her eyes. "I said, 'romance novel,' not *porn*. Why did you name yourself after your genitals?"

Her Rich Bitchiness was coming through again today, so I decided to mess with her. "Actually, it's a name that goes back generations. In my family, Dick is the name given to all the firstborn sons. My granddad was a Dick and so was my dad. But I'm the second-born son, so I missed out on getting to be a Dick in this life."

She seemed interested. "Really? Is that a true story?"

"Not at all." From what I'd heard, my dad *was* a dick, but it wasn't his legal name or anything. "Well, except that I *am* the second son."

Riley's angry forehead lines were back. And her nostrils were flaring a little too.

That was easier than it should have been.

She slammed her journal shut. "I know that while we're in this classroom we're supposed to be pretending like we've never met, but it's hard for me to even *talk* to you when everything you say to me is a lie."

Now I regretted opening my mouth at all. Jerking a bitchy girl's chain isn't all it's cracked up to be, especially when you're stuck there to suffer all the dirty looks afterward.

"I was making a joke," I said, trying to calm her down. "Maybe you've heard of this thing called 'humor'?"

She lifted her eyebrows. "I've heard of it. Like the other night when you said you hadn't been drinking and I totally fell for it. That was a pretty good joke. I wonder: If I'd taken you up on your offer, would you have driven me to the beach drunk?'"

Yeah, we were communicating now all right. What a low blow, reminding me of that corny ocean-trip thing I'd said. Riley—or whatever her romance-novel name was—fought dirty.

I didn't know how, but I needed to turn this around. It was going to be a long semester if we were going to be at each other's throats every time we got stuck together. Telling the whole truth was looking like my best—and only—option.

"First of all, I didn't set out to lie to you," I said. "I'm not naturally a liar. Not really. You got the wrong idea about the drinking stuff and I didn't want to have to tell you that you were wrong. Anyway, I ended up leaving my car behind and walking home that night. So I didn't drive anywhere drunk. It's not like a thing I do or anything."

She stared at me with her eyes open wide, but she didn't say anything, so I kept going: "Now I'm supposed to be telling you about a recent interpersonal exchange I had that didn't go well, right?" I took a deep breath and let it out slowly. "Well, I talked to a girl at a party and sort of got caught in a lie. A few days later, I was having a bad morning and almost ran that same girl over with my car. And then, like a real bastard, I yelled at her. I suck."

Riley put her hand over her lips, but not before I'd seen that she was covering up a small smile. "Tell me, Dick. Why do you think those exchanges might not have had your desired outcome?"

I shrugged. This was pretty hard actually, analyzing why a conversation went to shit. It had always seemed like a thing that just happens sometimes. Riley didn't offer any clues, so finally I said, "Maybe because I was being a jerk?"

She smiled at me in a strange way. Like she was getting over being pissed at me, even though she wasn't sure she was ready to be.

"I'll take my turn now." She opened her journal and read aloud. "We're supposed to give everyone a clean slate and not think of them or judge them as the person they are outside the class. But yesterday I ended up being really rude to . . . *someone* . . . because he'd been a jerk to me earlier and I was holding a grudge."

I was pretty floored that she'd written about me, but I didn't want to say anything about it and accidentally make her mad again.

She closed the journal and looked at me, biting her lip. "The exchange *did* have my desired outcome at the time, but I think I regret it now. A little bit, I mean."

A little bit was enough, I supposed.

"So what now?" I asked. "Mrs. D. said we need to talk about what we could have done or said differently?"

She nodded. "Yes. And we can do that if you want. But we both already know, so what do you think about giving that clean-slate thing another try?"

"Sounds good to me."

Smiling, she put out her hand to shake mine. "Hi, I'm Riley."

"Nice to meet you, Riley. I'm Dick."

7:59 P.M.

I pulled into the storage-unit lot, parked between Mikey's new truck and Daniel's motorcycle, and rushed to unit 43. I was late for band practice, which meant my brother was going to be pissed. He was never on time for anything—except band stuff—since he had to bum rides everywhere he went after his DUI arrest and losing his license. But that didn't stop him from taking other people's lateness, and especially mine, very personally.

The retractable door to our rehearsal space—which Mikey paid for, and we called Studio 43 to make it sound cooler than the ten-by-twenty-foot storage unit it was—was open about three feet when I got there, but there was no rowdy music coming from inside. I couldn't guess if that was a good or bad sign.

I reached for the door.

"We need to hurry up and decide on a name," Jared was saying. "It's going to be hard to advertise new shows without one."

I stopped short. Not *this* again.

Jared had recently decided that the name he chose when he was fifteen and just starting this band almost four years ago—the Real McCoys—had to go because there are too many others out there with the same name. The big debate had been going on for enough months now that only Jared was taking it seriously.

Daniel spoke next. "I'm telling you, I think we should go with the Fake McCoys."

Then Mikey. "And I'm all about Potts, Jackson, and the Motherfucking McCoys."

I knew he didn't seriously want that as our new band name, but I cringed anyway. And him not saying "Thomas" bothered the hell out of me. The rest of the guys seemed to be used to Isaac being gone, but I sure wasn't.

"Speaking of motherfucking McCoys, *where* is my brother?" Jared asked.

"I had him scheduled to get off at seven thirty," Mikey said. "But maybe my dad needed him to stay later?"

"Maybe you should call," Jared said.

Time to go in. Since I *had* to.

I slid the door up high enough to fit through. "I'm here," I said, ducking inside and pulling it shut behind me.

As always, the room—dimly lit by two small lamps and

strings of red Christmas lights snaking around the walls—smelled like pine-tree air freshener and stale cigarettes. Everyone was just hanging out and drinking beer: Mikey behind his drums, Jared at the mic, and Daniel on the ratty green couch we'd rescued from the side of the road at the start of summer.

"You look like shit," Jared said to me.

He was right, but Jared always thought I looked like shit. Compared to him, I usually did, I guess. It isn't like he got the better genes or anything. We look a lot alike: same medium build, dark hair, and sad excuse for an eye color that Mom called hazel. But I just threw on whatever decent clothes I could find, while he was always dressing in some retro James Dean way.

I ignored him and headed over to the wall to grab the doghouse bass. The sooner we got this rehearsal over with, the sooner I could get out of here. Away from my brother.

"Where've you been?" Jared asked.

"Tutoring, class, car wash, Good Times. Now band rehearsal," I said. Honestly, I was feeling as run-down as Jared thought I looked.

"That's too many places to be in one day, dude," Mikey said.

Jared frowned. "Good Times? You stopped for dinner after work when you knew we were waiting around on your ass?"

When Jared spent fourteen hours straight doing something besides sleeping, *then* he could criticize me for taking ten minutes to try to choke down some food. He seemed like he was in a mood to throw me against a wall if I said that out loud, though, so I focused on tuning instead of arguing.

Daniel got up and pulled another beer from the mini-fridge. "Hey, Dick!" he called out, motioning like he was going to toss it to me.

As a reflex, I started to put my hand out. But then I thought about the bullshit that had gone down at Daniel's that morning and let it drop. "No thanks."

"Really?" he asked.

"Yeah, I think I'll just pass," I said, looking straight at him. "I'm over it."

Daniel shrugged and cracked it open for himself while Jared and Mikey exchanged glances I couldn't quite interpret. My best guess would have been: *Right. Like* this *is gonna last.*

Maybe they were right. But I wanted to try *not* drinking for a while and see where it went.

Jared finished his PBR and tossed the can in the direction of the already overflowing trash. "Now that we're finally all here, I have some news," he said. "Will at Good Times gave me a heads-up that the Rat Rodders are going on tour, and they're talking about having us come along. I called up Owen to say we want to get in on it, so he's going to get back with me about dates and all that. Sounds like it's going to be cool."

Typical Jared, saying "we" would do it without asking the rest of the band first. The Rat Rodders were on an indie label and had a pretty good following, but they were also flaky with opening-band bookings. Their lead singer, Owen, promised us shows a few times before, but something always went haywire at the last minute.

Nothing could stop Daniel from getting caught up in it, though. Again. The crazy optimist, Isaac used to call him.

"Sweet," Daniel said, grinning. "Where are we going?"

Jared shrugged. "Everywhere. California, lots of Southern states. Like I said, they'll be getting back with me real soon."

"Sounds good," Daniel said.

It didn't sound that good to me, to be honest. Swear to God, some of these dudes made it their lives to argue whether you can call your band "rockabilly" if you don't play exactly the way they did in the fifties, if using an electric bass instead of an upright makes you the ultimate poseurs, if psychobilly is the crappiest subgenre ever to exist, and on and on and on. Basically—like most music scenes, I guess—rockabilly is overrun with know-it-alls.

"If it actually pans out this time, we'll have a lot to plan," Mikey said.

"Like our brand-new name," Jared said.

The rest of us groaned.

We got in our places and played through a few songs for the next hour or so.

After almost a year in the band, I'd done only a few rehearsals fully sober, and all of those had been long before this past summer. I can't say whether it was better or worse this way. Neither, maybe. Just . . . different. But it was kind of surprising how much the little screwups stuck out and how off Daniel's timing was.

Just before nine, Jared started having problems with his mic and Daniel broke a string. It was about time to pack it in for the night anyway, so I put the bass away and started to leave. Before I got out the door, though, Jared looked up from the box of cords and shit he was digging through and asked, "Hey, Seth, have you seen my other mic anywhere?"

I shook my head.

From his new place on the couch, Mikey said, "You know, I think I remember Isaac letting Kendall borrow it a few months back, after she got that karaoke machine."

"Well, I need it," Jared said, standing. He looked straight at me. "Can you get it?"

"What? Why me?" I asked. "I don't hang out with Kendall."

"You see more of her than the rest of us do, right?"

"No." The way he'd asked made me think he knew I'd slept with her or something. I hadn't told anyone, but that didn't mean it hadn't gotten out. Crap like this always seemed to get out. "I only see Kendall when she's with Mom."

Daniel gave me a weird look. "What are you talking about? You see her at school all the time. Just ask her for it the next time you run into her."

His way of being all casual about the chicks he fooled around with had always been a mystery to me, but never more than at that moment. Daniel hooked up with Kendall once at a party last winter. Things got screwed up for all of us when Isaac found out about it, beat the shit out of Daniel, and quit the band. After a month or so, Isaac and Kendall got back together, like they always did, and Isaac started playing music with us again, but things between him and Daniel were never cool after that. The thing I didn't get was that Daniel never even seemed sorry. There was no chance of Isaac finding out about what *I'd* done, but I felt like a bastard over the whole thing, anyway.

"You'll probably get your mic back faster if you give Kendall a call and ask for it," I said to Jared.

"Can't you just do it for me? I don't have her number."

As much as I didn't want to risk making these guys suspicious, I wanted to talk to Kendall even less. "Get it from Mom. I'm not your secretary."

Mikey rolled his eyes. "You know what? I'll call Kendall. It's only a microphone. No big deal."

"Cool," I said, lifting the door and heading out.

Mikey and Jared stayed put, but Daniel caught up with me and we walked to our parking spots. For a few seconds I wondered if he was figuring things out and was going to give me shit over Kendall, but instead he said, "That's pretty awesome news about that Rat Rodders tour, huh? I think it's exactly what we need."

"Yeah, if it even ends up happening," I said, shrugging.

And right then I wondered how I could *let* it happen. No one had said much about my sloppy, embarrassing performance at our show the week before, but I'm sure they'd have just told me to get over it and get back up there. What they didn't get was that I couldn't. Not without Isaac.

Daniel crossed his arms over his chest. "What's going on with you? Why do you have to be such a downer? You were never like this before."

Before? Did he mean before all the times the Rat Rodders screwed us over? Before Isaac died? Or maybe before I'd found him on the floor this morning.

"I'm trying to be realistic," I said. "Those guys never come through. Maybe we should just hold off on getting our hopes up."

"Whatever." Daniel climbed on his bike. "You keep being negative, Dick, but I'm going to think good thoughts. Like about how, soon, this is all finally going to be paying off. We're going to get out of this town. The four of us. We'll travel all over. Get paid to play music. What could be better?"

What he didn't mention were the parts he was looking forward to most: the partying, the booze, the drugs, the chicks. For Daniel, being in a band was about fun first and music last.

"You realize this isn't going to be tour buses and ritzy hotels," I said. "We'll spend half our waking hours driving in some van from one sketchy club to the next. And then we'll sleep on strangers' floors and live off convenience-store hot dogs and chips."

"Sounds like a hell of a great time to me." He started his bike and yelled over the engine, "Maybe you can try keeping an open mind?"

But it was way too late for that.

FRIDAY, **SEPTEMBER 10**

5:38 P.M.

Two days later. A thrilling afternoon at work. Mikey, who manages his dad's full-service car wash/gas station, had given me the crap job of scrubbing wheels, so I was on my knees finishing up a minivan. It was overcast, and with the wind redirecting the water from the hoses Trevor and Lyle were using, my sweatshirt and jeans were getting damp.

I was deep in concentration when someone touched my shoulder. I looked up to see Kendall staring down, wearing her orangey hair in those stupid pigtails again. "You're in luck, lover," she said. "I was here dropping something off for Mikey, and he just so happened to mention that it's time for your break."

So the missing microphone thing was over and done

with. It was good of Mikey to take care of it for Jared so I didn't have to, but it was really *not* cool that he'd sent Kendall out to harass me afterward. Especially since I was shaky and sweaty, and I hadn't felt much like eating ever since I'd started this no-drinking thing.

"I don't want to take a break," I said.

"Of course you do." As she put one hand on her hip, her fitted black shirt with too many undone buttons shifted so I could see the top of her lacy red bra. "Everyone wants to take breaks. And anyway, we need to talk."

Trevor and Lyle were watching. How could they not with Kendall's boobs hanging out? And her legs. With that skirt. *Jesus.*

I didn't think Kendall would say anything about That One Night in front of them, but I didn't want to risk it. "Finish this for me?" I asked Lyle.

He nodded, so I tossed him my brush and walked with Kendall until we were out of earshot.

"Have you ever considered that I don't want to spend my break with *you*?" I asked.

"You only get fifteen minutes. Don't waste it arguing."

Then she grabbed my arm and pulled me across the parking lot. I was too tired to fight her, and even if I'd tried, she'd only have blabbed loudly at me anyway. What was the point?

We sat together on a bench facing the busy street, and I could smell her gummy bearness. With the headache I had going, it made me kind of queasy.

"Our last conversation didn't work out the way I'd planned," she said.

It was weird that she was so calm about it. I'd expected her to go crazy on me for driving off without her. But even when I'd hurried to get past her in the halls at school, the worst she'd done was stick out her tongue.

I raised my voice so she could hear me over the traffic. "Yeah, I'm sure it was a real bummer having to find another ride to school."

"Actually, I drove myself."

"In what?"

She twisted her lips in this guilty-looking way. "My . . . car."

"It was an easy fix, then?"

"Very easy," she said, still making that weird face. "I stuck the key in the ignition and away I went."

"I don't get it."

She put her hands over her face and peeked through her fingers at me. "Don't get mad."

And *that's* when I got it. "You're unbelievable. You actually made up a lie about your car breaking down just so you could come over and tell me that you think my friend—your *boyfriend*—was a loser who deserved to die?"

She was frowning as she dropped her hands. "First of all, I never said that about the car. You assumed. Second, Isaac and I had been broken up for two months when he died. And third, I never said he deserved it."

"So you broke up for a while," I said. "Like that was

anything new. Everyone knew you'd get back together like you always did. Isaac said it was only a matter of time."

"Isaac was wrong."

I stood. "I'm going back to work now."

But before I'd made it two steps, she jumped up, grabbed both my hands, and squeezed so hard it hurt. Her eyes were intense, serious. Pleading, even. "We still have, like, twelve minutes left. There's something I've wanted to say to you and I need to get it out, okay?"

I pulled free from her grasp. "Hurry up, then."

We sat again. She let out a loud breath and started talking quickly. "I know that what I was telling you the other day about Isaac seemed a little harsh. But the only reason I said it is because I was hoping it would help you get some perspective—"

"This is a joke, right? Because I'm about to be pissed if you dragged me out of work to badmouth Isaac some more."

Kendall folded her hands in her lap and calmly said, "I'm trying to explain myself to you. I want us to be able to get past this."

Why she thought *we* needed to be getting past anything was beyond me. "There are things people with decency don't do," I said, focusing on the swaying evergreens beyond the railroad tracks to avoid looking at her. "Like stealing from the church offering plate. Or talking shit about people after they die and then calling it 'getting perspective.'"

"Oh, please. You of all people are indignant about someone robbing the offering plate?"

I wasn't sure what she meant by me "of all people." Because I didn't go to church? Because I was arrested for shoplifting in ninth grade? Either way, why would she even be going there right now?

"What is *wrong* with you?" I asked. "Did you even care about Isaac?"

In that instant Kendall's entire expression changed: eyebrows lowered, mouth turned down, shoulders slumped. She closed her eyes tightly, and when she opened them again, several seconds later, they were bright with tears. "Of course I cared. I *do* care."

"Well, you sure don't act like it."

She started blinking fast. "Seth, I don't know how to do this. I don't know the *right* way to be. I've been dwelling on every single thing that ever happened with Isaac, trying to figure out how I could have helped him, and blaming myself for the fact that the most memorable thing he did with his life was throw it away. It totally just . . . sucks!"

In all the time we'd known each other, I couldn't think of when Kendall had ever said something so honest, so dead-on to what I was feeling.

She went on. "I've been thinking that maybe the only way a person can feel how they want is by acting like they already feel that way. So I'm doing it. I'm pretending like I've moved on. I wish you'd try it too, because I hate seeing you depressed and drunk all the time."

This dealing strategy of hers sounded crazy, but Kendall lying to herself—and to everyone—was easier for me to handle than if she really were just some heartless bitch. "I can't fake nondepression," I said.

She used the back of her hands to wipe under her eyes. "It's easier than you'd think."

I had no idea how to respond to that, so I sat still, stared at the cars, and listened to all the whooshing they made as they passed. For once Kendall didn't push me. In fact, she managed to keep her mouth shut for about two solid minutes before finally saying, "Well?"

"Well, what?"

"Are you still mad at me?"

I shrugged.

"I wish things could be how they were before," she said, tugging on her pigtails. "I mean, you and I have known each other our whole lives. I'm over at your house all the time, so we're still going to be seeing each other. It doesn't even make sense that we can't get past everything."

By "everything," I assumed she was also including the drama she'd caused for all of us with the Isaac/Daniel thing—and, of course, the sex that *we* never should have had.

"It isn't like you've given me much of a chance," I said. "It's only been a week since my show and you keep turning up and being all 'lover' this and 'lover' that. I mean, maybe what happened was no big deal for you, but it's weird for me, okay? I feel like a complete dick."

She dabbed at her eyes with her fingertips and then wiped black makeup splotches onto her skirt. "You do? How come?"

There was no way to say the whole truth—that I'd never wanted her in that way—without pissing her off, so I admitted only part of it: "Because of Isaac."

"Oh." She seemed to consider this for a few seconds. "Okay, well, stop it. Because wherever Isaac is right now, I think he wants you to move on with your life. Isaac wants you to get some and be happy."

"Not with you, he doesn't."

Kendall sighed like I was a lost cause. "Look. I'm not expecting things to turn around instantly for you and me. But can't we try being nonenemies first and see how it goes at least?"

If someone had asked Isaac a question like that, he'd have taken out his Magic 8 Ball and gone with whatever answer floated up to the surface. I didn't have that kind of trust in a plastic toy, so I just shrugged.

Kendall looked at her watch. "Your break's almost over. If you say you'll give me a chance, I'll leave you alone now."

"I'll *think* about it."

To my surprise, she didn't ask for more. "See you soon, nonenemy!"

7:16 P.M.

I'd been waiting about fifteen minutes when my mom came rushing in and set a plate of tacos in front of me. I was at my usual corner table at Good Times, in the back area where no one else sits unless they have to. It's even darker back there than in the rest of the joint, hot air is always blasting down for no good reason, and the view of the TVs is nonexistent, but I like it.

"Still no sign of your brother, huh?" Mom asked.

I shook my head. Jared hadn't picked up when I'd called home, and he wasn't at the storage unit when I dropped by after my shift either. Not that this was anything unusual. For someone who didn't have wheels, a job, or anywhere to be, Jared sure did turn up missing a lot.

"Well, I'm too busy to take a break and eat with you tonight anyway," Mom said, turning to head back to the bar. "If he shows, tell him to just put his order in with the kitchen."

Technically, Jared and I weren't even supposed to be there because Good Times was a tavern and we were both underage—minors could get in for the occasional Friday or Saturday all-ages rock show, and that was *it*—but Mom had been bartending forever and let us in on the sly. I came down for dinner most nights that she worked. Jared dropped in when he wasn't busy doing whatever the hell it was he did.

A couple of minutes later I was eating when Jared came busting through the back door. He threw himself onto the heavy wooden chair across from me, snagged a taco from my plate, and crunched into it, letting lettuce and tomato chunks fall onto the table. "I have news," he said. "Big fucking huge news!"

Jared doesn't get excited often. Not like this. It could only mean one thing. . . .

"I'll give you a hint," he said, grinning. "It starts with a *T*, ends with an *R*, and has *O* and *U* in the middle."

Just like I'd thought. Shit.

He dropped the rest of the stolen taco back onto my plate and stood. "Come on, let's go tell Mom."

"Jared, hold on—"

But he was already on his way to the crowded main area. As I pushed myself up to follow, I had a sinking feeling in my gut. Jared went right up to the bar and stood behind the only empty stool while I squeezed in next to him. When he waved Mom over, she kind of frowned—she doesn't like us mingling with the customers—but headed our way.

"Whatcha doing out here?" she asked, tilting her head.

"Oh, I just wanted you to give a chance to guess who's going on a six-week band tour starting in mid-October," Jared said.

I think he was aiming for casual, but he blew it by breaking into a smile so big, his face looked like it was going to split in half.

Mom gasped. "*You*?"

"Yup," he said. "I was just with Owen from the Rat

Rodders. The Real McCoys—or whatever our new name is going to be—is now on the bill to open for them on their tour. They've got a ton of back-to-back shows lined up all over the U. S. of A. It's going to be *in*sane!"

Mom started squealing. "Oh my God! Baby, that's *great*." She came running around from behind the bar and threw her arms around Jared's neck. Then she did the same to me. "I'm so proud of both of you," she said, jumping up and down. "I mean, wow! Can you *believe* it?"

Honestly, I couldn't believe it and didn't *want* to believe it. But I couldn't make myself say so. I couldn't even open my mouth. All I was capable of was standing there, thinking dizzying, nauseating thoughts and feeling like I was going to pass out.

October? Back-to-back shows for six weeks?

It was impossible. *Impossible.*

"I told you, Ma," Jared said, still grinning. "I told you I could make this happen."

Mom reached up to try to mess with his hair, even though it never budges with all the crap he uses in it. "I never doubted you for a second."

She hadn't, either. Last year Jared got fired from three jobs in a row for (1) showing up late all the time; (2) stealing; and (3) getting high during his break, so Mom ended up having to pay for everything when he was arrested for drunk driving. His attorney fees and court fines pretty much cleaned her out, but she never got on his case too much over it. He promised he'd pay her back when he started making money from his music. And now it actually looked like it could happen.

Except . . . *I* couldn't go on tour.

All the people sitting around the bar and the tables were drinking their beers and fixing their gazes on us instead of the three big TVs overhead. Mom clapped her hands and announced, "Hey, everyone! I just found out my babies are taking their music on the road for a band tour next month!"

There was applause all around, and a few guys even got out of their seats to congratulate us.

This *was* big news. Huge. Just like Jared had said.

"You know, that's really something," old Bob said, breathing his stale cigarette breath in my face while he yelled to be heard over everyone. "Anita here looks young enough to be your sister, and *you* look young enough to still be in school."

Mom had Jared when she was sixteen and me a little more than two years after that. She's thirty-five, but she can pass for about twenty-five. I'm lucky to only get the little brother thing; Jared sometimes has to put with up with people thinking Mom's his girlfriend.

Some other guy shook my hand while his girlfriend or wife patted my arm. Bob kept talking—to me or to himself, I couldn't tell. "Folks sometimes wait their whole lives for a bunch of nothing to happen, but you kids are off to a jumping start with *something*."

I watched Jared under the dim lighting. He was eating

up the attention and smiling like this was one of his coolest moments ever. It should have been like that for me, too, but it wasn't. My stomach was going crazy and I could hardly breathe.

"I'll be right back," I said.

Then I moved past everyone to get to the bathroom, and locked myself in.

SATURDAY, **SEPTEMBER 11**

12:23 P.M.

I was in the fancy three-floor bookstore on the Hill, with a magazine open on my lap and a whole pile of others next to me. But I wasn't reading; I was hiding out in what was probably the last place anyone would look for me.

The no-drinking thing was finally feeling decent—I'd gotten some sleep, I was eating normally again, and my head had stopped throbbing and feeling cloudy—but everything else was sucking.

No one wanted to shut up about the band tour. Jared, Mikey, and Daniel kept talking about how this was by far the best thing ever to come our way. A chance to see more states than just Washington, Oregon, and Idaho! Great exposure! Fun, fun, fun!

Blah, blah, blah.

All of us understood that we probably wouldn't become rich and famous from it—except for Daniel, who was taking *his* optimism to the max. There was a chance we wouldn't break even, since opening bands aren't always paid a guaranteed amount. But we all knew it was an amazing opportunity anyway.

I should have been as excited as hell—I *wanted* to be—but deep down I knew I wasn't going to be a part of it. Maybe it could have worked if the tour had come up during summer vacation. Or if my brother and I could be trapped in a van together for forty-five days without killing each other. Or if I was capable of getting my ass onstage. Or if Isaac was going too. But this wasn't going to work. And if *I* bagged, the whole band would have to.

A loud voice interrupted my thoughts. "I'm crazy sick of my hair," she was saying. "It just, like, *hangs* there looking totally hideous."

When I glanced up, I saw that Vicki Lancaster and Riley were heading my way and carrying their own stacks of magazines.

"You don't look hideous," Riley said, taking a seat on the couch across from mine.

Vicki plopped down beside her. "I think I'll cut it all off." She slouched and pouted like she was having the worst day of her life. "Or I'll dye it black. I don't know. I hate it."

Then they both seemed to notice me at the same time.

Riley smiled; Vicki scowled and stood up. "Let's sit somewhere else."

Riley grabbed Vicki's arm and pulled her back down. "No, this is fine."

She was still smiling at me, but now she looked kind of embarrassed. I couldn't guess what she was up to. We'd decided not give each other shit in class, but we'd never said anything about extending our peace agreement to bookstore couches with Vicki. I still wasn't over that thing she'd said about Isaac at Pete's party; I'd never get over it.

I gave Riley a nod and focused on the *Bass Player* magazine I was holding. It seemed as good a time as any to turn past page four. I had more important things on my mind than Vicki's hair. Like how exactly I was going to get out of this tour.

"I didn't know that stoner knew how to read," Vicki stage-whispered. "Or is he only looking at the pictures?"

I didn't give her the satisfaction of glancing up.

"*We* should be looking at pictures," Riley said. "Your appointment is in less than thirty minutes, so let's see if we can find a cut you like. How short do you want to go?"

"I don't know. Like, my shoulders? Or chin? Or somewhere in between?"

I kept my eyes on my own magazine and tried to pretend the girls weren't there. It wasn't easy; Vicki's voice could carry across the entire town. Plus, I could feel Riley watching me.

So the band tour. Everyone was stoked about it, talking like it was a done deal. It was obvious that Jared expected me to drop out of school like him and Daniel. And while that wasn't an idea Mom had been thrilled about, she didn't seem to think it was the end of the world, either. I wasn't going to do it, though. And I couldn't just take off and miss a month and a half of classes; that would set me back so far I'd never catch up, never graduate.

A booming voice pulled me out of my thoughts again. "There you are! I thought I saw you come up here."

Riley and Vicki turned their heads toward Carr Goodwin, who was now behind their couch.

"Hi, Rosetta," Carr said, grinning down at Riley.

I was confused about why he'd called her that, but then I realized it must be her real name—the one she'd said had come from a romance novel. *Rosetta*. It wasn't prissy-sounding like she'd made it out to be. I thought it was pretty. Like her.

Vicki smacked Carr with her magazine. "Now you're supposed to say, 'Hi, *Vicki*.'"

Carr laughed, and I could have sworn he was trying to be an American James Bond or something. Such a phony fuck. "Hi, Vicki. And what are you lovely ladies up to today?"

He hadn't looked at me once—I wasn't looking straight at him, either—but I knew he'd seen me. I also knew that neither of us would say or do anything if the other didn't start something first. Sober, we're both pretty low-key.

I mean, a musician and a school politician. Could we be *any* less badass?

Still standing, Carr massaged Rosetta's shoulders all casual, like he was just being his friendly vice-president self. I had a hunch, though, that he was seriously perving on her. Rosetta wriggled out of Carr's grasp like she got that same feeling. "Vicki's getting her hair cut in a few minutes," she said, holding out a magazine. "You want to help us decide on a style?"

"Sure!" He said it like he'd been waiting all year for this, walked around the couch, and squished in next to Rosetta. Then, grabbing a small section of her hair, he twisted it around his finger. "You aren't cutting yours off too, are you?"

Rosetta watched her hair in Carr's hand with her eyes slightly narrowed. "No."

"Good." He let go, and the long, black strands unraveled and fell back in place.

I thought about moving to get away from them, but I'd been here first. I wasn't going to let them run me off . . . or keep distracting me from my problem. Which, I realized then, could be solved if the guys found a new bass player to take on the road. One who wasn't closely related to the lead singer/dictator. One who was out of school. One who was into the rockabilly scene. One who didn't have incapacitating stage fright.

Vicki was still yammering while I tried to think of someone who could take my place. No one was coming to mind. What Jared said was kind of true: good bass players can be tough to find because most dudes take up guitar instead to get all the glory, solos, and chicks.

There was movement across from me as Vicki and Carr got up.

"Thanks for the help," Vicki said, running her fingers through her hair. "Hopefully, the next time you see me I won't look like such a freak."

Rosetta laughed. "You don't look like a freak!"

Carr reached for Rosetta's hand. "How about joining me for lunch at the golf course?"

She smiled up at him but left him hanging. "No thanks. I have something to do this afternoon."

"Like what?" he asked.

"Just stuff for school."

"You're always so mysterious," Vicki said. "What are you up to?"

"It's *nothing*," Rosetta insisted. "You two go do your things. I'll see you later."

Carr looked like he wanted to keep bugging her, but Vicki pulled him to the escalator.

The second they were gone, Rosetta jumped up from her own couch and sat next to me. "I wonder who has it worse," she said. "Kids who are forced to move a lot growing up, or the ones who are stuck around all the same kids their whole lives?"

It was an off-the-wall thing to say, but I was getting the idea that this was how she usually started conversations.

"I have no clue," I said.

"Me neither. I've never liked moving or having to make all new friends. But I'm noticing that people who go from elementary school to middle school to high school with the same kids never get a chance to start over. Like, maybe a certain guy will always be seen as a troublemaker, while some new girl can move to town and be accepted because no one knows her. It doesn't seem fair."

After dealing with Kendall's lies—or *omissions*, as she would call them—for so many years, Rosetta's openness blew me away.

"If you're wondering if I'm jealous that you're in with Vicki and Carr, the answer is no," I said. "I figured out a long time ago that they're not worth my time."

Rosetta blushed. "Oh. I was speaking purely hypothetically, obviously."

"Obviously," I said.

So much for her being open.

We sat in a silence that can only be described as uncomfortable. Rosetta chewed her bottom lip and watched the couch cushion between us like she was worried it was going to come to life and attack her. I flipped the magazine to a random page to keep up with my fake reading.

"Do you want to go to the café downstairs?" she asked. "Maybe get some hot chocolate?"

I had no doubt that she was talking to me, but I looked over my shoulder anyway to see if someone was watching, if this was some kind of joke. "Hot chocolate?"

She smiled. "Oh, don't even try to convince me that you're a coffee drinker. You and me? We're nonconformists. And as nonconformists we don't give in to the Washington State coffee obsession. Right?"

She didn't look like much of a nonconformist in her pale blue shirt and khaki slacks; in fact, she looked like every prep I'd ever seen. But there *was* something about her, something not quite like the rest of them.

"I thought you had important school stuff to do," I said.

"Exactly. That's why I need your help."

12:54 P.M.

There were four mugs on the table in front of us for the taste tests Rosetta wanted to do. Two had black coffee and two had hot chocolate covered with three-inch-high piles of whipped cream. As I grabbed my cocoa, chocolate ran down my hand. "This makes me feel like a five-year-old," I said, licking it off. "If I ordered a sandwich at this place, do you think they'd cut the crusts off?"

Rosetta used her spoon to scoop a big bite of whipped cream. "Don't be so stuck-up."

It was too funny having a chick from Rich Bitch Hill calling *me* stuck-up, but I didn't mention it. Instead, I took a swallow of the super-sugary drink, which scalded my tongue and the roof of my mouth. I was going to be regretting that move for days. "What do you have against coffee, anyway?"

"Nothing, really," Rosetta said. "Except it's gross."

"Have you given it a chance? Because, yeah, at first coffee's disgusting. But if you make yourself get through a few cups, you'll start to realize it isn't so bad. And then, next thing you know, you'll be craving the stuff."

Only then did I realize that Isaac had described beer in almost that same way in seventh grade.

"I'll be testing your little theory very soon," Rosetta said. "But first I have to ask the thing I've been psyching myself up for since I saw you today. Will you do the 'secrets' assignment with me?"

At the end of IC class on Friday, Mrs. Dalloway had announced that our weekend homework was to go outside our comfort zones and tell someone a secret. Then we were supposed to write about how we felt after the big breakthrough.

I shrugged. "I was kind of planning to invent a conversation to put in my journal for that one."

"Come *on*, now, Dick," Rosetta said in a chipper, Mrs. Dalloway-ish voice. "You don't want to deny yourself the chance to communicate interpersonally and reveal your darkest secrets! I'll tell you mine if you tell me yours."

I got a nervous twinge in my stomach. "You don't have to do this with me just because we're both in the class. Mrs. D. said we could tell our secret to anyone." I pointed to an old guy sitting a few tables away. "You can tell *him* if you want."

Rosetta laughed. "I don't even know that man. Besides, I was thinking you'd be a good choice since you have to do this assignment too."

"Why? So we can blackmail each other?"

She smirked. "*May*be."

As much as I didn't feel like spilling my guts, I *was* curious about what kind of big, dirty secret she had that she'd rather tell me than of one of her friends. "You first," I said.

"Okay." She pushed her hair behind her ears. "No one at school knows this, but I haven't ridden in a car since I moved here over six months ago. The therapist I was seeing diagnosed me with motorphobia, which is the fear of motor vehicles."

Therapist? So the pretty, rich girl was a mental case. I hadn't seen *that* coming. And I also couldn't wrap my head around motorphobia. Fear of heights, crowds, even spiders I could understand. But motor vehicles? It sounded like something made up.

Then I realized she probably *was* making it up, doing that whole persona thing. Which was a relief because now I didn't have to tell her anything real either.

I laughed. "That's a good one. Now I can see why you were so mad at me on the first day of school. The thing that scares you the most was trying to mow you down at the crosswalk."

She picked up her hot chocolate and took a sip. "My

fear of being run over is usually pretty minimal," she said slowly. "My real panic about cars comes when I try to get inside them. *That's* why I didn't accept a ride from you."

Okay, so she wasn't laughing with me here. She was kind of frowning, actually, and looking like she was regretting starting this whole conversation. Which was making me think she *hadn't* been kidding.

"So what happens if you try to get in a car?" I asked, trying to play off that I'd been making fun of her real-life freaky phobia.

She looked suspicious, but went on. "I get these uncontrollable feelings where I can't breathe and my heart beats like it's going to explode. And for an even *more* fun time, sometimes I'll start sweating and shaking and feeling like I'm going to throw up."

Intense. And yet . . . familiar. Like me thinking about getting onstage.

"Can you be cured?" I asked.

"I don't know. My shrink said I could. But he was making things worse, so I quit going to him. Since then I've been walking everywhere and avoiding all motorized modes of transportation. Seems to be working out fine."

I couldn't imagine living like that. From home to school to work and back home again would add up to more than five miles a day for me. "You said nobody knows about your motorphobia. But what about when you're out with your friends?"

She shrugged. "It's pretty easy. I meet them wherever we're going and then say that my uncle's picking me up so they don't expect to drive me home. I do whatever I can to keep anyone from noticing."

"Wow." It was all I could think to say. She hardly knew me, and a few days before, she hadn't even *liked* me. But now she'd told me something—on purpose—that she was keeping from her friends, from everyone.

"Well, this has been embarrassing," Rosetta said brightly. "But liberating nonetheless."

"Sorry about that."

She shook her head. "No, it's okay. Now you tell me your secret while I try to choke this down." Then, instead of drinking from the cup like a normal person, she sipped coffee from her spoon and made a face like a little kid being forced to take cough syrup. "This is *not* good," she said, shaking the spoon at me.

The coffee was terrible. It tasted like it had been sitting for a week, which actually made her reaction truer and her taste test less accurate than she knew. She was cracking me up with all the weird faces.

"Keep drinking. You're going to love it by the time you finish," I said.

She wrinkled her nose and kept loading her spoon up while I tried to decide on a secret to tell her. There was one thing I didn't ever discuss, but I was feeling like maybe I could talk about it with her. Maybe I even wanted to. And I did feel like I owed her something real after laughing at her.

"I have a phobia too," I said. "I'm in a band and I've played probably over twenty live gigs, but I have stage fright. Like, bad. I mean, maybe not quite as bad as your car thing, but still. It's crazy."

She gave me a small smile and I imagined that she was thinking: *My phobia is* so *much worse than* your *silly phobia*. Then she said, "It sounds like you're working around it if you've played onstage over twenty times."

"Yeah, well, my friend Isaac had these pregig rituals that would get my mind off things and make me feel ready to play," I said, purposely leaving out the part about how those "rituals" usually including sitting in a car with the stereo blaring, passing Isaac's flask back and forth until it was empty, and swallowing a pill or two. "He died over the summer, and about a week ago, I had to play my first gig without him. It was so bad, I don't think I can put myself through it ever again."

Rosetta nodded, and I could tell she totally got it. "I used to see your friend around sometimes," she said. "But I didn't know him at all."

"We started hanging out when we were twelve. He played guitar and I play bass and we ended up joining my brother's band together." That same queasy feeling I got whenever I remembered what happened to Isaac was kicking in, but I needed to tell her the rest. She was the first person I'd actually *wanted* to talk about it with. "In July there was this one night when we both got pretty wasted. When I went inside for bed, he said he was just going to crash out under the stars. The next morning I found his body under a rosebush in my front yard. I was the last person to see him alive and the first to see him dead."

Rosetta was biting her lip; gnawing it, actually. "I think I know what that felt like for you."

I couldn't guess how she could know anything about it, but she was looking at me like she did understand, like she wanted to help.

"Was it alcohol poisoning?" she asked.

I took a big gulp of coffee. "No. And it wasn't a drug overdose either. The official cause of death was asphyxiation. He was on his back and threw up while he was unconscious. So, basically, he drowned on his own puke."

"Oh!" She stared at me so intently that I had to look away. "That must have been *horrible* for you."

Horrible. Yes.

"If I'd thought to go out and check on him, if I'd made sure he was lying on his side or his stomach, he'd probably be alive right now," I said.

Rosetta reached across the table and squeezed my hand. "It isn't your fault."

I didn't want her to let me off the hook. "I screwed up and now he's dead."

"You didn't know it was going to happen like that. You couldn't have guessed."

No, I couldn't have. But still, I couldn't shake the feeling that somehow I *should* have.

I waited for Rosetta to say something else, but she seemed to be waiting for me. Finally she squeezed my hand one more time and let go.

MONDAY, **SEPTEMBER 13**

7:24 A.M.

Two days later. My tutoring had been canceled for the morning, so I should have been able to take my time before school. Instead, Jared and Daniel had come stumbling home in time to rope me into dropping them off at Denny's for breakfast.

Jared was spacing out in the front seat. Daniel was talkative as hell in the back. And me? I was driving along, having mad beer cravings from smelling it on their breath. Their *breath*, for Christ's sake.

"I have to get me one of those scrambled-egg sandwiches," Daniel said. "What do they call that shit again?"

I wasn't in the mood, but I played along. "Moons Over My Hammy."

Daniel started howling, and even though it wasn't

funny to me, I got why it was to him. There's nothing more hilarious than someone saying "Moons Over My Hammy" when you're drunk, stoned, or sleep-deprived; Daniel was all three.

"Where were you guys last night?" I asked.

I didn't want to know what I'd missed. Except, for some weird reason, I *needed* to know.

"Out at CJ's," Daniel said, scooting all the way forward so that his face was between Jared and me.

I rolled down my window to breathe some nonbeer air while Daniel put his arms around our seats and started shaking us. "We were celebrating like the rock stars we will soon become!"

"Chill, dude," Jared said.

"Yeah, sit down." I nudged Daniel's chest with my elbow. "And put your seatbelt on before a cop shows up and gives you a ticket."

All Daniel's talk about becoming rock stars was adding to my guilt. I was still stressed over how to tell them I wasn't going on tour. Knowing that *I* was going to be the one to kill Daniel's good mood wasn't making it easier.

"Goddamn seatbelt laws," Daniel said. But he scooted back and put it on anyway. It was a good thing, too, because a police car came swinging around in the rearview mirror less than a minute later.

"Shit," I said.

Jared startled upright. "What?"

"Cop!" My heart was kicking up to high speed already.

Jared sighed. "Swear to God, you're killing me with this cop-scare bullshit."

You'd think he'd have taken this seriously. I mean, if he'd been more careful back when he still had his license, he wouldn't have been relying on his little brother to drive him around in his own car.

"Do you think they're after me?" I asked.

Daniel laughed. "I think you have bad karma, Dick. Get it? Karma sounds like 'car.' Cops stalk you because of your *car*-ma—"

"Yeah, I get it."

Drunk Daniel was kind of annoying when I was dead sober.

"You're not breaking any laws, bro," Jared said. "Calm down."

I probably *was* breaking laws. Laws I didn't even know existed. Not to mention the things my passengers were up to. But I couldn't get busted for what they were doing, could I? Unless I got pulled over, they stashed their stuff somewhere, and then the car got searched.

Okay. Jared was right; this paranoia was getting out of hand.

"Hey, check it out," Jared said. "The speedo's working."

I looked away from my mirrors to sneak a glance at the dash. Sure enough, the speed gauge was up.

"How fast are we going?" Daniel asked.

Jared said, "Looks like twenty-seven. Twenty-eight."

"Dick, I *told* you!" Daniel said. "You're going almost ten under the speed limit. No wonder you've always got pigs after you."

I hit the gas, annoyed that he might have been right. "You know, this might not be about my driving at all. Maybe there's a warrant out for your arrest or something."

"Ri-ight," Daniel said, laughing. "You really don't know much about the cops in this town if you think they'd just follow us around if they had a warrant." Then he turned around and yelled, "You looking for me, piggy?"

"What the hell are you doing?" I asked.

Daniel kept it up. "You want me, you come and *arrest* my ass!"

I had to stop him before he did something insane. It's all fun and games until your friend riles up the cops, right? I flipped my blinker on and yielded for a left at the next light.

Seconds later the cop breezed on by in the right lane like he hadn't even noticed we were there.

Daniel busted up laughing again.

"New theory, Seth," Jared said. "Cops are always driving on the same roads as you because they don't have a lot of other roads to choose from."

"Whatever."

We were close enough to see the Denny's sign by now. Daniel started singing in falsetto: "I need your moons over my hammy, baby. Moons over my hammy toniiiiiight!"

Then he took off his seatbelt again, lunged forward, jerked the wheel, and steered us toward a curb, then a utility pole, and then oncoming traffic.

"Will you fucking *stop*?" I yelled.

Jared shoved Daniel back so I could get control again. But not long after, the ride went from feeling like smooth sailing to 4x4ing through the Grand Canyon. With all the bouncing and shaking and lurching, I had a tough time turning into the restaurant parking lot.

"What just happened?" Jared asked.

"Hell if I know," I said, bringing the car to a crooked stop across three spaces.

The problem was obvious as soon as I jumped out of the car. The rear passenger-side tire was not just flat; it was completely shredded. This wasn't going to be another one of those quickie patch jobs at the tire place. I was going to need to come up with cash for a new one; there was no getting around it. In the meantime, I wasn't going anywhere until I threw the spare on. So much for keeping up with my school-on-time-every-day streak.

"What'd you hit?" Daniel asked as he fell out of the car. Jared helped him up and closed the door.

"I have no clue." I unlocked the trunk to pull out the tools and trusty doughnut spare. "I was too busy trying *not* to hit anything to notice."

Jared shook his head and looked at me like I was the biggest loser on the planet. Like this was somehow *my* fault.

Like he hadn't been sitting right next to me when Daniel commandeered the wheel.

For the next minute or so I loosened the lug nuts while Jared and Daniel waited around being as unhelpful as possible. Bastards.

"You're taking great care of my car," Jared said. "The tires are balder than eagles."

Right. Because he'd had them in *such* pristine condition that they must have gone bad on my watch. I glared up at him, but was he too busy pulling a pack of smokes from his jacket to notice. He lit two and passed one to Daniel.

"Maybe we can head in and you can fix this later," Daniel said. "I'm starving."

I dropped the tire iron and started jacking up the back. "Go ahead. I told you, I'm not staying. I have school. Which is where I'd be right *now* if I'd left your asses at home."

"Nah," Jared said. "That tire would have gone bad no matter what. You'd be doing the same thing you're doing now, only on the other side of town."

"And you wouldn't have the pleasure of our company," Daniel added.

I flipped him off, which made them both crack up.

"Hey, when did you start caring about school, anyway?" Jared asked. "You trying to impress some chick?"

In the world according to Jared and Daniel, getting into a girl's pants is the only reason for doing anything.

"No," I said. But for some reason, I thought of Rosetta for a second.

"Then why even go?" Daniel asked. "We're leaving in a few weeks and this shit won't matter ever again."

Okay. I had to deal with this. I had to tell them. It was time.

I stood up. "I'm not dropping out of school to tour with you."

"How's that going to work?" Jared asked, blowing smoke toward me. "You planning to do all your homework on the road?"

Daniel shook his head, flicked his ash. "I don't think they actually let you come back if you miss that many days. Unless you were in the hospital or something."

They weren't getting it.

"No, I mean I'm not dropping out because I'm not going on tour."

That shut them both right up.

Jared said, "Is this a joke?" at the same time that Daniel asked, "Are you kidding?"

"No," I said, in answer to both of them.

Daniel stood there with his eyes wide open, looking like he'd been shocked into silence, but Jared picked up the slack by yelling so loudly that people could probably hear him inside the restaurant and the grocery store across the parking lot. "What the hell are we supposed to do without you?"

I opened my mouth to answer, even though I didn't exactly have an answer. But it wouldn't have mattered anyway, because my brother wasn't in the mood to let me get a word in. "Something good actually came our way for once, and you're bailing?" he shouted, throwing down his less-than-half-smoked cigarette. He ran his hands over his messy, greasy hair. "And you wait to tell me until after I've already committed to doing this tour? I can't fucking believe you, Seth! I mean, *what*? We're supposed to cancel because you're in love with school all of a sudden?"

"You have over a month," I said. "That's enough time to find someone to replace me."

"Sure," he said, glaring. "You think we're going to find someone who plays well, who can learn all our songs, *and* who is going to be able to tour with this short notice? The only reason I put up with you in the first place is because I couldn't find a decent bassist who wouldn't flake out. Look where that got me."

"I'm sorry."

And I was. Not enough to change my mind. But still, I knew how much this sucked for him. For them. I really did hate that it was because of me they were high and dry.

"Whatever," Jared said, shaking his head.

He stomped toward the restaurant without looking back. Daniel gave me a pissed-off/confused/stoned look and stumbled after him.

Algebra was well under way when I got to school. I grabbed a late pass from the office, but I decided to wait the fifteen minutes for the bell to ring before seeing about turning in homework and getting my next assignment. I'd get hassled by the teacher for skipping, but at least I wouldn't have to deal with it in front of all the freshmen.

The halls were empty. I ducked into the stairwell where Isaac and I used to go whenever we felt like ditching. It was a great spot because the stairs partially covered an area near the heater, so no one knew we were there, but we could still see them. It was depressing to be there without Isaac, to remember that we'd never hang out there together again. Just like we'd never again hit the McDonald's drive-thru at 3 a.m., go camping on the coast, or float down the river on inner tubes.

As I leaned into the corner, I heard the echo of footsteps and loud breathing. I wasn't alone.

I poked my head out and saw a girl against the railing, holding on with both hands. Her head was down, so I couldn't see her face, but I could tell she was Rosetta from her long, black hair. It was the first time I'd seen her since we talked about our secrets stuff at the coffee place two days ago. I hadn't realized until that moment how much I'd been looking forward to talking with her again.

But now her body was shaking from her shoulders down, like half her bones were missing. It wasn't loud breathing I'd heard before; it was uncontrollable sobbing and gasping.

I couldn't even begin to guess what would make her cry like that. Physical pain? Or maybe someone had died. What would I know about it? I'd cried more when I found Daniel *not* dead than when I'd found Isaac.

It was obvious that she'd left whatever class she was supposed to be in for a good and upsetting reason. She probably didn't want me of all people to get in her face about it. She probably wanted her privacy. Still, chances like this didn't come up all the time. I could go over there, put my arm around her, let her get her tears all over my shirt.

On second thought . . .

I grabbed the Magic 8 Ball hanging from my belt loop and asked it telepathically if using the fact that Rosetta was having a bad day as an excuse to touch her made me a bigger asshole than Carr.

It is decidedly so.

I asked if I should do it anyway.

My reply is no.

The 8 ball was right. I was useless at emotions and crap anyway; I'd probably make things worse. Hopefully, she'd be calmed down by the end of the day and we could talk in IC.

I leaned against the wall to stay hidden and felt like a total bastard as I listened to her sobs getting quieter over the next few minutes until they faded to silence. I checked to see if she'd left, and she was still at the railing with her eyes closed and her face screwed up like she was in pain. That type of violent crying would do a number on anyone. Then she wiped her eyes, took a hair band off her wrist, pulled her hair into a ponytail, and let out a few loud breaths before turning to go.

As I watched her walk away, all I could think was that Rosetta's ugly cry-face was somehow the most beautiful I'd ever seen.

2:40 P.M.

Alex/Xander and I were supposed to be building our empathy skills together. Mrs. D. had said empathy was going to change our interactions in so many unbelievable ways. She made it sound like our lives would become magical if we were able to listen and *feel* what another person is feeling.

Everyone else in class was working in groups of three, but Riley/Rosetta was a no-show so the numbers were off and Xander and I were stuck on beanbags in the corner on our own. We'd been at it for ten minutes, making junk up, trying to "understand," "ask questions," and "paraphrase" to become active, empathetic listeners or whatever. With still another ten minutes to go of this torture, all Xander and I had mastered so far was sounding like complete tools, and my mood was getting worse and worse.

I'd had a sick anxiety all day about what was going to

happen when I got home. Jared and Daniel were pissed at me for quitting the band, and Mikey was going to be too.

Xander turned the pages of his textbook in his lap, searching for tips on the crap we were supposed to be discussing. "On page twenty-two it says that we shouldn't be discouraged if this feels uncomfortable and awkward. The more we practice, the better we'll get at it."

I couldn't have cared less about this shit, but he wouldn't give up. The dude was *out* of control. "I'm not feeling it," I said, slamming my own book shut and dropping it on the floor next to me. "These fake conversations are the worst."

"Maybe we shouldn't use them," he said, pushing his hair out of his eyes. "Maybe if we talk about regular stuff, it will come up naturally."

"Whatever."

He closed his book too. "So. What's been new with you lately, Dick?"

Like he had any idea what was *old* with me.

"Nothing, *Alex*," I said.

"Did you have a good summer?"

"No."

He laughed and rubbed his hands together. "All right. What didn't you like about your summer?"

He did *not* just ask that.

"A few things," I said. "You know, too much rain, not enough sun. Food poisoning at the Fourth of July barbecue. Oh, and my best friend, you know, *died*."

He turned red and looked away. "Sorry. I wasn't thinking."

Even though he'd brought that on himself, I felt like kind of a jerk anyway. Why did he have to be so goddamn cheerful and talkative all the time?

I looked around at the other groups. As always, they all seemed to be getting shit done. I was starting to think it wasn't a coincidence that whatever group I ended up in was lame. Maybe *I* was lame. Of course, now that Rosetta had stopped hating me, we'd probably be decent at this. If only she'd shown up.

"Have you seen Riley today?" I asked Xander.

"I have physics with her," he said, all perked up again. Things sure did roll off his back easily. "I'm pretty sure she was there this morning, so I don't know why she isn't here now."

"Is your physics during first period?" I asked.

He nodded.

That explained it, then. Sort of. She must have left physics to cry. And then what? Went home?

"I guess we can forget empathy and talk about whatever we want for the last five minutes," Xander said, glancing at the clock. "I was wondering, does your band have any gigs coming up? I had fun at your last one."

"Actually, we were supposed to be going on a six-week tour with the Rat Rodders next month." I sounded like I was bragging. Maybe I kind of was. "But I quit the band this morning and things are up in the air."

"Why'd you quit?" He frowned. "I mean, if you don't mind talking about it."

I didn't mind. So I gave him the lowdown. Well, the low-down about not wanting to drop out of school.

He nodded like he was working out how to turn this conversation into another empathy exercise, but all he ended up saying when I was done was "Bummer."

It was almost disappointing.

"What are they going to do about the tour?" Xander asked. "Take another bassist in your place?"

"That's the plan, I think. If they can find one in time."

The bell rang then. We grabbed our stuff. Got off our beanbags. No more need to talk to each other today.

But as we were standing there putting our bags over our shoulders, I said, "Hey, Xan—I mean, Alex. Sorry for, you know, how I was being before."

He smiled. "It was my fault." Then he pointed at my DICK tag. "And anyway, you give fair warning."

3:17 P.M.

After class I was feeling kind of worried and guilty for not saying something to Rosetta in the stairwell. Spotting Vicki walking past, I realized that she was my best shot at learning where to find Rosetta. I also realized that it was like having no shot at all; she wasn't going to tell me anything.

Maybe I was starting to lose it, but I decided to try

the Magic 8 Ball again. "Should I even bother asking for Vicki's help?"

The answer was as simple as they come: *Yes.*

I hurried to catch up.

"How's it going, Vicki?" I asked, putting on a huge a smile as I'm capable of so she might forget for a second that we couldn't stand each other.

She continued walking without a word.

I kept up with her. "Can you tell me where to find Rosetta?"

Vicki stopped suddenly and turned her head so fast, her blond hair—now in kind of an angled cut—swung in front of her face before falling back where it belonged. "Hmm. Let me think." She tapped her chin with her fingertip for a second. "Hell. *No.*"

Then she started almost sprinting to get away from me.

"It's really important," I said, speeding up to follow. "We're working on a project together. For a class."

Not entirely true, but Vicki would never know.

"That's a good one. You doing a school project is the best joke I've heard today."

Her little jabs were getting so old.

"I'll bite. What's with all the hostility?" I asked as she pushed open the glass door that leads to the parking lot.

She let go once she was through so I had to catch it quickly before it slammed into me. Then she laughed—one of those mean laughs like a crazy cartoon villain's. "I've changed my mind. You playing innocent is an even better joke."

We'd never gotten along, but I couldn't think of any specific thing I'd done to her to make her act like this. Was I supposed to know what her problem was?

"Quit looking so clueless," she said before I'd said a word. "I told you I'd never forgive you for what you did to me on Halloween and I meant it."

Halloween?

Wait . . .

I chased her down the stairs. "Wasn't that in sixth grade?"

"Seventh," she said over her shoulder. "But I still wouldn't forgive you even if it had happened in kindergarten. You and your rotten eggs ruined my night and my princess costume."

We were at the edge of the parking lot now and she still wasn't slowing down. Couldn't she stay in one place for a minute?

"It was an accident," I insisted.

"Like I'm going to believe that."

Okay, she was right; it had been no accident. Isaac and I had sure gotten a good laugh over it at the time. The shocked look on Vicki's face as she got pelted six times—once on the back of the head and five on her frilly pink dress—had made it even better. We had some seriously good aim. And, yeah, looking back, it was kind of jerky, I guess. But isn't that what you're supposed to do on Halloween? Eat candy all day, play some tricks, bust shit up, ruin things for the kids who have everything that you don't have?

"You really aren't over that?" I asked. "It's been four years."

"Wow! You can count that high?"

Talk about bitchy. Getting Rosetta's location out of Vicki was going to be way more work than I wanted to put in. Time to walk away, right? I didn't need this bullshit. But then I remembered Rosetta's cry-face and I decided I would give it one more try. With empathy this time. It sure couldn't hurt.

Step one: Consider how *I* would feel.

That was pretty easy to figure out. I think it would suck to get blasted with rotten eggs.

Step two: Ask questions to better understand.

"You thought it sucked having rotten eggs thrown at you, right?" I asked.

Vicki stopped her minijog and turned to me with her hands on her hips and rage all over her face. "Are you *threatening* me, Seth McCoy?"

"No, I'm asking you a question."

"Yes, it sucked," she said, still scowling. "Duh."

That wasn't enough to work with, and since I didn't know what to ask next, I tried Mrs. D.'s favorite question: "How did it make you feel?"

She held out the tiny remote on her keychain and pressed a button. The headlights flashed on a silver BMW right in front of us. "It made me feel like you're a dickhead."

All righty, then. Enough questions.

Step three: Summarize the information.

"So it sucked," I said, feeling like an idiot. "And you felt like I was a dickhead."

Vicki gestured impatiently. "Hasn't this been well established by now?"

She was right about that. I'd have to make sure to ask more probing questions if I ever tried this again.

Step four: Summarize how I think she's feeling about the information.

This was the hardest part—trying to put myself in Vicki's place—but probably the most important. "So I think what you're feeling is that the Halloween egg thing was embarrassing." I tried to see her face to guess if I was getting it right, but she had turned to open the Beemer's driver's-side door. "And it was probably pretty gross?"

She threw her bag inside without a word or a look my way.

"And you feel like I was a dickhead because I wasn't sorry about it. Is that right?"

She turned then, with her super-skinny eyebrows raised high. "You are such an *ass*."

"Look," I said. "I'm trying to, you know, feel what you feel or whatever. Can't you just work with me?"

In answer, she got in the car, slammed the door, and started the engine.

What a waste of time this had turned out to be. Fuck empathy. Seriously.

I headed across the lot and was almost to the Mustang when Vicki rolled up beside me. "Rosetta plays golf at the country club almost every day," she said, peering out at me over the top of her sunglasses. "She's probably there."

I could have fallen over from the shock of Vicki Lancaster doing something decent for once, but I didn't let on. "I've never been there. Will she be on the grass stuff?"

"Yeah, the *grass stuff*, Seth. Park at the pro shop and then head out to the course. You'll find her if you walk around for a while."

"Cool. Thanks for helping me."

That had worked out pretty sweet in the end. If using empathy could get someone like her to chill, maybe Mrs. Dalloway was really on to something here.

"Actually, I'm not helping *you*," Vicki said. "I just don't want Rosetta to get a bad grade on her project."

Or maybe not.

3:29 P.M.

After driving through a winding tunnel of trees to the good old Rich Bitch Hill Golf and Country Club, I spotted the pro shop sign. I bypassed the circular drive and parked in the adjoining lot between a BMW and a Mercedes; you know, your *standard* rich-folk modes of transport. There were plenty of even nicer cars around, though, and I recognized at least half from having washed and detailed them.

I got out and stood next to the Mustang, looking around. There was a lot to take in: grass everywhere—green and bright like it had been spray-painted—and all these ponds, fountains, and white buildings so fancy they looked like they belonged on postcards or something. I'd driven past this golf course tons of times, but the property is surrounded by such tall, thick evergreens that I'd never had any idea all this was going on.

Finding Rosetta was going to be harder than Vicki had made it sound. I could see from here that with all the trees on these hilly grounds, it could end up taking hours. I wasn't sure I was up for it, but figured I might as well get started.

As I made my way across the parking lot, I passed some old guy getting out of his Jag and three women—probably in their fifties—wearing cheesy visors as they wheeled bags of golf clubs behind them. I don't know what I expected, but there was something weirdly normal about these people. Like they were hanging out in this unreal place and were unfazed by all of it. That's what it's like when you have this kind of money, I guessed. The only way I'd ever know is if I wound up in a super-successful band or won the lottery someday. I figured my chances for either were about one in fifty million. Approximately.

I was about to start up a hill, but just then I caught sight of a girl standing about fifty feet ahead of me. She was wearing dark pants and a red jacket, and her black ponytail kind of moved with her as she hit golf balls into the distance.

Rosetta.

Seeing her now, I wasn't entirely stoked anymore about this plan to bust over and save the day. Maybe she'd think I was some kind of stalker. Maybe leaving her alone had been my best choice all along. I mean, she was okay. I could see that from here. Maybe I should go home without her ever knowing I'd come.

Home: the place where my unemployed brother and dropout friend had been sitting around all day waiting to rip me a new one. Home: where nothing but good, good times were waiting.

I sighed. Screw *that*.

I made my way over to Rosetta, trying to ignore my crazy-fast heartbeat. I didn't even know what I was so nervous about. As I got close, I noticed a wire bucket of golf balls tipped over on the ground beside her. One by one she was sliding the balls forward with her club and thwacking them hard to join the hundreds of other balls that dotted the grass in front of us.

"Looks like a strong swing," I said. The truth was, all I knew about golf was that watching it on TV was the best insomnia remedy I'd ever found.

Rosetta whirled around, looking the exact opposite of happy to see me. "What are you doing here?"

The girl had made an excellent point. I should turn and walk away. Maybe if I was fast enough, she'd forget I'd been there at all.

So I did.

"Wait!" Rosetta came running after me and touched my arm. "Sorry. I didn't mean to sound so rude. You appeared out of nowhere, and it kind of scared me."

I glanced back at where she'd been standing before. She'd actually thrown her club down to chase after me.

"Oh," I said. "Sorry for scaring you."

We stood there watching each other. Her face was pale and her nostrils were kind of red, but she wasn't anywhere near as wrecked as she'd been in the stairwell. She bit her lip. "Um. So what *are* you doing here?"

I went straight for the truth. "You weren't in IC class, so I thought I'd see if you're okay."

She opened her eyes wide, and I could tell she hadn't expected me to say that. Then she smiled and pointed to a bench about six feet back from where her spilled golf balls were lying. "You want to sit for a minute?"

As I followed her over, she said, "I'm fine, actually. I bombed a physics quiz this morning and had to get out of there."

I didn't believe her—no one gets *that* worked up over science—but there was no way I was going to let on that I'd seen her crying if she was going to try to play the whole thing off.

"What did I miss in IC today?" she asked as we sat on the bench. "Did you have to hang upside down and communicate like bats?"

"No, no bat stuff. Just empathy. Alex and I were empathy-practicing *fools*."

She laughed. "I'll bet you were. I can totally picture that disaster."

"Hey. My mad empathy skills worked on Vicki. She told me that you come here every day."

Except, she hadn't said it because of my empathy. But whatever.

"Actually, I'm not here *every* day," Rosetta said. "I boycott this place on Wednesdays."

"Why?"

She waved her hand toward the white buildings behind us. "Oh, they have this stupid thing where men can play on the actual golf course on Wednesdays, but the women are confined to playing at the driving and putting ranges only. The whole deal is such old-boys' club sexism. Basically they're saying we aren't good enough, that we get in their way. It makes me so mad that I boycott every Wednesday to make a statement."

The way she saw herself as this nonconformist statement-maker while playing golf at a country club was hilarious, but also pretty cute.

"So you play here all the time except the one day a week you aren't allowed," I said. "What kind of statement are you making? 'I'll show you guys! If you don't want me here on Wednesdays, I just . . . won't come!'"

She looked at me, shocked that I was making fun of her,

I guess, but then she burst out laughing. "When you say it like that, it makes me sound ridiculous!"

"Sorry," I said, still messing with her. "You're a total rebel. A revolutionary. Don't ever let anyone tell you differently."

"Shut *up*!" She was so adorably embarrassed and just so *pretty* that when she gave my arm a playful push, my head and my entire body started tingling like I was high.

Rosetta shifted on the bench and brought her arms over her head to stretch. "I have to say, I'm glad this isn't weird," she said, popping one of her shoulders. "I was afraid of what it would be like to see you again after we skipped from level two to, like, level four and a half on the self-disclosure scale the other day."

"The *what* scale?"

"We learned about it in class, remember?"

I shrugged. Did she really think I memorized—or even listened to—everything that went on in there?

"The self-disclosure scale," she said. "It has five levels, and the more people tell about themselves to one another, the higher their relationship moves. It says in the textbook that skipping or moving through levels too quickly can make things uncomfortable. So I was saying that I'm glad it isn't like that with us."

"Gotcha," I said, feeling kind of . . . uncomfortable, actually.

"Oh, *no*." She put her hands on her now-red cheeks. "I

just ruined everything by talking about it, didn't I? Forget I said any of that and let's"—she jumped up, grabbed a golf club, and held it out for me—"hit balls until the awkward moment has passed!"

I took the club from her, but only because she looked like she wanted me to so badly. "Golf isn't my thing," I said as I stood.

"You've played?"

I shook my head. "It seems boring. No offense."

"None taken." She started rushing around to set out some balls for me. "I think everyone thinks that way before they try it. It reminds me of something someone once said to me about coffee. You know, the idea of it might not appeal, but if you give it a try, you might find that it's tolerable. And then one day when you've stopped paying attention, you'll realize you're hooked."

It was weird having my own idea thrown at me like this. Somehow she'd made it sound kind of smart.

"So golf is like coffee. I had no idea."

"It's an acquired taste," she said with mock seriousness. "Nowhere near as horrible as you expect. Of course, I still think coffee's gross, but that fact shouldn't affect your enjoyment of golf in any way. Go ahead and give it a try."

I stepped up, raised the club behind me, and brought it back down to the ball as hard as I could. Instead of popping up and sailing through the air like Rosetta's, it kind of rolled along the grass in a diagonal line.

"You connected with the ball on your first try," she said, clapping her hands. "That's really good!"

But she'd gotten excited too soon, because then I missed on my second try. Swung again. Missed. Swung. Missed. "I suck," I said.

"Maybe it will help if you watch me a few times so you can see how you should be moving. Then I'll come over and help you, okay?"

I stood behind her—far enough back not to get hit—and watched her square her shoulders, bend her knees a little, wiggle her ass, and then swing. Her ball sailed off, and then seemed to disappear. "Do you see what I'm doing?" she asked. "With my hips and keeping my head down?"

Oh, I saw, all right. "So whose head are you imagining hitting when you do that?"

She glanced at me over her shoulder. "Dick, I'd have to have a good imagination to picture a ball this size as a human head."

I started cracking up.

Just then some middle-age dude came rolling up behind us in a golf cart and about scared the hell out of me. He was eyeing me in a way no one would call friendly. "Rosetta," he said in this voice that sounded so polite he *had* to be putting on an act. "I'm here to remind you that your guests need to follow the dress policy when they're with you, and that includes on the driving range. If he needs a change of clothes, we have plenty of choices available for purchase in the pro shop."

Rosetta had turned to look at him, then me, then back at him. "I'm sorry. I wasn't thinking. We'll leave now."

He gave a quick nod. "Have a nice afternoon," he said, shooting me another dirty look as he turned to drive away.

After he was out of earshot, I asked, "Is that guy the country club fashion police?"

"Kind of. He's one of the pros here, so I guess he thought he needed to talk to me before one of the other members complained and turned your dress-code violation into a thing."

"I hate it when people turn stuff into 'things.'"

"Me too," she said, giggling. "The big rule is that you can't wear denim. You're also supposed to wear a shirt with a collar and golf shoes. So your jeans, hoodie, and Chucks look is every kind of rule breaking. "

"That's what I'm good at." I stuck the club I was holding back in her golf bag. "You know, you don't have to quit because of me. I was only stopping in to make sure you hadn't run away from home."

She shook her head and knelt to put the rest of the golf balls back in the bucket. "It's okay. I've been here for hours and my wrists are sore."

I bent to help her. We weren't much closer than we'd been before, but the wind was blowing around a few strands that had come loose from her ponytail, and everything felt different somehow. I breathed in her flowery shampoo until we'd dropped all the balls in. Then I reluctantly stood and helped her up.

"You'll have to come here again sometime," she said, grabbing her bulky bag of clubs. "I'll teach you how to play. I think you're going to be great."

I doubted it, but it was cool that she'd asked, that she seemed to be kind of into me maybe? "I might be up for that. But only if we can make a *real* statement and do it on a Wednesday."

"Ha!"

We got to the parking lot, and I was struck by how run-down the Mustang looked. I can safely say it was the biggest—and only—piece of junk in the lot. "Three guesses which one's mine."

She nudged my arm. "I know your car very well since you almost ran me over with it."

"How could I have forgotten?"

I leaned on the driver's-side door while Rosetta propped her bag up. "It was sweet of you to come here for me," she said. "It means a lot."

The look on her face—a mix of shy and adoring—made me feel unworthy. Especially since she didn't know I'd seen her crying at school. "I'm sure most people would have done the same," I said, shrugging. "You need a ride home?"

As soon as the words were out, I felt like an asshole. But Rosetta smiled. "I'd love that, but I didn't manage to cure myself of my wacky phobia yet. Rain check?"

"For sure. Is it a short walk to your house at least?"

She gestured back toward the golf course. "I live up by

the tenth hole, and it isn't far at all. But, you know, I *like* walking. I get in anywhere between three and ten miles a day. And—bonus!—I don't contribute to air pollution."

I made a face and opened my door. "Okay, that's enough sexy talk."

She laughed. "Are you sure? Because if you want we can take it back to self-disclosure level three and discuss our thoughts about global warming. Or 'climate change' as the cool kids are calling it these days."

I covered my ears like I couldn't take any more, but she *was* kind of hot when she was nerdy. "See you tomorrow. Unless you're going to flunk more tests and skip out again?"

"I'll definitely be there, Dick."

I don't know why, but I didn't want her to call me Dick anymore. It was feeling kind of fake. "Maybe we should use our real names outside class. Yours is Rosetta, right?"

"Yes. Rosetta Vaughn."

"All right," I said. "Well, mine is—"

"Seth McCoy. I know." She kind of wrapped her arms around herself like she was getting cold. "I've known since February fourteenth, actually."

She'd memorized the date she found out my name? What the hell?

She laughed. "Don't freak out! I only remember because it was Valentine's Day."

As if that explained it. "And *why* do you remember learning my name on Valentine's Day?"

"Kendall Eckman was running after you in the hall screaming, 'Seth McCoy, if you don't buy a rose from me, I'll kill you!' She was doing that Valentine's drama club fund-raiser. Remember?"

"Actually, yes."

What I was remembering was getting stoned with Isaac before school, and Kendall harshing my mellow the minute we walked in the door.

Rosetta was looking at me like there was more to this story. "And after she kept asking, you bought a red one?"

"Right. And I passed it off to—" I'd been about to say "some chick," but with how intently she was watching me, I was getting a different idea. "—*you*, right?"

She extended her arm to pass me an imaginary rose in the same way I must have handed her the real one. Then she imitated the corny voice I must have used. "Here, beautiful. Have a wonderful Valentine's Day."

Oh, Christ. The stupid shit I said sometimes. "No wonder you thought I was such a loser."

"I didn't think that at all."

She was smiling and looking like maybe she had more to add. My heart started knocking around again while I waited. But she didn't say whatever it was, and after too many seconds of silence, I couldn't take it anymore. "All right, I'm out of here for real now."

"Me too," she said.

She grabbed her bag and moved to the sidewalk while

I got in the car and started it up. I kind of fiddled around with the radio and pretended to adjust my mirrors so I could hang around and watch her leave. She didn't go anywhere, though; she just stood in that same spot redoing her hair and digging through a pocket in her bag.

Finally it got too weird and I had to drive away.

THURSDAY, **SEPTEMBER 16**

2:28 P.M.

Three days later. Mrs. Dalloway was in the hall, blocking the classroom door. "Hi there, Dick. Are you prone to seizures?"

"Uh, no."

Thirty minutes later I was wishing I'd said "Uh, yes," because then she'd have had to turn off the strobe light. Then again, it might not have made a difference; the loud electronic music and Mrs. D.'s yelling probably would have been enough to do me in anyway.

The classroom theme was "rave party," and Mrs. Dalloway had gone all out covering the windows for maximum darkness, setting up black lights along with the strobe, passing out multicolored neon glow bracelets and necklaces, and arranging the tables to make a nine-by-nine dance floor where we all had to stand because there was "No sitting allowed!" for the whole period. The only detail she'd missed was the hallucinogens, but what can you do, right?

From what I could figure out, the point of this torture was to show that you can't learn to communicate properly at a party. I think most of us could have figured it out on our own—and if not, a five-minute demonstration would have done the trick—but Mrs. D. was getting a kick out of driving her point home. Three people had asked her to turn the music down, but she'd just smiled and pretended she couldn't hear them.

The twelve of us students were standing together in a close, uncomfortable bunch. With all the noise going on, I'd managed to make out only about half the lecture—which, come to think of it, was probably more than I heard on a regular day, when I was able to sit and zone out.

"I have a new project for you all!" Mrs. D. shouted over the music after wrapping up her talk. "Your homework for tonight is to make a list in your journal of things that are outside your comfort zone. I'd really like to see you dig deep. This is going to be an ongoing project where you'll be challenging yourselves to try things you never thought you could or would want to do. Have fun, but remember none of it should be easy for you. If you don't feel *un*comfortable about putting something on your list, it doesn't belong there!"

I couldn't help glancing toward Rosetta—who was standing about five feet away from me, the yellow and orange necklaces she was wearing on top of her head glowing like a halo—and I wasn't surprised to see that she was looking right back at me. We were probably both thinking about the thing she'd be putting on her list.

Rosetta had been on my mind pretty much nonstop since our conversation at the golf course. Every time I'd have myself convinced that I was a dumbass for thinking this could lead to something, she'd show up smiling or saying hi or whatever, and I'd get even more distracted.

Mrs. D. went on. "Just to be clear: I'm not advocating anything illegal, dangerous, or damaging for this project. Do *not* rob a bank and say that it was a homework assignment. Understood? Now please mingle for the rest of the period! This is a party or something, right?"

Or something. Right.

I was closest to Jezebel/Tara and Jade/Brittany. They'd been swaying the whole class, so now that Mrs. D. had given the go-ahead, they started twirling around and laughing in that obvious way girls do when they know—or at least *think*—everyone's watching them. The strobe effect made it so that I couldn't predict where their glow bracelets were going to be from one flash of light to the next.

Brittany scooted close to me and started doing these weird dance moves while I stood totally still. "Hey, *Dick*," she said, moving in and tugging on my name tag. "You got any E on you?"

"Sorry, fresh out."

"That's too bad." She flashed this huge smile, and the black light made her teeth look purply white and freaky.

I'd only done ecstasy twice, and, embarrassingly enough, the first time was at a party freshman year where Brittany and I had fooled around and then pretty much never spoke again. The second was a week after that and the trip was so bad it had turned me off uppers for good.

Tara and Brittany started dancing together right beside me, and, I have to say, I probably would have thought it was super-hot if I couldn't see Rosetta a few feet away, talking to Xander. Compared with her, they were only mildly hot.

"You know what I heard?" Brittany asked, leaning toward me again. "Cat pee glows when you shine a strobe light on it."

Okay. Not hot at all now.

"You mean a black light!" Tara yelled. "Black lights make cat pee glow, not strobe lights!"

Then they started arguing about it. About *piss*, for Christ's sake.

At an actual party I'd have been looking for an escape, so I decided to head for an empty spot on our little dance floor. Rosetta and Xander followed me over. Together.

"This has been an interesting class," Xander called out to me.

"I must have missed the part where she went over what the point of it was," I said.

I was talking to him, but I was looking at Rosetta—the IC

class rave-party angel—who was smiling at me with glowing purplish teeth that, of course, looked anything but freaky.

"I couldn't quite hear everything either!" Rosetta yelled. "But I got the idea that it was an extreme demonstration of the communication-as-a-simultaneous-transaction concept to show how noise—whether it's literal or psychological— keeps people from having a perfect understanding of one another."

"Yeah, that's what Mrs. Dalloway was saying." Xander nodded his head slowly. "I kind of thought she'd go into that thing about spaces themselves affecting the conversations that take place in them. The crazy stuff that goes on at parties is all wrong in the classroom. And vice versa."

I looked back and forth between them. "Huh. You don't say."

They glanced at each other and then burst out laughing at the same time. I knew it was stupid, but I was kind of jealous. Not because they were both school smart in a way that I never would be—even though that was true too—but because geeking out was one of the probably many things Xander had in common with Rosetta. And, well, I didn't have *any*thing.

Rosetta kept smiling at me. "I know what you're thinking, and you're right. Alex and I are complete dorks."

"I, personally, think the correct term in this case is 'nerds,'" Xander said.

Rosetta laughed again. "You're right. Nerds it is."

She was killing me here.

Luckily, Mrs. D. ended the music and strobe light crap and turned the lights back on, which was nice and jarring in its own way. "You can keep the glowing jewelry," she said as she collected our name tags. "I'll see you all tomorrow with your lists!"

Everyone grabbed their stuff and started shuffling out. But I was taking my time, hoping Rosetta would walk with me to the parking lot like she had the past two days. Instead, she gave Xander a thumbs-up and said, "Good luck!" before rushing out.

Strange. And disappointing. I started for the door too.

"Hey, Seth. Dick. Whatever," Xander said, still planted in his same spot. "You aren't playing with the Real McCoys anymore, right?"

I stopped. "Right."

Did he think I'd changed my mind about quitting during the past three days? Well, he wouldn't be the only one. Jared and Mikey were already scrambling and making phone calls to find my replacement, but Daniel was in all kinds of denial, thinking if he harassed me enough I'd give in and decide to tour.

"My band doesn't have a bass player," Xander said, looking at the floor and talking in a rush. "So I was wondering if you'd be interested in playing with us. We're doing a pop-punk sound—heavier on the punk—but if you're looking for a change, maybe you'd be into jamming with us sometime?"

Oh, yeah, this would go over *great* with Jared, Daniel, and Mikey. Still, it wasn't the worst idea in the world. I'd wanted to try something new for a while. And now, for the first time, there wasn't anything holding me back. You know, *except* Jared, Daniel, and Mikey.

"Who else is in your band?" I asked.

"Taku Endo. And also Brody Lancaster," Xander said, pushing his hair out of his eyes. "I already talked to them, and they're down with having you come out."

Taku was my math tutor, and he seemed like a cool guy in that same dorky/friendly way as Xander. Brody, however, happened to be Vicki's twin brother.

"I don't know," I said, trying to think of an excuse so I could get out of it without sounding like a dick. "I've been on upright bass for a year now, and I haven't even picked up an electric in that time. In fact, mine's in storage."

All our equipment was in storage because that's where practice was held, but Xander wouldn't know that.

"You don't have to worry about gear," he said, waving his hand. "We rehearse at Brody's. His dad set him up a studio downstairs that has everything. Seriously. You can use his bass and amp if you want. In fact, you could *steal* them and he wouldn't notice."

Xander was sort of smiling and shaking his head in a "damn those rich kids" kind of way, and I didn't know what to say. It was the first time I'd ever realized he wasn't one of them.

"Think about it," he said, handing me a sheet of paper

he'd been holding. "This has my phone number and Brody's address. I'm heading over right now, and we'll be at it for a few hours. So if you want to stop by, feel free. Or if today isn't good, we can shoot for some other day. We're there all the time, so it's up to you."

"Cool, thanks." I folded the paper and shoved it in my back pocket, but there was no way I was going to need it. I mean, me in a band with Brody? *Please.*

3:20 P.M.

When I got out to the parking lot, Rosetta was waiting by the Mustang, still wearing her neon halo. Amazing. The one person I'd hoped would turn up, and here she was. I could get used to this.

"Let me guess, you're cured and you want a ride somewhere?" I asked.

She laughed. "That's a big *no*. I wanted to hear how it went with Xander. He was nervous all day about asking you to meet his band. It was pretty cute."

Xander. Cute. Ugh.

"Yeah, he talked to me about it, but I don't think it's going to work out," I said, dropping my bag next to the car.

"Why not? You need a band, right? And they really need a bassist." She set her backpack next to mine. "They've been playing together for almost a year. Two guitars, drums, vocals. No bass. Xander says it's ridiculous."

She sure knew a lot about Xander and his band's goings-on.

"It's not that simple," I said.

"Well, Xander told me that you're good—better than they are—so you don't need to worry about that. Or are you thinking that you'll be wasting your time because they aren't good enough?"

Strangely, it had never occurred to me to wonder about either of those things. "It's not that."

"Then, what?"

If she wanted the truth, I'd give it to her. Whatever. "I just don't see myself spending time with an asshole like Brody Lancaster."

She frowned and lines formed between her eyebrows. "Brody? He's nice. Quiet and moody sometimes, but not an asshole."

"Uh-huh," I said, rolling my eyes. "This coming from someone who hangs out with his evil sister."

Rosetta squinted at me like she was trying to figure out if I was serious. "What are you talking about? Vicki's snobby sometimes, sure, but she isn't evil. And anyway, Vicki and Brody are nothing alike."

"Are you *kidding* me?" I asked. "At that party at Pete's, Vicki said what happened to Isaac was a 'nontragedy.'"

Rosetta opened her eyes wide, all surprised. "She *said* that?"

"Yeah, she said that. She also said she hoped the same

would happen to me. If that isn't evil, I sure don't know what is."

"I don't understand why she'd be like that," Rosetta said, biting her lip. "That's really, really awful. She isn't usually flat-out mean to people."

"Yes, she *is*."

Rosetta stared at the ground. "Let's think about this. The night she said that to you. It was a party and she was drinking a lot, right? So I'm positive she didn't mean it. Drunk people are always saying and doing terrible things they wish they could take back later. It's just part of being a pod person. I'm sure she feels bad if she remembers."

She was saying this to calm me down, to make me feel better, but I hated that she was making an excuse for Vicki's bitchiness. "She doesn't care that she said it," I said. "That's how she is all the time. It isn't like there's just one time, *one* thing with Vicki. She is always starting some—"

"This is getting so far away from the subject," Rosetta said, cutting me off. "What I was saying is that maybe you should give *Brody* a chance. Check out the band; see if you want to do it. That's all. I don't want to have an argument over which of our friends is a bigger jerk or should be dead or anything like that."

Which of our friends *should* be dead?

Unbelievable.

I grabbed my bag and headed to the driver's-side door.

"Seth, hang on," Rosetta said.

But I couldn't. Even though I knew I was probably blowing it with her, I didn't care; I needed to get away from this screwed-up conversation.

I opened the door. As I was about to get in, Rosetta said, "Damnit."

She didn't yell in frustration like most people—including me—might have. She just sort of sighed it. And yeah, it's tame, but it was such a surprise coming from her that I stopped and turned.

"I'm sorry," she said, meeting my gaze. "I didn't mean that the way you think. I don't know what I was meaning or why I said it at all. I'm just . . . sorry."

"Okay," I said.

And that was it. Fight over.

We leaned next to each other on my car, close enough that her shoulder was touching my upper arm. I thought about making a joke about how it was good that we'd gotten our first argument out of the way on the first day of school at the intersection, because now we were already getting to be experts at it. But I knew it would only come out lame, so I didn't bother. Instead, I said, "Psychological noise sucks."

"I know. Do you mind if we rewind this conversation and record over it?"

"Rewind to which part?" I asked.

"How about to whichever part where I can say, 'I'm not an expert on these things, but maybe playing music with these guys is what you need. It's a fresh start. What's it going to hurt to try?'"

"So then what's my line?"

She pulled one of the neon glow necklaces off her head and stuck it on mine. "Maybe you don't have a line. Maybe at this point you decide not to think about it, not to try to talk yourself out of it. You get in your car, go to Brody's house, and play bass. And then, even if you decide it's something you don't want to do ever again, at least you'll have a jump start on the 'challenge yourself to do things you find uncomfortable' homework, right?"

That gave me an idea. "How about this: I'll do it if you come with me. In my car."

She laughed. "I don't think so."

The more I thought about it, the better it was sounding. "You're going to put it on your list for the homework, right? Getting past your motorphobia?"

She nodded.

"Then you should take your own advice. Don't think. Don't talk yourself out of it. Just get in the car."

She laughed again. A nervous laugh, but maybe it was an excited one too, like she was considering it? "I *can't*," she said after a few seconds. "I have a clinical disorder, you know."

"Excuses, excuses. You chicks with phobias are all the same."

I smiled a little so she'd know I was teasing.

"I know you can do this," she said. "And no matter what happens with the band, I think you'll be glad if you try."

Now *she* was the one changing the subject. If anyone else had pressured me with the "you can do this" crap, I'd have probably been annoyed. But because it was her, it was working. I actually wanted to. Just to show her I could, I guess.

"Fine," I said. "I'll go. And then afterward we'll get started on *your* challenge. Deal?"

"Deal."

3:41 P.M.

I stood on the steps at Brody's, waiting for someone to answer the door. It seemed quiet for a house with a band practicing inside. At Studio 43 people could hear our music from a block away.

Finally, the door swung open and Vicki was standing in the doorway, staring at me. I was *so* sick of running into this chick. She felt the same because she said, "This is getting ridiculous."

I didn't want to get into it with her. "I'm here for a band thing."

For about a half second she looked like she was going to argue or ask questions, but then she just walked away, leaving the door open. I took that as my cue to go in.

Everything, from the floors to the furniture to the walls

to the high ceiling, was white and beige. The only actual color was a red flower arrangement on a short table and a large red painting on the wall. I followed Vicki through the front room and hallway and into the huge, chrome-filled kitchen. Then she opened a door and pointed down a flight of stairs. "They're in there."

"How do I know this isn't a dungeon where you torture your enemies?" I asked.

"Because if it were, I'd have put you in there years ago," she said over her shoulder as she stomped away.

I headed down, and I could just make out the drums. At the bottom of the landing, guitars kicked in very faintly. I pulled opened a heavy door and the noise level increased. There was yet another door behind it. When I pushed *that* open, the music got so loud I could feel it. This place had some amazing soundproofing.

As it turned out, the practice room itself *was* sort of dungeonlike—if the Rich Bitch Hill version of dungeons has dark walls covered with acoustic foam and thick black carpet on the floor.

Brody was standing at a mic with a vintage Fender strapped over his shoulder. He had his usual Kurt Cobain look going on, except his sweatshirt and jeans were very obviously clean and expensive. He looked at me through his blond hair for a second, and then ceased playing and turned toward Taku, the other guitarist. Taku stopped too and gave me a nod. With his spiky hair, industrial cartilage bars in both ears, and black shirt with black jeans, Taku didn't look like he belonged in the same scene, much less the same *band*, as Brody. In fact, with Xander's laid-back pseudo-surfer look, they were all kind of mismatched, which—I have to admit— was kind of a nice change after all the pressure to look the rockabilly part with the Real McCoys.

Xander got up from behind his drums. "Hey, Seth. Glad you could make it. I was just saying I didn't know if you were going to show."

Brody was looking past me, and I wondered if maybe he was wishing I *hadn't*.

I shrugged. "I thought I'd check it out."

"Cool," Taku said.

Xander started rushing around, getting the bass plugged in and ready, while I stood there feeling out of place. "'Scratching at the Eight-Ball,'" I read aloud from a banner that stretched across the back wall.

"That's the name of our band," Taku said.

Weird. Not Magic 8 Ball. Just plain 8 ball.

I said, "It sort of makes me think of someone scraping their fingernails over a few grams of coke. But I'm guessing that isn't what you're going for."

Xander started laughing so hard he looked like he was about to fall over. "See, these guys didn't believe me when I told them that 'eight ball' would make people think of drugs. But Taku is so straight-edge we have to get on him to use his asthma inhaler, so he has no clue."

I'd noticed that Taku coughed a lot in the mornings.

"For the millionth time. I *don't* have asthma. I have bronchospasms," Taku said. Then he turned to me. "Our name came from a Social Distortion song. You know how knocking the cue ball in the pocket is called 'scratching'? And when you scratch trying to sink the eight ball, you automatically lose on what should have been your winning shot? So yeah. Scratching at the Eight Ball. I guess we were feeling cynical when we chose it, right, Brody?"

Brody nodded. "Always."

It was the first word he'd said since I'd walked in.

Xander handed me Brody's Gibson Firebird bass, which looked like it had never been played, and sat behind his drums. "Let's do this," he said. "Seth, jump in whenever you feel comfortable."

Then he hit his sticks together several times and started pounding away on his drums. Brody and Taku started playing too.

I'd never auditioned before. This wasn't quite how I'd expected it to work, but I could handle it. And as anxious as Xander seemed, maybe in some ways it was more like they were auditioning for *me*.

I listened, and it didn't take long to figure out that even though they were inexperienced, with very little stage presence, they were all decent musicians. Xander had called their style "pop-punk," but, for some reason, I'd kind of thought I was going to be dealing with a boy band that cussed. But there was nothing bubble gum about the loud, fast guitars and drums. It was obvious they'd been inspired by old Green Day or the Offspring, but Scratching at the 8 Ball was doing something much heavier, more complex.

After several minutes of getting a feel for the song, I started messing around until I came up with a bass line. For the past year I hadn't touched anything but gut strings and I knew my fingers were going to be sore as I got used to steel again, but at that moment it felt good. *Really* good.

We kept going like that for an hour. They'd play a song through while I listened, then I'd play with them until we were ready to move on to the next. We made it through about five songs, and I found myself getting more and more into it. The songwriting was interesting. Whoever was responsible for the arrangement was pretty gifted.

"That was awesome," Xander said, standing and wiping his forehead on his sleeve afterward.

After getting past the kinks, I'd played well—at least I thought so—but there was more than the music to consider. For one thing, Brody Lancaster was in this band, and he wasn't giving off any good vibes. He'd been staring at the floor the whole time, as if he couldn't even stand to look at me.

I didn't expect any of us to make a decision right then. I needed to think; they needed to talk it over. But then, right in front of me, Xander said, "If that didn't convince you guys that this bass-free thing has gone on way too long, I don't know what will. Are we going to beg Seth to keep playing with us, or what?"

"He's good," Taku said, coughing. "And he picks things up super-fast, too. I think it can work."

"I. Told. You. So." Xander stabbed the air with a drumstick at every word.

Brody set his guitar on a stand and walked over to the black leather couch, looking like he was deep in thought.

"What do you think, Brode?" Taku asked.

"I think Xander was right," Brody said quietly. "And he *is* good. Really good." Then he looked me in the eyes. "Are you into it? I mean, would you want to play with us?"

Actually, I *did* want to. This band could definitely be the low-pressure thing I needed. They'd been playing together for more than a year without ever performing live, so there was a good chance that I'd be able to keep off the stage for a good, long while.

I kept my answer for Brody simple so I wouldn't sound too gung ho. "I think it could be cool."

"In that case," Xander said, "do you need to consult your agent?"

Brody and Taku exchanged confused glances.

"My what?" I asked.

Xander laughed and pointed at the Magic 8 Ball hanging from my belt loop. "You always carry it with you, right? If I had one, I'd want its opinion about something like this."

My face got hot. Asking the Magic 8 Ball questions had

been Isaac's thing. But me, most days I just kept it close and fidgeted with it.

"I think it would be cool to get one of those for the band," Taku said. "It goes well with our logo and name."

Xander nodded. "Totally. Seth, I hope yours doesn't tell you not to join us. I've always had this crazy dream of one day being part of a rhythm section that's made up of more than just me."

The three of them were watching me, obviously waiting for me to ask the question. So, taking a seat next to Brody, I did it. "Should I play with Scratching at the Eight Ball?"

As I turned the Magic 8 Ball over, Taku read the answer aloud. "Without a doubt."

5:15 P.M.

I'd never really paid attention to how much drum crap Mikey collected until I was forced to start moving it on my own. I'd been so stoked when I'd left Brody's that I'd busted on over to Studio 43 to pick up my bass and amp. Brody's were nice, of course—nicer than mine by most people's standards—but I prefered the feel of my Fender and was itching to get my hands on it. I hadn't been this keyed up about music in a long time.

Unfortunately, my speedy grab-and-go plan didn't work out. My bass was zipped up in its soft case, leaning against the wall and collecting dust right where I'd left it last year.

But my amp was behind Mikey's drum kit with cymbals, stands, and other garbage blocking it in.

I spent several minutes clearing a path. Then I wheeled my amp to the middle of the room and got to work putting everything back in some kind of order. Just as I was finishing, Jared, Mikey, and Daniel walked in. An hour earlier than their usual rehearsal time.

"Dick, I knew you'd come crawling back," Daniel said, grinning. "I *knew* it." Then he turned to Jared. "We can call off that Craig guy, right?"

Now I was going to make everyone all pissed off at me again. Total buzzkill.

Jared was glaring at me. "In or out, Seth. You can't be changing your mind like this all the time."

"I'm *not*," I said, quickly. "I'm here to get my stuff out of your way."

Daniel's smile turned to a scowl. Jared sent more dirty looks at me.

"Don't worry about it, Seth." Mikey threw his jacket over the back of the couch. "You can keep your shit here. It's not like we need that section of wall for anything."

I shrugged. "I think I'll just take it anyway."

Daniel stalked over to the minifridge and pulled out a beer.

"Don't be like that," Mikey said to me. "Just because you quit the band for now doesn't mean you have to clear out for good. We don't hate you or anything."

"Speak for yourself," Daniel said between gulps from his can.

Jared crossed his arms over his chest. "All I have to say is that you're not taking that amp anywhere. We've got a guy coming out here to audition any minute, and I already told him he can use our stuff if he ends up joining us."

"That's great," I said. "He can use *your* stuff. But the amp is—and always has been—mine."

I gathered up my cords and strapped my bass over my shoulder. Maybe I could get this all out to the Mustang in one trip and drive away before this conversation really went to shit.

Daniel spoke up then. "What do you need the amp for? Why can't you leave it here?"

They were all looking at me, waiting for my answer.

I hadn't expected to be having the "I Joined a New Band" conversation this soon. In fact, I'd been hoping like hell to avoid it until they'd found my replacement and had things under way. For a second, I considered keeping the truth from them and just using Brody's amp for a while. But Daniel was my friend. I wasn't going to be a dick and *lie* to the guy. "I had another music thing come my way, so I'm going to try it out," I said.

I braced myself for their reactions.

Mikey stood there looking shocked.

Jared headed out of the storage unit without another word.

And Daniel?

Well, he threw his beer at me.

The good news was that Daniel's aim sucked, so the can slammed full force into the wall next to me instead of my face. The bad news is that it kind of exploded on impact.

I stood there with beer dripping from my hair and clothes while Daniel paced a small patch of cement floor. "What is *up* with you? All you're doing is screwing everything up for me lately."

Maybe I should have argued or tried to explain my side. I was just so *tired* of it, though. And it wasn't like he cared what I had to say. "I'm sorry, dude," I said.

"Fuck *you*, dude."

And then he walked out.

THURSDAY, **SEPTEMBER 30**

7:37 A.M.

Fourteen days later. Taku and I finished our zero period math stuff early, so I had time to kill before my first class. Just as I was putting out my hand to get Rosetta's attention down the hall, Carr Goodwin shoved past me. He made his way over to Rosetta, holding out a ridiculously huge bunch of red and white flowers for her. In a voice loud enough that I could hear him even over the morning hallway noise, Carr said, "Roses for my Rosetta!"

His Rosetta? This was news to me.

During the two weeks since I'd joined up with Scratching at the 8 Ball, Rosetta and I had been sitting together in IC class almost every day, talking between classes, and had even met at her country club driving range once. The phobia curing was going nowhere, but I was getting the feeling that things with *us* were leading somewhere.

Rosetta looked from the roses to Carr's face. Then she bit her lip, took the bunch, and held it like a baby against her. Carr ran his fingers over his preppy-boy hair, probably to make sure his hairline hadn't receded farther in those few seconds. He started talking—rambling, from what I could see—and when he shut up, he raised his eyebrows like he was waiting for an answer. Rosetta nodded slowly and tipped her face forward to sniff the flowers.

My mom once told me that girls like it better when guys give one rose instead of a dozen, but I couldn't see how that would be true. Single roses come from lazy, poor jerks like me. I mean, you can get a single rose at the gas station when you're filling your tank. Or even at, you know, stupid school fund-raisers. Big, fancy bunches like what Carr brought had to be planned out in advance and shit. And, loser that I was, I'd never thought to do something like that.

Rosetta started talking. From where I was standing, I thought she looked like she was being sort of stern, but it was hard to tell because Carr was grinning and giving his stupid Carr laugh the whole time. He pulled an envelope from his jacket and gave it to her all businesslike.

My view was blocked as Kendall came straight toward me. Just what I needed right now.

"What are you doing two Saturdays from now?" she asked.

I leaned to see past her. Rosetta was trying to hang on to

all those flowers and rip the envelope open at the same time while Carr stood there.

Kendall waved her hands in front of me. "Focus. Right here," she said, gesturing at her own face.

I forced myself to look at her for a second. "Two Saturdays from now? I don't know. Probably nothing."

Now Carr was talking again while Rosetta frowned at the card in her hand. I wondered if he was upsetting her. If I should go over and casually interrupt.

"Perfect," Kendall said, clapping her hands. "We'll go to the homecoming dance together."

"What?"

"My dress is red, if that helps you plan. And don't worry, I won't wear heels that make me tower *too* far over you. Do you want to drive or should I?"

I shook my head. "Kendall, I'm not going to any dance."

"Why not?"

"Why *would* I?"

She pouted. "We're supposed to be nonenemies, but you totally suck at it. You don't return my calls. You never want to hang out."

I had no idea where this was coming from. No one had told me she'd been calling or wanting to hang out. Not that I would have been interested anyway, but still. "This isn't about you. I've been hella busy."

It wasn't an exaggeration, either. I'd been spending all my time sitting in class, working at the car wash, keeping up with my homework, playing music in Brody's dungeon, staying away from Daniel, and making time for Rosetta. For once, my avoidance of Kendall was unplanned.

"Prove it." Kendall put her hands on my shoulders. "Show me you're serious about being my nonenemy by taking me to the dance."

There was no way. No *way*. My brother and our friends had taken chicks to a few dances over the years, but I hadn't bothered to go to one since middle school. I'd never heard of a single good thing happening at a dance.

"I can't," I said, pushing her hands off. "Besides, you know you'd have a better time with someone else."

She rolled her eyes. "Whatever, lover."

And then she walked away.

Whatever indeed.

After she was gone, I glanced back toward Rosetta. Carr had taken off, and Rosetta was opening her locker, so I headed over.

"If those roses are for me," I said, coming up behind her, "I have to say, you shouldn't have."

Laughing, she turned to face me. Such a nice change from moody Kendall.

"That's what I told the person who gave them to me," she said. "Can you give me a hand?"

I helped her force the flowers into her locker. When she slammed it shut a second later, some fern stuff was sticking out the door. "Good old Carr," I said. "What's he up to?"

Rosetta leaned against her locker. "Oh, just bringing me flower arrangements almost as big as I am. Writing disturbing notes. The usual Carr stuff, I guess you could say."

I didn't know this was "the usual Carr stuff." Since our semiargument about Vicki and Brody, Rosetta and I hadn't talked about any of her friends. Or my friends either. And whenever we hung out, it was only the two of us—which was exactly how I liked it.

Rosetta handed me the envelope he'd given her. "Read this. Tell me what you think."

So I read.

DEAR ROSETTA,

YOU PROBABLY DON'T REALIZE THAT THESE FLOWERS ARE SYMBOLIC, BUT THEY ARE. RED AND WHITE ROSES REPRESENT UNITY AND TOGETHERNESS, WHICH IS EXACTLY WHAT YOU AND I SHOULD HAVE. YOU'LL UNDERSTAND LONG BEFORE I'M PRESIDENT AND YOU ARE THE FIRST LADY. I HAVE BIG PLANS FOR OUR FUTURE. YOU'LL SEE.

ALL MY LOVE,
CARR

P.S. HOW DOES A ROLLS-ROYCE LIMO SOUND?

I didn't know what Rosetta expected me to say, so I went with "Huh."

"Creepy, right? But Carr thinks he's being charming. I've told him I like being his friend, I like golfing with him, but that's all it's going to be. I don't know what else I can say without being rude."

"Maybe you should add 'telling Carr off' to your personal challenges list," I said, trying not to let on how much I liked the idea.

"I'm hoping it won't come to that."

I didn't want to be uncool, but I had to ask. "What's the Rolls-Royce thing about?"

"Oh, it's Carr's idea of a great ride to the homecoming dance. He asked me to go with him back when he was still acting normal. I'm kind of regretting saying yes now. Especially since I told him that I want to meet him at the dance, but he won't give up on the hired car idea."

Even though she didn't seem to be looking forward to it, it bugged me that she'd agreed to go with him. I didn't even want to think about what it could mean. "I can help you solve your Rolls problem in time for the dance," I said. "I'll borrow a van and get a bunch of guys together. When you're out walking somewhere, we'll pull over and grab you. You'll be so freaked out about being abducted, you won't care that you're inside a motor vehicle. See? Instant motorphobia cure."

As far as jokes go, it wasn't funny. Luckily for me, Rosetta just kind of scrunched up her nose and said, "Okay, I think you've given me a whole new white-van phobia with this idea. Please, please tell me you won't try it."

"Of course I won't."

"Promise?"

"I promise."

She smiled big then, leaned closer, yanked the hood on my sweatshirt over my head, and pulled the strings hard so that my eyes were covered and the opening was tight around my face. "Just for saying that," she said, "*you* should have to go to homecoming in a Rolls with Carr."

There a little bit of light coming through, but I couldn't see much. "Can't. I'm allergic."

She burst out laughing. "To Rolls-Royces? Or to Carr Goodwin?"

"Both. School dances, too."

"What do you think would happen to you?" she asked, letting some of the tension out of the strings so I could see again. "Hives? Rashes?"

"I'm not sure. It could be serious though."

"That's too bad. You could have added 'going to the dance' onto your list of challenges. And maybe you'd even have fun?"

"I guess we'll never know," I said.

8:38 P.M.

Trevor and I had just finished putting the hoses and scrubbers away at the car wash and were about to leave when

Mikey said, "Seth, don't clock out yet. I need to talk to you."

Trevor gave me a questioning look. I shrugged in response. If I was in trouble for something, I had no clue what.

After Trevor took off, Mikey locked the door. "I'm leaving on tour in about two weeks," he said, switching off the neon OPEN sign. "My dad's stressing about me not being here since he's busy with the other store and doesn't want to have to run both on his own. And he doesn't want to hire someone new to take over, either, since I'll be back in six weeks."

"Oh," I said, trying not to let on that my insides were feeling a little twisted all of a sudden. If they were going to close down the car wash until Mikey came back, I was going to be *so* screwed. My car was falling apart around me; I needed all the money I could get.

Mikey kept talking. "So what I'm hoping for is that between you and a couple of the other guys, we can work something out to keep things running smoothly so my dad doesn't have to go too crazy. I'm thinking I'll adjust the schedule so you can all pick up a few more hours to cover me. And you'll take turns being in charge of opening and closing, balancing the register. Stuff like that. Lyle's already trained, so I'm thinking maybe you and Ian can give him a hand."

This idea was sounding way better than having to lose a month and a half of pay. Except for the me-being-in-charge-sometimes part.

"I suck at math, you know," I said.

He rolled his eyes. "Dude, it's simple addition and subtraction. Nobody's going to make you find the square root of x divided by y or anything like that when you're putting together the day's sales here." He walked around behind the counter and tapped the computer screen. "Besides, the register does most of the work for you. If you've got time, I can show you right now."

So I watched and listened to him explain the closing procedures while he pressed buttons on the computer, counted the till, and took all the paperwork to his office to get it in order.

"Think you can handle it?" he asked afterward as he piled up the receipts on his desk and stapled them together.

From where I was sitting on the chair next to him, I shrugged. "There's lots to remember."

"Don't worry. I'll have you practice a bunch of times before I leave. And I'll put together step-by-step instructions you can follow if you ever run into a snag."

"Well, if you're *sure* I won't screw anything up."

"I'm sure. I know I can trust you with this. Which is more than I can say for most of the *other* dildos I've hired on this crew."

"Thanks a lot," I said, letting out a short laugh. "Seriously, though, I'm glad to do it. And I'm even gladder that you're not pissed anymore. Jared and Daniel have had the hate going for two weeks straight now."

"You knew that was going to happen, though, right?" he said, swiveling his chair to put the deposit in the safe. "Especially with Jared. He made a plan and he was fully expecting all of us to go along with it. I'm putting off my night classes at the community college until next quarter. You really chose a hell of a time to quit on us."

"I can't make all my decisions based on what my brother wants."

"You're right," Mikey said, spinning back around and facing me. "And I guess I'll give you a pass for not coming on tour. I mean, if it's really about you finishing school like Jared was saying. I can't say I get why it had to be this way, though."

"What way?"

"Come on. You joined another band without even telling us. You, me, and Daniel, we've all been tight forever. And Jared's your brother. You just bailed like you didn't give a shit anymore."

I shook my head. "That isn't how it was."

"Well, that's what it seemed like."

"Xander and those guys had nothing to do with it. I didn't even know they were looking for a bass player until after I'd told Jared and Daniel I was out."

Mikey didn't respond. He just busied himself by separating slips and paper-clipping things together in an order that made sense only to him.

I went on. "Look, playing with you guys hadn't been the same for me since Daniel and Isaac's fight. And with Isaac not even here anymore, everything's just . . . way different."

"Well, that's true," Mikey said. "Now we only have to worry about Daniel getting into fights and passing out in random alleys."

He was smiling when he said it, but I didn't find it funny. Yeah, Isaac did used to get hard-core wasted when he was bored or pissed off or having too good a time. But was that seriously the only thing Mikey could say about him?

Mikey sighed, obviously picking up on my mood. "We've had a lot of good times in this band. That weekend trip to Portland where we spent more at the strip joint than we made at the gig. Camping on the way to and from Boise during spring break because we couldn't afford a motel. The parking lot duels with those swords from the truck stop. And a lot of it was because of Isaac."

I nodded, glad he could at least admit that Isaac was fun and not just some pain in the ass.

He went on. "But we've got to keep going. Isaac isn't here anymore, but we are. And now we're gearing up for our biggest adventure yet."

Right then I had a pang: doubt, regret, and a tiny bit of jealousy all rolled into one. There was nothing I could do about it, though, and nothing I *wanted* to do about it. "And while you're having your adventure," I said, "I'll stay here and solve the square root of *x* divided by *y* for you."

"You can handle it," Mikey said. "And Seth, you and me are cool, okay?"

"Thanks."

"No problem." He locked all his paperwork into the filing cabinet, then grabbed his jacket off the hook and motioned that I should get up too. "You know what I was thinking the other day?" he asked as he flipped the lights and set the alarm. "With you gone, there's only one real McCoy left in the band. How stupid is that? I think Daniel's on to something with his Fake McCoys idea."

I couldn't help laughing as I followed him through the store in the near darkness. "How have things been working out with my replacement?"

"Craig—he said he's having a hard time figuring out my go-to beats, but he's doing good and having fun with it. And so far your brother gets along with him. Which means a lot less arguing and bullshit at practice. I'm thinking in that way, you might have done us a favor."

"Cool. You should tell that to the other guys."

Mikey turned to me with raised eyebrows. "Maybe *you* should."

THURSDAY, **OCTOBER 7**

7:25 P.M.

I was finishing my dinner at Good Times when cold hands covered my eyes. I didn't even have to wonder who it was.

"Hi, Kendall," I said, twisting out of her grasp.

Her shiny peach lips formed into a pout. She looked trashy as always, but also kind of hot in a tight top and denim skirt. "How'd you know it was me?"

"Because I don't know anyone else who goes around smelling like a pack of gummy bears all the time."

"Gummy bears?" She sniffed her hands. "All I smell is my mango lotion."

"Mangoes. Gummy bears. Whatever."

She took a seat across the table from me. "You can't hide, you know. I know where you live, where you work, where you hang out. I'll always find you, driving around on that ridiculous spare tire."

So dramatic. So Kendall. But in spite of the threatening words, I wasn't worried; she was looking a lot friendlier than she had during our last conversation.

"Was I trying to hide from you? Because I don't think I was." I looked over my shoulder toward the bar. "Does my mom know you're here?"

"She's the one who told me where you sit." Kendall pushed some orangey strands from her face, all serious. "Anyway, I've decided that you've had enough time to think things over, so we're going to come to an agreement now."

Kendall could stand to learn a thing or two about communication. Based on our past conversations she should already know that her ordering-Seth-around strategy was guaranteed to fail.

"If this is about that dance, my answer is still no."

She clasped her hands together and stared at me pleadingly. "Please? If you do this for me, I'll do anything you want! *Any*thing."

I could think of very few things I wanted from her. "I'm getting the feeling this doesn't have much to do with you wanting to be better nonenemies with me like you said before."

She sighed. "Well, of *course* it doesn't."

"So what's the deal?"

Kendall grabbed my Coke and sucked on the straw.

"I didn't want to get into this with you, but the truth is, I've kind of been hooking up in secret with someone from school. I figured we'd finally be going public at the dance. But as it turns out, he *likes* keeping me hidden. He's taking someone else, if you can believe that. We can't let him get away with it."

Typical Kendall, getting herself mixed up in something like this and then trying to make it *my* problem. I wondered if the secret-boyfriend thing was about her moving on after Isaac, or if she was still just trying to convince herself that she was over him. "Who is this guy?" I asked.

"I can't tell you."

If she was hoping I'd try to get it out of her, she was about to be disappointed. "Why do you want to go with me so badly?"

Kendall laughed. "Oh, Seth. Fishing for compliments! I never thought I'd be seeing *this*."

"I'm not—"

"No, it's okay. I'll do it." She grabbed a steak fry from my plate and shoved it into her mouth. "My plan is to make him jealous," she said, chewing and talking at the same time. "So whoever I go with has to be hot, right? You happen to be the hottest single guy I know, *and* you don't have a date. That makes you the one I need."

She was laying it on a little thick.

"What do you think's going to happen?" I asked, wadding up my napkin and throwing it at her. "He'll drop the other girl in the middle of the dance when he sees us together?"

"That would be the best thing *ever*." She grinned and threw the napkin back. "But don't worry. No matter what, you'll still get your payment."

My payment. When she said it like that, it sounded sketchy.

She went on, taking another fry. "Now, this is the part where we negotiate a deal. If you spend the evening of the homecoming dance looking like a sex god and pretending to lust madly for me, I'll do something for you. Whatever you need, *lover*," she said, winking.

Good thing I could tell she was messing with me, because there was no way I was going to go *there*. But the more I thought about the dance itself, the more I was realizing that it might not be all bad. I could keep an eye out for Rosetta and make sure Carr wasn't harassing her. I'd surprise her.

Of course, I still couldn't make things easy for Kendall. This was a big favor, after all. "Yeah. You know, I'm not so sure about this."

"I'm willing to spend money," she said quickly. "How about if I buy something you need for that rust bucket you call a car? A new tire, maybe?"

"Perfect. You give me a hundred bucks for new tires and I'll go to the dance with you."

She dropped the fry she was holding into the ketchup glob on my plate. "You think I'm made of money? How about fifty?"

I could tell I had her, though. Making her loser secret boyfriend jealous was obviously important to her. "Seventy-five. And you have to knock off the 'lover' bullshit too."

She nodded slowly. "Deal."

We reached across the table and shook on it. Then, as I tried to let go, she gripped tighter and wiped her oily fingers all over my hand.

I jerked free and grabbed a fresh napkin. "You suck."

Kendall laughed and then, looking past me, said, "I wonder what those two are doing."

I turned. Next to the bar, Xander and Taku were talking to my mom. "They're probably looking for me."

With nosy Kendall following, I headed over to see what they wanted. I was sure I hadn't told them I eat here, and I park out back so no one sees me coming and going. But I guess it wouldn't have been too hard to find me if they were looking. Kendall had proven that.

I was still a few tables away when Taku handed Mom a folder. "We stuck a band biography, lyric sheets, and a CD with three of our songs in there for you to check out," he said. "Is that all you need?"

It wasn't looking like they were there to see me after all. No, it was looking a lot like they were there trying to book a gig. For their band. Their band of which I was also a member.

Shit.

Just like that, my heart was racing, and the cheeseburger I'd eaten was wreaking havoc on my insides. Kendall pushed her way through to stand next to Mom and grabbed the folder. Like I said, *nosy*. "'Scratching at the Eight Ball,'" Kendall read from the cover. "Kind of a long band name. Cool logo though."

Taku and Xander stared at each other like they were trying to figure out what Kendall was doing there and why she'd busted in on their conversation. I couldn't say I blamed them.

Since they still hadn't noticed me off to the side, I stayed back and tried to decide how to handle this. They'd played together for a year before even bothering to find a bass player. What was the rush to play a live show all of a sudden?

Xander started rambling. Like he does. "We did the demo in a home studio, but it's good quality. Oh, and you'll see that we don't have any press clippings. And our bio doesn't have much going on either. But I know we can get a bunch of people here to see an all-ages show if you'll give us a chance."

Kendall looked across the way at me and raised her eyebrows, as if to ask if I'd known they were going to do this. I shook my head in answer.

"I don't schedule the shows or have any say over which bands play here," Mom said, smiling at Xander and Taku in an "oh you poor kids" kind of way. "But I'll be sure to pass this on to the guy who does."

"Thank you," Xander said. "We really appreciate that."

Kendall laughed. "Are you guys serious? Do you *really* not have any idea who you're talking to here?"

Xander and Taku looked at each other and then at Mom, trying to figure it out, but they had no clue. I decided it was probably time I got Kendall to stop torturing them, so I went over.

"Oh, hey, Seth," Xander said when he saw me. "What are you doing here?"

"Eating dinner."

"What a weird coincidence." He grinned at Mom. "This is Seth McCoy, our bassist. He's played here with the Real McCoys, and they've pulled in a good crowd on quite a few occasions."

Kendall laughed some more, and Xander and Taku gave each other questioning looks again, this time tinged with annoyance.

"Oh, I know Seth McCoy all right," Mom said, smiling. "He's one hell of a bass player, I tell you what. He took a few lessons when he was a kid, and then taught himself the rest by sitting in his room listening to the radio and playing along to every kind of song out there. Or so I've *heard*."

"Yeah, yeah," I said. The radio thing is true, but it's embarrassing when she talks about it. "This is my mom, you guys."

"What?" Taku said at that same time as Xander managed a *"Huh?"*

I went on. "Mom, Xander and Taku are in the band I've been playing with."

"I kind of figured that out," Mom said.

Jared was the one who told her I'd quit the Real McCoys and joined a new band. She hadn't said much of anything about it to me, but I could tell she didn't get it. She kept smiling, though. Mom pretty much always kept smiling. "Baby, you could have told me your new band was looking for a show. You know Will can get you on without all the usual hoop jumping."

"I might have if I'd actually known we were doing this." I gave Xander a pointed look. "Can I talk to you guys for a quick second?"

They followed me over to a booth.

"I must have heard you wrong, because I thought you said that was your *mom*," Xander said, shaking his head. "You meant to say 'sister,' right? Because there's no way she could be *anyone's* mom."

"Except, maybe, like, an infant's," Taku said.

"You didn't hear me wrong," I said.

"Why didn't you tell us your mom worked here?" Xander asked.

"It never came up." Which was true. When *would* it have come up? "Why didn't you tell *me* you were going to book shows for us? It's kind of something I'd need to know, don't you think?"

"We thought you'd be glad if we did all the legwork," Taku said. "But I can see now that it would have been smarter and saved us some steps if we'd had you do it."

I was on the verge of losing it. "I've only been in the band a few weeks. Why are you in such a hurry?"

"Taku and I have wanted to do this for a while," Xander said. "Then the stuff we're doing in IC class gave me the push I needed to stop waiting around for something to happen. Now that we've brought you in, we can move forward."

"Does Brody know?" I asked.

"Brody is what you might call 'resistant to change,'" Taku said. "But he'll come around. He always does."

Xander nodded. "We aren't going to commit to anything unless you and Brody agree. This whole thing is just about us putting some feelers out there and seeing what kind of response we can get."

"Well, I don't think we're ready," I said.

"Most places book a few months out, right?" Xander said. "So you don't have to worry. You already know our songs almost as well as we do. By the time our first show comes along, you'll know them even better."

He was missing my real issue, but I didn't want to spell it out. If I was lucky, Will would take his time about giving us a show. And if he didn't?

Well, I had no idea what then.

SATURDAY, **OCTOBER 9**

7:17 P.M.

Kendall and I hadn't even left my driveway yet, and the whole homecoming deal was already a pain in my ass.

"You're going to be talking about me every chance you get, so you'll need to remember to use the words 'hot,' 'sexy,' or the equivalent," Kendall said as she followed me down the steps. "Also, you have to seem jealous when other guys hit on me. But not *too* jealous. It might get complicated if people believe we're a true couple. And anyway, I don't want anyone to think I have bad enough taste to be with some controlling asshole, you know?"

I was starting to think it would have been better just to pick up extra shifts at the car wash instead of putting myself through this dance crap.

"You don't care if *I* think you have bad enough taste to

waste your time trying to make some douchebag jealous who won't even go out in public with you?" I asked.

Kendall wrinkled her nose. "Make sure you don't have *that* expression on your face all night. People need to think we're having a good time, or this whole thing is pointless."

"Whatever," I said, pulling my keys out of my pocket.

Mikey's truck came kicking up gravel around the corner. His headlights shone in my eyes for a temporary blinding, but not before I'd seen that there were three people in the cab.

*Fan*tastic. Now I really was wishing Kendall had stuck to our original plan and met me at the dance instead of having her mom drop her off here to ride with me. Jared and Daniel had both chilled out some since I'd talked to them after my first night closing with Mikey, a little over a week before. Still, I could have lived my whole life without them finding out about this. As far as I knew, no one had a clue about That One Night, and I wanted nothing more than to keep it that way.

Mikey gave me a wave while Jared and Daniel climbed out. Then he drove off, leaving the four of us in the driveway.

The light on our porch was bright enough to show the surprise on Jared's and Daniel's faces. "You two going to a dance or something?" Jared asked.

I would have thought it was obvious from our clothes. I mean, I was just wearing black pants and a button-down shirt Kendall had forced on me, but it was still a big step up from ripped jeans.

"It's homecoming," Kendall said, hooking her arm carefully through mine as though she didn't want to squish the flower thing on her wrist that she'd bought for herself. "Seth asked me to be his date at the last minute."

I glanced at her, trying to try to figure out why she'd said that, but she seemed to be making a big effort not to make eye contact with me.

"Oh Jesus," Daniel said, laughing. "Dick sure is getting good at doing weird and unexpected shit lately, isn't he?"

"I don't exactly take 'weird and unexpected' as a compliment," Kendall said.

"You're right," he said, checking her out. "What I should have said is that he's lucky you were free. You're looking hot tonight, Eckman."

Kendall did look good, all done up like some glamorous old-time film actress in a slinky red dress. She'd changed her hair again, and it was the first time since freshman year that I'd seen her with her natural dark brown color. During her on-again/off-again thing with Isaac, her hair had always been Marilyn Monroe blond.

Jared lit a cigarette and smirked at Kendall. "What kind of blackmail did my loser brother have to use to get you to go out with him?"

"Ha-ha," I said.

I was *really* ready to leave now. But then Kendall made things worse by starting to laugh for real. "No blackmail. Just lots of begging. Right, Seth?" she said, elbowing me.

I moved away from her. "Yeah, right."

Daniel was still looking at Kendall. "You should come see me after the dance."

She raised her eyebrows. "*You* should keep dreaming."

"Every night, Eckman," he said. "*Every* night."

I expected Kendall to snark at him, but she just rolled her eyes and headed for the Mustang. I followed and climbed into the driver's side, leaving her to open her own damn door. This wasn't a real date, even if she was suddenly faking like it was.

7:31 P.M.

I managed to keep my mouth shut until after I'd backed out of the driveway. Then I turned to Kendall. "You didn't say anything about this acting shit. And you definitely didn't say you'd be trying to make it sound like I'm desperate for you."

She reached over and patted my arm. "Yes, I did. And you had to have known that I wasn't going to let anyone think *I* was the pathetic one here."

"Would it have been so pathetic for you to just say that you asked me because we're nonenemies or whatever?"

"Yes!"

I pulled out onto the main road, and Kendall started messing with the stereo. It drove me crazy when people changed the music in my car—especially without asking—

but I didn't bother saying anything. It wasn't like she was going to stop, anyway.

"Why do you care so much that I told them you asked me?" she asked, still scanning through radio stations. "Are you that embarrassed to be seen with me?"

One thing you could say about Kendall: the girl never had a problem coming up with ways to make *me* sound like the jerk in any given situation.

"I don't want anyone getting the idea that I'm trying to get with Isaac's ex-girlfriend."

She left it on some hip-hop crap. Typical.

"Isn't it about time you stopped thinking of me in relation to Isaac all the time?" she asked in a sad-sounding voice. "Isaac and I first got together a year and a half ago, but you knew me a *decade* and a half before that. To me, you're not Isaac's friend. You're my former neighbor and nonenemy. Can't I be those things to you?"

Kendall did have a point; we'd known each other practically since we were born, and Isaac hadn't moved to town until sixth grade. Changing my thinking wasn't as simple as she made it sound, though. "We can't go backward just because Isaac isn't around anymore," I said. "If he were alive, I know you wouldn't be in this car hanging out as my former-neighbor/nonenemy right now. You'd have found some other guy to help you make your secret boyfriend jealous or—more likely—you'd be back with Isaac and heading to this dance with *him*."

"You're wrong about that last part," she said, shaking her head. "When I broke up with him, it was for good."

I couldn't tell if she believed that or if it was another lie she was telling herself. But Isaac hadn't believed it.

"Quit looking so skeptical," Kendall said. "Isaac cheated on me a bunch of times, which I'm sure you know. With one of my so-called friends, even. I kept taking him back, but the last time it happened, I was so exhausted and pissed off that I decided I couldn't do it again. And that was *it*."

This was the first I'd heard about *Isaac* cheating. "But *you* messed around with Daniel before that, right?"

She sighed. "No. When the Daniel thing happened, Isaac and I had just broken up for the third time because I'd found out about him and some girl at a party."

It sounded like their relationship had been way more screwed up than I'd ever known.

"So was Daniel your way of getting back at him?"

"You can call it that if you want," she said, shrugging. "I think of it more as me trying to move on and get over Isaac. Which was the whole reason I went to that party in the first place—to hook up with Daniel."

The idea that Kendall had preplanned hooking up with Daniel floored me. Daniel was into Kendall in the same way that he was into all hot chicks, but Kendall walking away from him in my driveway was a classic example of how *non-seriously* she seemed to take him. "How did that even happen?" I asked. "I mean, why Daniel?"

She covered her face and laughed a little, like she couldn't believe we were having this conversation. "Okay, this isn't going to make me sound honorable, but I guess part of it was because I was thinking I wouldn't mind if it got back to Isaac so he could feel what I was feeling. And since I was rebounding—and Daniel *is* rebound guy—I thought I'd see if it was true what everyone says about him, you know, having all the moves down. As it turns out, he totally does. So, yeah. Um. *That's* why Daniel."

I stared at the taillights in front of me, feeling anxious all of a sudden. If Kendall could talk about what sex had been like with Daniel, what was she telling people about me? What was there *to* tell?

While I was trying to figure out whether I wanted to know, Kendall started talking again. Calmer now. "You probably don't believe me, but I want you to know that I honestly thought Isaac and I were over when everything happened with Daniel. I'm not a cheater."

I waited a few seconds before saying, "I believe you."

The thing was . . . it seemed like she really was telling the truth. I just had no clue how I could have had things so mixed up.

I turned into the school lot—which was about half-full—and pulled into the first empty space. Kendall switched on the dome light and flipped the visor down to look in the tiny mirror. "I'm glad I finally got to tell you my side," she said as she touched up her lipstick. "Thanks for listening."

"What else was I going to do? I'm trapped in a car with you."

She laughed and punched my arm. "Prick."

Peaceful times between us had been rare, and I didn't know when the next would be coming. So I decided to just throw the subject out there. "I've been wondering about that night. You know, when I played my last show with the Real McCoys?"

She stopped puckering her lips at herself but didn't take her eyes off the mirror. "What about it?"

"Well, all I remember is getting wasted and then waking up next to you. You're the only one who knows what went on during the hours in between. I kind of want to know how it happened. I mean, not a play-by-play. Just the basics."

"There's honestly not much of a play-by-play to relay for you."

"Meaning what?" I asked hopefully. "Nothing really happened?"

Kendall closed her eyes for a long second, and then turned to face me. "Is right now really the best time for us to relive this?"

Shit. Now it was obvious what she'd been getting at. "Not much of a play-by-play" equaled one miserable play.

My face got hot. Actually, I was warm all over. And, God, was I ever wishing I'd kept my mouth shut. "That bad, huh?"

I tried to laugh it off, but I sounded like almost as big of a loser as I felt.

Kendall shook her head. "It's just—"

I cut her off. "You don't have to tell me," I said, talking fast. "I'm sorry if it sucked for you. I was trashed and it was my first time. Not that I'm trying to make excuses. But I thought you should know. In case you want to cut me a break if you ever tell anyone about it?"

So pathetic.

Silence.

Kendall stared at me, her eyes open wide. "Wait a second. So you're telling me you'd never been with a girl before?"

"No. Not all the way."

"Oh!"

She was surprised. Which was . . . maybe an okay sign. I don't know.

"So what about *after* that night?" she asked.

I didn't see how that was any of her business, but I told her anyway. "No."

A slow smile spread across her face. "Wow, Seth. That has to be the sweetest, most adorable thing I've ever heard."

I looked away. "Shut up."

She pushed the visor back up and shifted in her seat. "I'm *serious*," she said, leaning close to me. "You're in a band, and you have that 'wrong side of the tracks' thing going that the good girls love. I always figured you were getting action all the time. Just, you know, more discreetly than your friends."

"Okay. But weren't you just saying it wasn't . . . decent?"

She shook her head.

"So you really had no idea, then?"

"None," she said.

Relief. And then I didn't want to talk about it anymore. "Are you ready to go to this stupid dance now or what?"

She raised her eyebrows like she wasn't sure how she felt about the abrupt end to the conversation, but then she smiled. "If you're going to get your ass out of the car and open my door like a gentleman this time, then yes, I am."

"I can do that."

8:32 P.M.

"You better not have been making a dumb face just now or I'll kill you," Kendall said two seconds after the photographer's camera flashed. "I'm going to be cherishing these pictures for the rest of my life, you know."

"Oh, me too," I said. "Me too."

She laughed and pulled me away from the backdrop. For almost an hour now, she'd been dragging me all around the gym, which looked about the same as always, except for the dimmed lights and the homecoming banners. She wanted to make sure her secret boyfriend saw us together in every possible place, I think. My face was aching from all the fake smiling, and she'd been holding on to me so tightly while we walked that I'd almost forgotten what it felt like *not* having her left boob mashed against my upper arm. Making her guy jealous—whoever he was—was exhausting work.

"Where are we off to now?" I asked.

Kendall flashed a beauty-pageant smile. "Does it matter, darling?"

I sighed. "Well, I'm getting kind of tired of walking around. Maybe we can sit down and chill for a while?"

I'd been keeping up my end of the bargain, acting all cozy with Kendall and complimenting her every chance I got while she paraded me from group to group. Maybe some people would have been entertained watching Kendall put on this show, but I was wishing like hell not to be a part of it. Especially since it was putting a big crimp in my plan to surprise Rosetta. I still hadn't been able to spot her—and believe me, I'd been looking—but I was getting paranoid that she might have noticed all this close contact going on with Kendall and me and was getting the wrong idea.

"I think we'll dance now," Kendall said, letting go of my arm just long enough to grab my hand and tug me toward the dance floor.

I was about to make a smart remark about how I'd thought she'd *never* ask, but Pete Zimmer chose that moment to stroll up in all his football-god glory and block our way. The smell coming off him was like beer cologne. I have to admit, right then I probably would have just about killed for a drink or two . . . or seven.

"You look good, Kendall," Pete said in a low voice.

Kendall smiled and somehow managed to snuggle against me even closer than before. "Thank you."

"No," he said, looking her up and down slowly. "I mean, you look *really* good."

Kendall giggled. "Again, thank you. I am having such an amazing time with Seth tonight. Do you know Seth McCoy? He's in a band."

She was so *weird*. Of course he knew me; we'd been going to school together all our lives.

Pete acknowledged me with a nod and then went back to staring at Kendall's cleavage. If Kendall had been my girlfriend and he was pulling this shit, I'd have wanted to kick his ass. But I remembered having seen them together at his party at the end of summer, and I started figuring out what was going on here. She was *his* girl, even though he got his kicks by refusing to go out with her in public.

"Vicki isn't having fun," he said. "I can't figure out why, and she isn't telling."

Vicki was the girl Pete had brought to the dance so no one would know he was secretly screwing Kendall. It was all coming together.

Kendall's smile didn't slip. "That sucks."

I got the feeling Kendall's plan was going to pay off in about thirty seconds: Pete would be ditching Vicki; Kendall would be ditching me. All as it should have been.

While I waited for it, I went back to scanning the area for Rosetta and Carr. Still no luck. Maybe Rosetta hadn't been able to figure out a way to avoid the Rolls-Royce and had to pretend to be sick at the last minute? This was the first time in my life I'd ever been disappointed *not* to see Carr.

Then a strange thing happened. Kendall didn't let go of me. She didn't disappear with Pete. Instead, she elbowed me in the ribs. My cue to say my thing.

Caught off guard, I looked at Kendall.

She stared back at me.

And then there was that elbow again.

I cleared my throat and said, "I'm really stoked that Kendall came to this dance with me. She's one of the sexiest chicks here."

Kendall's eyes narrowed ever so slightly.

"Uh. Yeah." Pete looked at his feet. "I'd better get back."

And just like that, he was shuffling away.

Kendall turned to me, frowning. "Thanks a lot. That was your most uninspired performance yet. Even as drunk as he is, he *still* noticed that you sounded like you were reading from a cue card."

"Sorry."

But, really, I *wasn't*.

It was hitting me just how ridiculous this whole deal was. In the car Kendall had talked about what a bad boyfriend Isaac had been, but what she had going on now was just as screwed up. All this stupid drama. And for what exactly?

A couple of Kendall's friends walked by right then, so

she turned the smile back on for them and kept it going even as she looked at me. "Do *not* flake out on me, Seth. I'm paying you to help me sell this. Remember?"

9:27 P.M.

Kendall and I were right in the thick of things on the dance floor, and she was going crazy bouncing around with the crowd to a rowdy old country song that even all noncountry fans know. I'm not much into dancing—especially not while sober—but I was faking it to keep her happy. It seemed to be working too. Her cheeks were pink, her eyes were bright, and her smile might even have been real.

"If you weren't with me, who would you have wanted to come to this dance with?" she asked.

Yeah, she was all about the nosy questioning too.

"No one, remember? And I would have been fine with it."

The DJ switched to another slow song, and I silently cursed him. So boring. I moved in close and put my arms around Kendall's waist while she wrapped hers around my neck. One thing was for sure, I was getting good at going through the motions while feeling absolutely nothing.

"I know you weren't *planning* to go," she said. "Let's put it like this: If you had to ask someone and were guaranteed a yes, who would you have chosen?"

I shrugged, even though I did have one person in mind, of course. "Why are you asking me this?"

"No real reason," Kendall said, propping her chin on my shoulder. "It's just that there's a girl who keeps staring at you, and I think she's your soul mate. I'm sensing that you're going to fall in love and it's going to be romantic and intense. Probably tragic, too, but it will be worth it because it will change your lives forever."

"You're sensing all that because some girl looked at me a few times?"

She lifted her head and grinned. "Yes."

I couldn't help laughing. "You are one strange chick, you know that?"

"I'm going to assume that what you meant to say is that I'm nice to watch out for my nonenemy like this," she said, patting my cheek. "Here, let's rotate slowly so you can look at her. But don't be obvious about it like you always are. Be cool. Be casual."

We kept doing our slow-dance swaying, then Kendall started leading me into a turn. A very, *very* slow turn. Cool and casual, that was me.

"Who am I supposed to be looking at?"

"We're not there yet," Kendall said as we moved what felt like only a fraction of an inch at a time. "Okay. This should be right. Straight ahead of you, way over at the edge of the dance floor. Under the clock?"

In that second, I forgot all about this soul mate joke. Because, after looking all night for Rosetta, there she was. She had on a strapless silvery-blue dress and her black hair was hanging loose in thick waves. There must have been twenty feet and more than twenty people directly between us, but she was looking so beautiful over there that I could hardly *breathe* over here.

"Do you see her?" Kendall asked, jolting me back to reality.

"I see Rosetta Vaughn having a conversation with Carr Goodwin." I sounded much calmer than I was feeling. "I don't see any girl staring at me."

Kendall forced me to move so that Rosetta out of my view again. "That's who I was talking about. She probably looked away while we were turning."

Something weird was going on here. Maybe at some point Kendall had seen me with Rosetta at school? And maybe I'd been obvious, like I supposedly *always* am, and now Kendall was making up this whole Rosetta-staring story to mess with me? "I kind of doubt she could have been looking at me through all these people."

Kendall rolled her eyes. "Seth, I know what I saw. Now, why don't you go give the girl a thrill and ask her to dance?"

"Because I'm dancing with you. Just like you're paying me to do."

"It's okay. You've done a good job tonight, all things considered. I don't mind if you take a break from me and dance with her for a few minutes. Really."

My heart started thumping away. Seeing Rosetta was what I'd been waiting for—and the main reason I was here—

but I now realized I hadn't made a plan for what I'd say or do once it happened. Whenever I'd imagined it, Rosetta had been the one to come to me, I guess.

"How am I going to keep making your secret boyfriend jealous if I'm with another girl?"

Kendall smirked. "For all you know, he already left the building. Now, I'm giving you permission to go talk to the hot girl over there who totally wants you. You aren't seriously going to be a wuss about it, are you?"

I whipped my head around to look at Rosetta again, ruining the cool and casual thing I'd had going on before. Rosetta had no clue, though; she was too busy smiling up at Carr to notice what *I* was up to.

Ugh. Maybe I'd be a wuss after all.

9:35 P.M.

At any point between Kendall grabbing my arm, nudging people out of our way, and marching me to the edge of the dance floor, I could have tried to stop her. But as nervous as this was making me, I didn't try. Kendall had the balls that I seemed to be lacking at the moment, so I let her make my decision for me.

Now here we were. Standing in front of Rosetta and Carr. And for the first time since I'd helped Kendall out of my car, she'd let go of me.

Up close, Rosetta's dress was more blue than silver

and made her eyes look even prettier than usual. Whether she'd seen me before that moment, I couldn't tell, but she was seeing me now. Somehow, her face was communicating most of the feelings our IC class had listed for Mrs. D. after the first day: confusion, nervousness, curiosity, surprise.

I couldn't quite pick up on whether she was thinking the surprise was a good or bad one.

"Oh, hi there!" Kendall said in a weird, shocked way, as if they'd appeared in front of us instead of us coming to them. "It is *so* nice to see you two here tonight."

"Hi," Carr said, looking at Kendall as if she were speaking a language he couldn't—and didn't want to—understand.

"Isn't this DJ great?" Kendall asked. "Like, every time I want to hear a certain kind of song, he just happens to play it next. It's almost as if we have a connection or something. You know what I mean?"

It isn't every day that I get to see Carr at a loss for words or Kendall babbling like an airhead, but I couldn't enjoy the moment; I was too busy trying to send messages to Rosetta with my eyes: *This isn't what it looks like. Unless it looks like I'm here to see you. Then it's* exactly *what it looks like. Okay?*

But Rosetta's forehead was still creased in confusion; she wasn't getting the message.

Kendall kept it up in that same loud, phony-friendly way. "Anyway, we just wanted to come over and congratulate you on the great job you and your little group did organizing this dance, Carr. Seth doesn't even like school dances much, but he's *loving* this one. Aren't you, Seth?"

If we'd been talking to anyone else in the gym, her comment would have segued into the part of the Kendall & Seth Show where I gave my "Kendall is sexy" speech and Kendall pretended to be embarrassed. There was no way I was going to say any of that to Rosetta, though. And it wasn't what Kendall wanted me to do either, right?

Bracing myself for Kendall's elbow from hell, I decided to wing it. "Well, me loving the dance might be an exaggeration," I said, looking only at Rosetta. "But since I get to cross something off my 'challenges' list and haven't broken out in hives yet, I'd say things are going fine."

The elbow didn't come. And even better than that, Rosetta seemed like she might be getting it now. "That's really great," she said, smiling. "You aren't allergic after all."

Carr seemed to have had more than enough of this interruption. "I'm glad you're enjoying yourselves." He aimed his politician smile at us all and put his hand on Rosetta's shoulder. "We were waiting for a good song to come on so we could dance. So I guess we'll see you—"

"Hang on," Kendall said, flashing that freaky beauty-pageant smile again. Then she stepped forward to link her arm in his. "We should mix it up a little here, Carr. Seth and Rosetta. You and me."

Carr shook his head. "I don't think—"

"Come on!" Kendall said, in a voice like Carr was a

puppy and she was offering up treats. "Just for one quick song. It'll be fun!"

And before he got a chance to argue again, she pulled him away, leaving me standing there alone with Rosetta.

9:38 P.M.

This was my moment—the only one I was likely to get tonight—and I had to make it count. There would be roughly three minutes before the song ended. Three minutes before Carr came back for Rosetta. Three minutes before Kendall came for me. Which meant I had *three measly minutes* to do or say something that would make Rosetta realize I was the guy for her.

Since I was always so great under pressure, I jumped into my big moment by stating the obvious: "You look amazing."

Like she hadn't been hearing that all night from Carr. Like anyone with working eyes and vocal cords would have been able to *keep* from saying it to her.

But she didn't seem to mind hearing it again. "Thanks. You too."

So far, so good. We'd used up about ten seconds. Time to move on to the me-being-really-smooth part. "I'm here as a favor to Kendall. But the main reason I agreed to come is because I wanted to surprise *you*."

She smiled at me in that way she has that gets me all wound up, but somehow calms me at the same time. "I'm so glad you did. I know you said you weren't coming, but I've still spent the whole night wishing you'd change your mind. And here you are!"

I don't know how she did it, how she could say cool stuff so easily like that. Even if she didn't speak again before our three minutes were up, those words had already made all the Kendall and Pete crap worth it. Because that—*that* right there—was the best thing a girl had ever said to me.

I was basking and trying to work out something non-corny to say back to her when Xander came over all breathless. "Seth, I just got a text from that booking agent dude your mom set me up with. And get ready for this! Will said he'll put us down for an opening slot in two weeks if we want it. We'll go over the details at rehearsal tomorrow so I can give him an answer, but I wanted to let you know about it right away. Now I'm going to go find Taku. And Brody. Well, *maybe* Brody."

Then he ran off again, leaving me with a tight knot in my gut to go along with all the rest of my tension. Could his timing have been *any* suckier?

"I might need to quit that band," I said to Rosetta.

I'd tried to make it sound like a joke, but I was dead serious.

She touched my arm gently. She got it. Of course she did. She was probably the only one who could. "Maybe it will be fine if you make up an elaborate lie like I did tonight," she said, wrinkling her nose.

"What did you lie about?"

"Remember how I asked Carr *not* to hire a car because I was going to meet him here?"

I nodded.

She pushed her hair back. "Right. So I'm coming out my front door to walk here, and there's Carr in my driveway jumping out of some stretch Mercedes. And he says, 'Surprise! I know you didn't want a Rolls-Royce, so I got this instead!'"

I looked out at Carr and Kendall on the dance floor. The moves he was busting were stiff and dorky as hell. Kendall looked amused. "That guy just won't give up."

"I *know*," Rosetta said. "I was panicking because there was no way I could ride with him. But I didn't know how to avoid it since, I mean, the car was *right there*. I ended up telling him I've taken a pledge for the environment and I can't ride in any vehicle that burns fossil fuels for the rest of the year. He fell for it and then decided to be nice and walk here with me."

A pledge for the environment. It was a good cover story, really. The bizarre sort of thing Rosetta might do even if she wasn't trying to hide her phobia. Still, it bothered me that she'd gone there. Now she had this excuse ready, so wouldn't she have even less reason to try to get over it?

"Maybe I should come up with some fake pledge to tell the guys," I said. "Like, 'Sorry, I can't do the show. I've made a pledge on behalf of starving musicians everywhere to never accept money for playing music.'"

"Xander would just tell the place not to pay you to get around that. Maybe you should say you've developed a new type of allergy."

I rubbed my chin, pretending like I thought she was being serious and I was considering it. "Maybe I *should*."

Right then the music changed to a boy band song. Our three minutes of alone time were up. But Kendall and Carr weren't racing right back to us. I had no problem taking advantage of that.

"Do you feel like dancing?" I asked Rosetta.

She was looking toward Kendall and Carr too. "You know, I'm kind of thirsty."

I caught Kendall's eye, pointed in the direction of the far-off beverage table, and made a motion like I was drinking from a cup so she'd know where we were heading. She waved.

Another surprise. When Kendall wanted to be, she was pretty damn cool.

9:47 P.M.

Rosetta and I were next to each other at a table far from all the dance action, sipping watery punch from plastic cups. "I have to tell you," she said, "for the first few seconds after you came over with Kendall, I was wishing you weren't here tonight."

There aren't a lot of ways to take that, but I figured she was making some kind of joke. I mean, she *had* to be, right?

"Fine. This will be the last time I ever risk an allergic reaction to surprise *you*."

"Oh, you know what I mean," she said, laughing. "I thought maybe you were *with* Kendall. Like her boyfriend. But then I realized that you're definitely not her boyfriend." She bit her lip. "I mean, you're not, right?"

I shook my head, probably much harder than necessary to get my point across. "Not even close. We've known each other since we were kids, but we're more nonenemies than friends, even."

She smiled. "Good to know."

And that's when I knew. It was time. Time for me to tell Rosetta how crazy I was about her. Time to just *say* it.

I set my cup down.

She set hers down too.

I looked into her eyes.

She looked into mine.

This was big. A big, huge moment. Or, it had the potential to be if I didn't screw it up.

Time for me to lay it all out and stop waiting around for whatever I'd been waiting for all this time.

I reached over. Took her hand. Gave a light squeeze.

Okay. Now.

She squeezed back and held on tight.

Now.

And then she pushed back her chair and stood.

Panic.

This was my moment. I couldn't just let it pass. "Rosetta—"

"Come on," she said, pulling me to my feet. "Let's get out of here."

9:50 P.M.

Rosetta was barefoot. She was holding the straps of her high-heeled shoes in her left hand and my hand in her right. We were running. Not *from* anyone. Not *to* any specific place that I knew of. We just ran.

It had started with fast walking as we'd gone past Mrs. D. and Ms. Naylor at the chaperone table, and we'd switched to a jog as we headed out of the gym. Then, in the hall, Rosetta had pulled off her shoes and the full-on running had begun. Past the lockers. Out the glass double doors. Down the steps. Like we couldn't get away fast enough.

I didn't know where we were going. I didn't *care* where we were going.

It was cold. Not so much that I could see my breath, but there was enough bite in the damp air to burn my lungs a little. Switching from the noisy gym to the silent outdoors was as jarring as it was peaceful. My brain kind of hummed as I took it all in.

The whole thing—the running, the darkness, the air, my lungs, my heart, being with Rosetta—was making me feel . . .

well, "alive" sounds dumb, but it's the only word I can think of to describe it.

I felt more alive than I had since Isaac died.

9:54 P.M.

The stadium lights at the football field were turned off, but there was still enough light spilling over from the parking lot for Rosetta and me to find our way to the stands. We slowed down. Way down. My pulse was throbbing in my neck, thundering in my ears. At least I could blame this rare exercise for the effect instead of my nervousness alone.

I was still holding Rosetta's hand. "I've never run away from a dance with a barefoot girl before."

She looked up at me, smiling. "And I've never been a barefoot girl who's run away from a dance before."

We headed up to the back row with me panting all the way. Rosetta put her shoes down and we settled next to each other on the cold metal bench. Sitting so close—probably closer than we had ever been—I was hyper-aware of every little thing: the warmth of her hand in mine, the pressure of our arms lightly touching, the mere inches that separated our legs, the slight rise and fall of her breasts in that satiny dress, the incredible fresh, flowery scent of her hair.

With my big moment in the gym delayed, I was back to worrying, wishing now that past Seth had already gotten this over with so that present-time Seth could calm down.

We sat there, neither of us saying anything for a few seconds. My breathing was the only sound going on, and it was kind of embarrassing. She was so in shape and I was like a winded old man. I closed my mouth tight and started with slow in-and-out breaths through my nose only. Much better.

Rosetta pushed her hair behind her shoulder. "I just love that feeling when things are about to change. Like when you know that in a few seconds you're going to do something and become someone different."

I had no idea what she was talking about. What was she about to do and become? Or was this not really about her but some, like, poetry thing instead? The stuff she thought and said was sometimes so beyond me that I couldn't keep up.

She shifted ever so slightly on the bench so that her shoulder was against my arm. "A while back, I started really focusing on what it feels like before and after I do new things," she said. "Last year, my parents and I went to this suspension bridge over a river in Canada where people can pay to bungee jump. My mom chickened out, but once I'd gotten it in my mind that I was going to do it, I had to."

"Are you serious?" I asked.

It wasn't like I thought she was afraid of everything in the world. But it did seem backward that someone who couldn't ride in a car had done something like that. I was pretty sure I couldn't do it.

"I know. Weird, right?" she said, smiling. "I remember, I had the harness on, the cords were hooked up and ready, and I was standing there on the platform thinking, 'These are the last seconds in my life that I'll ever *not* have jumped off a bridge.' It was such an intense moment."

I still didn't know why she'd started talking about this, but it was kind of feeling like maybe she was just making conversation. Which was okay with me because I was starting to relax for the first time all night.

Well, okay, "relax" is pushing it. Especially since, while talking, she'd lifted our hands from my knee, intertwined her fingers in mine, and then let our hands drop back onto my leg again. Kind of high and inside on my leg, actually.

Jesus.

"You know," I said. "When people jumped off bridges back in the olden days, those seconds standing on the platform were some of the last that they lived at *all*."

She scooted a tiny bit closer to me. Which made our hands move a tiny bit higher.

"That's why bungee jumping is such a rush," she said, seeming not to notice what she was doing to me here. "Because you know that the jump should kill you. They say the people with the most fear of jumping are the ones who end up loving it the most. So I went for it. I stepped over the edge. And in that split second, I went from being someone who hadn't jumped off a bridge to someone who had. It was one of the most amazing things I've ever done."

"You're crazy," I said, shaking my head. "I had no idea how crazy you are."

She laughed. "Well, that's my most extreme example, but there's stuff like that happening every day. Like the first time you fly in an airplane, eat cashew cheesecake, play a round of golf, listen to a new song. The first time you have sex. Which, I don't know what that's like, personally. But, the thing is, for your whole life, you're someone who *hasn't* done a particular thing. And just like that"—she snapped her fingers—"you're someone who has."

I was in a strange place with the sex thing. After having been a virgin for sixteen years, I was mostly able to accept that I wasn't one anymore, but it still didn't feel real. Not like Rosetta's hand on my leg.

"So what's next?" I asked. "Are you and your thrill-seeking parents going to go skydiving or something?"

And just like that, the easy vibe was gone, and Rosetta was letting go of my hand and sitting up straight. She'd moved only four inches, maybe five, but it felt like five feet. I had no clue what I'd missed.

She was looking at me questioningly. "I thought you knew."

"Knew what?"

She bit her lip. "Well, my parents. They aren't around anymore. They passed away."

Shit. How could I have known that? Or maybe it was more like, how could I *not* have known?

"I'm sorry," I said, feeling like a jerk. "I had no idea."

"They died right before I moved here in February." She

started smoothing her dress over her legs. "Which is *why* I moved here. I live with my aunt and uncle." She looked at me again. "You really didn't know that?"

Rosetta and I had been hanging out for several weeks. We talked to each other a lot. At least, I'd *thought* it was a lot. But not about her family. Which I hadn't noticed until this exact moment.

"I should have picked up on it," I said. "I'm really sorry, Rosetta."

"It's okay," she said, shaking her head as if she was trying to clear her mind. "When I first came to town, my busy-body aunt made sure to tell everyone at the country club about taking me in. I assumed there wasn't anyone left who hadn't heard about Little Orphan Rosetta."

"Yeah, I'm not really part of the country club crowd."

She smiled at me. A tiny, tiny smile. "That's probably why I like you so much."

Then she moved close again, took my hand, and held it in both of hers while she stared down at her lap some more.

I didn't know what to say. What to ask. What to *do*. But I couldn't just sit there and say nothing. She hadn't left me hanging when I'd told her about Isaac. And this thing with her parents explained why she'd understood so well about Isaac. It might explain even more than that.

"You don't have to talk about this if you don't want," I said. "But when you were crying in the stairwell at school a few weeks ago, did it have something to do with your parents?"

"You saw me crying?"

"I'm sorry. I should have said something at the time. I'm really sorry."

"You don't have to keep apologizing," she said softly.

But I kind of *did*. It felt like the only thing I could do.

"The reason I was in the stairwell is because I was upset about my quiz," she said. "In the middle of crying my eyes out, I thought about how if my mom found out I'd been sobbing over physics like that, she'd tell me I needed to chill so I wouldn't give myself ulcers. For a few seconds, I felt better, like I'd really be having that conversation with her when I got home from school. But then I *remembered*, and it felt like both of them had just died all over again."

Her words hung there, but I totally got it. I was sure it would be worse when it's your parents—it *had* to be—but I still knew what she meant. "That happens to me sometimes with Isaac. There have been times that I've thought about calling him up before I remember that I can't anymore. The remembering part sucks."

"And the dreams are even worse, I think, because of how they mess with your mind." Rosetta sighed. "I'll have them where my mom and dad will appear, and I'll be all, 'But I thought you guys were dead!' And they'll say stuff like, 'We had no choice except to fake our deaths, but now it's safe so we're back for you.'"

I nodded. "Sometimes Isaac will show up in mine like that too. It will all come out that him dying had been a trick. And even though I know I should be pissed that he played me, I'm so relieved about him being alive that I don't even care."

"And then you have to wake up and find out that the *dream* was the trick," she said.

"Exactly."

"Which can throw off your whole day before it even begins."

"Or the whole week," I said.

And with that, Rosetta and I shut up and just sat there looking at each other.

We were both screwed up; we'd already figured that out weeks ago. But I think we were both just realizing that we were screwed up in the same way.

I put my arm around her. Rubbed her goose-bumpy arm. Pulled her close.

She tilted her face up. Touched my cheek. And kissed me.

10:18 P.M.

Rosetta's lips were on my lips, her cheek was against my check, her tongue was touching my tongue, and her hand was gently stroking my face. Every single part of me was responding. I held her body against mine, as close and comfortably as our sitting-on-a-bench position would allow. One of my hands was on the cool, satiny material at her waist, and the other was high on her back, running over her hair and soft skin.

If I had kept track of all the minutes I'd spent wondering what it would be like to kiss Rosetta, they would probably total hours. I'd pictured it wrong, though. In my imagination, kissing her hadn't made everything feel like it was happening in slow motion and at lightning speed at the same time. And all these small movements, touches, and feelings hadn't added up to something so intensely huge.

The real thing was *awesome*.

Too soon, Rosetta and I were two people whose lips, cheeks, and tongues weren't touching anymore. I opened my eyes and looked into hers, and I could tell she'd felt it too, whatever *it* was. All I was thinking was *Amazing*, but I didn't want to say it aloud. That one word described what I honestly meant, what I honestly felt, but it wasn't enough somehow.

So I didn't speak at all. I kissed her again.

10:26 P.M.

Loud voices had moved to the outdoors. Car doors were slamming and engines were starting up in the parking lot. Which meant people were starting to leave the dance.

Reluctantly, I paused in kissing Rosetta to look at my watch. "Uh-oh. We've been gone half an hour."

Her jaw dropped. "We should get back!"

"Kendall's going to kill me for ditching her. And Carr's going to kill me for running off with his date."

Rosetta stood up. "I can't believe how fast that went. It seemed like ten minutes."

I grabbed her shoes and put my arm around her as we headed down the bleacher steps, feeling let down by this not-making-out-anymore-and-heading-back-to-our-dates thing we had going on now. But when we got to the bottom, Rosetta smiled shyly at me. "So . . . that was nice."

"*Yeah*, it was."

And then we both laughed. I don't know about her, but for me it wasn't because of embarrassment or nervousness or anything. It was more like I was just so *psyched*.

"My bungee metaphor kind of got lost back there," Rosetta said as we kept going in the direction of the parking lot. "But it did make me think of something else I want to tell you."

I vaguely recalled hearing about metaphors in English class. So Rosetta *had* been talking about poetry, then?

"What was your metaphor?"

She glanced up at me, still shy. "It was supposed to be about you and me. And specifically about how I was *really* ready for you to kiss me for the first time."

Okay, that had all gone right over my head.

"I see," I said.

Rosetta burst out laughing again. "You know, now that I

just said that out loud, I can tell that it was very corny and heavy-handed. Sorry about that."

"No, it's cool. Definitely the first time a girl's ever talked about trying to jump to her death to get me to kiss her."

She laughed even harder, so that we had to stop walking for a few seconds until she calmed down. "Okay, so I have another metaphor for you. This one's better, I think. Wasn't Xander saying that the band thing he wants you to play is in two weeks?"

"Yeah. You think I should jump off a bridge to get out of it?"

"Actually, I think you should play the gig."

That was kind of a buzzkill.

I shook my head. "Rosetta, I can't—"

"Just hear me out." She stopped walking again and turned to face me, looking all happy and beautiful. "You think you can't play a good show onstage without Isaac because you've never done it. Maybe for this stage-fright deal it's going to come down to how badly you want it."

"If it was that easy, we would never have had a conversation about it in the first place, would we?"

"Oh, it *definitely* isn't easy." She grabbed my free hand and started swinging it. "But maybe it's like free-falling. You feel like you'd rather do anything than have to face it, but once you do it you realize it's the best feeling you've ever had. Music is something you're good at, something you like doing. And, I mean, if *I* can jump off a bridge, you should be able to play bass in front of a room full of people, right?"

I sighed, suddenly not a fan of Rosetta's metaphors or of her laying them on me when I'd been feeling so good about everything else that was happening with us. "You know that every single thing you're saying to me is true about you too right? Even more because you're the one who did jump off that bridge. If you can do something huge like that, you can do something small like get in a car."

Her smile faded and she shook her head. "It's not the same thing."

"It is, Rosetta. It's exactly the same. Facing your fear or whatever and just pushing through. You're saying *I* can. I'm saying *you* can. It's easy to say to each other. It's not so easy to actually do it ourselves."

Her shoulders slumped and now she was frowning a little, but she nodded. "You're right. I shouldn't pressure you like this. I'm sorry. I won't do it again."

I thought I'd be relieved, but instead I was disappointed. I guess deep down I wanted Rosetta to get on my case. I liked how she challenged me, how she had so much faith that I could do things. And I liked turning it around on her, too. I didn't even know why, but I wanted so badly to be the one to help her get over her phobia.

It was way past time for us to get back to Kendall and Carr, but I was getting an idea and knew that if I didn't blurt it out right then, I'd wuss out entirely. "You know what? I'm going to do it. I'll commit to playing the gig. But only if you end your fake pledge and ride there with me."

She had the wide-eyed look of someone who'd been backed into a corner, but I didn't let up. I needed her help. She needed mine.

"Please," I said. "Do this with me."

She shook her head. "I can't."

"You *can*."

"Seth, no."

"We have two weeks. We both have the same thing to work through when you think about it. We can use it as our ultimate IC class challenge or whatever, figure it out together, and make it happen."

She was chewing on her lip. Considering, maybe?

"Come on, Rosetta. You know I can't do it without you."

And that's when she nodded. Slowly, hesitantly. But it was a nod.

10:35 P.M.

In front of the school, Rosetta and I were the only ones heading in instead of out. A few people were getting into limos and crap like that, but a bunch more were on their way to the parking lot we'd just come from. Pete and Vicki were passing by, and Vicki was staring at us so hard it looked like her eyes were going to pop out. Rosetta waved at her, and Vicki did that phone gesture thing by her ear that girls do and mouthed all frantic, *Call me*.

From the bottom of the front steps, I could see Carr and Kendall waiting together up top. Carr looked pissed, but like he was trying to hide it; Kendall just looked pissed. I didn't blame her. Even though I hadn't meant to, I'd totally dicked her over.

"Here we go," I said to Rosetta, wishing I could kiss her one more time before having to leave her for the night. Instead, I followed her up.

Carr stepped forward when we got there. I could tell that he was very deliberately *not* looking at me. "Are you okay, Rosetta?"

"I'm great, actually," she said.

Carr nodded, and, as big an asshole as he was, I almost felt sorry for him. I mean, his date disappeared with some other guy at a dance. That *had* to suck.

"If you want to go change now, I'll walk you home," he said.

"That's classy," Kendall said. "You're making her walk?"

"Actually, I hired a car," Carr said in an overly patient way. "But Rosetta has strong political beliefs and recently made a pledge to the environment, so she wasn't able to ride in it."

Kendall gave Rosetta a once-over. "A pledge to the environment? All righty, then!" she said with that false brightness she was so good at. "You two have fun with your walking. I'm ready to use up some fossil fuels, Seth. *Now*."

"Okay," I said.

"*Great,*" Kendall said. "Rosetta. Carr. It's been real."

She turned and started down the steps, her heels clicking hard like she was imagining stomping through my skull the whole way.

Rosetta looked at me, apologizing with her eyes. Then she disappeared inside.

I went after Kendall, trying to think of something I could say to make this up to her. But three steps down, I headed back to Carr, who was watching me with no expression on his face.

"Can you give these to Rosetta?" I asked, holding out her shoes.

He took them without responding.

But then, after I'd made it down a few steps again, he said, "A word of advice, McCoy. Stick with sluts like Kendall. Rosetta's way too good for trash like you."

FRIDAY, **OCTOBER 15**

9:47 P.M.

Six days later. I pulled into the Kenburn Lanes lot, parked in a big hurry, and rushed to get inside. I was late. So late.

Any other year, I wouldn't have bothered showing up for the annual bowling shindig on the one game-free Friday night of Kenburn High's football season. Obviously, I didn't care about the football bullshit or the big rah-rah get-together. But I was there to see my kinda-girlfriend. Whom I'd kept waiting for almost an hour.

The nearly full parking lot should have been a clue, but I still hadn't expected the place to be so packed. Students, teachers, parents milling around. Balloons and crap all over. And the *noise*. The usual sounds of balls hitting the floor and crashing into pins, and pins slamming against one another, the back wall, and the floor were pretty much drowned out by everyone's talking, laughing, shrieking, and yelling.

From the main level, I looked toward the lanes and seating areas below for any sign of Rosetta. No luck right off, but I spotted Brody, Taku, and Xander bowling with a group of chicks, so I headed to them first.

"Hey, the band's all here!" Taku called out from where he was standing near the automatic ball return. "Have a seat, Seth, and we'll add you in for the next game."

I shook my head. "I'm just looking for Rosetta. Anyone seen her?"

"She's around," Brody said, glancing up from his bolted-down chair in front of the computer. "I saw her with my sister earlier."

"Cool. Thanks, man."

I started to leave, but Xander tugged the back of my jacket to stop me. "We were talking about adding a rehearsal Sunday night. Can you make it?"

"Sure."

"And while we're on that subject," Xander said, turning back to the girls and raising his voice, "you're all coming out to see us next Saturday night, right?"

"See you where?" one of them asked.

Xander clutched his chest all dramatic. "Did you hear that? She doesn't know what I'm talking about!"

Brody gave him a hard look. We were confirmed to play

the show in exactly one week, and the closer it got, the pissier Brody was becoming.

"What?" Xander laughed, clearly not quite picking up on the seriousness of Brody's hate vibes. "All I'm saying is that if *someone* I know would get around to making those flyers like he keeps saying he's going to do, Megan here would already know that Scratching at the Eight Ball has a gig on Sat—"

"Shut up, Xander," Brody interrupted. "Give it a rest or we're going to call the whole thing off."

Right then I spotted Vicki several lanes away. This was as good a time as any to bail, so I did. When I got close, I saw that Vicki was taking a bow after having lobbed her ball into the gutter. Pete and a bunch of the football crowd were laughing with her, but Rosetta was nowhere to be seen.

"I'm giving up on that stupid ball and getting a new one!" Vicki announced.

"Oh, sure," said Pete. "Blame the ball."

I'd never been Pete's biggest fan, but he made me sick now with whatever he was doing to Kendall. I stepped wide to avoid him—and walked straight over to *my* biggest fan, Vicki, who was heading to a ball rack.

"Hey, where I can find Rosetta?" I asked.

Vicki shoved her thumb and two of her fingers into an orange ball and held on to it with her arm hanging loose. "Probably at her house."

"Nice try," I said. "Brody already told me he saw her with you."

Vicki met my gaze. Her expression was one that she hadn't directed my way for years, if ever: not friendly, but not *un*friendly, either. Just neutral, I guess. "That was true like half an hour ago," she said. "But she's gone now. Past nine o'clock is late for her."

I could tell she wasn't messing with me.

And that's when the disappointment hit. *Hard*. It had been a stressful week with all the crap I'd had going on with work and the band. Rosetta and I had hung out in the halls at school whenever possible and in IC every day—of course—but the thought of just getting to be with her tonight had been the thing keeping me going all afternoon. All week, even. And I'd missed her by thirty goddamn minutes.

"Did she say anything before she left?" I asked. "Was she was pissed about me being so late?"

"She isn't pissed. Her uncle just said she needed to get home, so she went."

A booming voice cut in. "Or maybe Rosetta's avoiding you, McCoy. You ever think of that?"

I turned, and there was Carr, laughing his fake-friendly vice-president laugh. I don't know who he was trying to fool. I haven't been in a ton of fights—mostly just Jared kicking my ass when we were kids—but after putting up with so much of Carr's shit, I was about *this close* to throwing down so he could see exactly what kind of trash he was dealing with here.

"Goodwin, why don't you mind your own fucking business?" I asked.

He smirked in response.

Vicki sighed loudly, pulled her phone out of her back pocket, and handed it to me. "Here. Call her."

So I did. Rosetta picked up on the second ring.

"I'm sorry I didn't get here soon enough to see you," I said. "Vicki said your uncle told you to come home?"

"Yes. He says there's some crazy storm coming and he doesn't want me walking around at night in it."

"I really wanted to see you tonight," I said, trying to keep from sounding whiny—and only halfway pulling it off.

"Me too. Do you want to meet me at the golf course after you get off work tomorrow? Then we can see each other all afternoon."

"That sounds good."

Which it *did*. But even if she'd said "Do you want to meet me on the surface of the sun?" I'd still have agreed to it.

9:56 P.M.

I was almost to the exit when Kendall came in. She lunged straight at me, jumped up, and wrapped her legs around my waist and her arms around my neck. The collision knocked me backward, but I managed to keep on my feet. Barely. I held her ass with both hands to keep her weight from pulling me to the floor.

With her face inches from mine, she said, "Hi, nonenemy!"

"Damnit, Kendall," I said, looking over her shoulder and see who was paying attention to this ridiculous scene she was causing. I have to say, *everyone* was. I tried to set her down, but she squeezed tighter. So tight, I could hardly breathe.

"Don't let go," she said in my ear. "Please, please, please. And if you don't mind, can you try to make it look like you're enjoying this a little?"

The only thing I wanted to do was let go, but she wasn't allowing it, and I knew we'd both end up on the floor if I tried to force her off. "I'm not playing this game to make your douchebag boyfriend jealous anymore. That was a one-time deal."

"Oh, really? Whatever happened to 'I'm *so* sorry, Kendall. I'll make this up to you somehow'?"

Despite how pissed Kendall had seemed at Rosetta and me after the dance, she'd been pretty decent about it, actually. In the car ride to her house, I'd kept apologizing and offering to let her keep her money, but she'd kept insisting that she wasn't mad at me and that she wanted me to have the cash so I wouldn't drive on my "sketchy" spare tire anymore.

Standing like this, my back was killing me now. I tried pushing Kendall's legs to get free, but she wasn't budging. Christ, she was strong. "You aren't the lightest thing I've ever had to hold up," I said.

"And your breath isn't the freshest thing I've ever had to smell, so I guess that makes us even. Doritos, right?"

Fuck.

I opened my mouth and breathed full on in her face. She shrieked so loudly, I swear to God, everyone in the place could have heard—which is really saying something—but at least she jumped down and let me go.

"Kendall, you can't do shit like this. I'm with Rosetta now."

She straightened her skirt and looked around. "Weird. Does she have one of those magic invisibility cloaks?"

"You know what I mean. We're getting together. Seeing each other. Whatever you want to call it."

"Well, the only reason you have this 'whatever' going on with her is because of *me* setting up you two at the dance," Kendall said, putting on her biggest smile. "Can't you just do me a favor and stand there looking fascinated by everything I say for a few minutes?"

"No."

I headed for the door, expecting her to chase after me, to try to drag me off somewhere like she always did. But this time she let me keep on walking.

I don't know what made me do it; I glanced back. Kendall was watching me, and her eyes were bright with tears.

Fuck *again*.

I'm 99 percent sure a real Ferrari 246 Dino has only one steering wheel, but the video game version Kendall and I were in at the bowling alley arcade had two. Kendall was gripping her wheel with both hands and venting loudly enough for me to hear over the revving engines/squealing tires sound effects while I was resting my elbows on my own side.

For the first time in our lives, I'd dragged her off somewhere, and we'd now been *not* playing this racing game for about a minute. The arcade was empty, which is why I'd chosen it.

"I don't know what's wrong with me," Kendall said.

Her whole breakdown-crying thing was about her secret boyfriend, naturally—the secret boyfriend she was still semidefending and refusing to name even though I'd already told her I'd figured out who it was on my own.

"I don't know what's wrong with you, either," I said.

It came out sounding harsh, but she didn't seem to mind.

She wiped her eyes, and if it wasn't for the black streaks from her makeup—and you know, her boobs—she would have looked just like she did after her dog was hit by a car when we were kids. "I hadn't even spoken to him since the dance. But then I see him here, and the next thing I know we're hooking up in his car. And, of course, when he's done, he just goes back to his friends and acts like I don't exist."

Now I was clenching *my* steering wheel. This Pete situation was getting way past annoying. And Kendall was letting it be that way. "It isn't like it was an accident. You chose to go out with him, right?"

She sighed. "Right."

"So if you don't want to do it anymore, then don't."

"That's the thing, though. I do want to. I like him. Or I *did* like him. I just want him to give a shit about me and stop acting like I'm not good enough. More and more it seems like it isn't going to happen, though."

The demo game on the machine was running on its constant loop, and I almost wished I had a few quarters to throw in just to make something different happen on the screen in front of us. "You should have realized he was using you when he told you he didn't want anyone to know you're together," I said.

"That part was my idea in the beginning," Kendall said, shaking her head. "I didn't want Isaac to find out I was with someone else, because it would make him try harder to win me back. I knew I'd give in and get with him again if that happened."

I turned to stare at her. Every time she talked about how things had been with her and Isaac, it sounded worse and worse. "Jesus, Kendall."

She looked away. "I know. I'm as bad as my mother. Jim is the best thing to ever happen to her, and she's always worrying about what's going to happen if he leaves. I don't want to be like that. Like *her*. I want to be like your mom."

I snorted. "That's a good one."

"I'm serious."

And the weird thing is, I could tell she *was* being serious. She didn't get it.

"You know that dumb poster of rabbits in a basket we have hanging in our living room?" I asked.

"I think it's cute!"

"Well, Mom put it up to cover a hole one of her ex-boyfriends punched in the wall. In fact, I'd say about half the crap you see hanging on our walls has a gaping hole behind it."

"I know that. But what I'm saying is—"

"Have you seen that broken TV under our carport?" I interrupted. "That's from when that asshole we call the Psychopath threw a bottle of whiskey right through it. All the restraining-order stuff with *that* guy made for some good times."

"Okay, but—"

"And, of course, there was also that dickhead who got my mom knocked up twice by the time she was eighteen and then skipped town for good before the second kid was even born. You see what I'm getting at here? She isn't known for picking winners."

More sighs from Kendall. "I'm telling you, it isn't *who* she picks that I admire. It's that, unlike my mom, Anita kicks them to the curb and then doesn't let them come back. I want to be like that."

It didn't seem like much to aspire for, but what the hell did I know?

"Do it, then," I said, shrugging.

She nodded. "Yeah."

I couldn't tell whether she meant she was going to take my advice or if she was just acknowledging that she *should*. But with her calmed down and finished with the crying, I climbed out of our race car. "I'm taking off now. You gonna be okay?"

She looked up and nodded again. "You're a decent non-enemy sometimes, you know that? Keep it up and I might have to start calling you my friend or something."

"Oh no," I said, laughing a little as I took her hand and helped her up. "Anything but that."

SATURDAY, **OCTOBER 16**

7:38 A.M.

The next morning. If the Three Stooges had a van-loading company, it would have been a lot like what was going on outside Studio 43: guys bumping into one another, almost dropping things, and cussing as they tried to pack all the gear while still leaving enough room for everyone to ride in semicomfort.

"It's not too late to change your mind, Dick," Daniel said, yawning big. This was the earliest he'd dragged himself out of bed since he'd been in school last June. "Craig won't let us use his van if we kick him out of the band, but you can come along as my roadie if you want."

The big day was here, and my former band was about to hit the road for the Rat Rodders' tour. I'd driven Jared and Daniel over to meet Mikey and Craig and stayed to help with the packing and hauling, but it was about time for me to head to the car wash to get the morning crew going.

"Daniel, if anyone needs his own personal roadie, it's me," Mikey said. "You have only a guitar and amp to move. I have a bunch of drums and cymbals and stands and—"

"Is it *my* fault you're bringing all that shit?" Daniel asked.

Jared pushed past carrying his pedal board. "Nobody's getting a roadie here. Sorry, Seth. No room."

"Aw, shucks," I said, snapping my fingers. "Way to stomp on my dreams, big brother."

Mikey and Craig started cracking up as they heaved Jared's amp into the back.

I followed Daniel over and stood next to him while he leaned against the building and lit a cigarette, which was right in line with his never-do-manual-labor-if-someone-else-will-do-it-for-you philosophy. "Dick, be honest." He was using a quiet voice—probably so Craig couldn't hear. "You're regretting it now, aren't you? You wish you were coming on tour with us."

I nodded. "A little bit."

Which was kind of downplaying it. I mean, I had no idea how I was going to get onstage for Scratching at the 8 Ball's gig at Good Times here in town, and the thought of trying it in other towns at clubs I'd never been to was even freakier. Still, like everyone had been saying from the start, chances like this didn't come up all the time. And it was kind of an ego thing too. I'd been the bass player who helped get the band to this point; it sucked that Craig would get the credit. If things had been different, if Isaac were still alive, maybe we all would have been going on this trip.

"I knew you'd be kicking yourself," Daniel said, shaking his head. "You wouldn't listen to me. I still want to kill you for bailing on us. But I did figure out one good thing that's going to come of it."

"What's that?"

Still talking in his quiet voice, he grinned and said, "You may have noticed that the dude we got to replace you isn't much of a looker. Which means, of course, that more chicks are going to be keeping their eyes on *me* while we're playing."

I laughed as I pulled my keys out of my pocket. "All right," I said, loudly enough so that they could all hear. "I'm out of here, you guys. Have a good trip. Make sure you break your legs and all that stuff."

Mikey and Craig were arranging the amps in the back, but Mikey shot his hand out to wave. "Try not to run my dad's business into the ground, Seth."

"Sure thing."

My brother walked with me to the Mustang. "What do you think of 'The Jared McCoy Band?'" he asked.

After all this time, the guys hadn't been able to agree on a name, so it was looking like they were stuck touring as the Real McCoys after all. But Jared still wasn't giving up on his search for something new.

"I think Mikey might have a problem with you trying to name the band after yourself again."

"Yeah, good point. I hate this band-naming shit." Jared pulled out his cigarettes. "Anyway, you take care of Mom, okay?"

As I was nodding in answer, he reached over and patted my back for about two and a half seconds. I almost could have sworn it was supposed to be some type of tiny partial hug thing, but I guess it's also possible that there was an insect on my jacket he was trying to squash.

4:45 P.M.

If I'd made a list of the places where I wanted to spend time alone with Rosetta, behind the cart barn at her golf course wouldn't have come to mind. I was happy with whatever I could get, though, so if it turned out that she wanted to stand here all day like this, I had absolutely no problem with it.

"I told the guys in the pro shop," Rosetta said between kisses, "that we'd be teeing off"—*kiss*—"as soon as you got here."—*kiss*—"So we should"—*kiss*—"probably go do that."—*kiss*—"Don't you think?"

"Definitely," I said.

Then we went back to kissing.

Yup. *This*. All day. More than fine with me.

But after only a couple of minutes, Rosetta gently pulled

back. "You know, it might be kind of awkward if someone finds us here."

I doubted that was going to happen. The storm her uncle had been talking about was on its way now, and no one except Rosetta and I seemed to be braving it. And anyway, I was dressed in the country-club–legal clothes I'd brought to work with me that morning, so there was nothing to worry about—unless they had some rule against making out behind the cart barn. Which, come to think of it, wouldn't surprise me at this place.

"Okay, okay," I said.

We headed over to the first tee. Without the building blocking the wind, the cold stung my face. Huge gusts pulled at our clothes, thrashed through the trees, and ripped over the flags. It sounded like we were surrounded by dozens of cracking whips. A round of golf didn't seem to me like the best thing we could or should be doing right now, but it was important to her so I kept my mouth shut.

Using my borrowed driver, I hit a terrible shot—my specialty—and waited while Rosetta took her turn. Then we trudged to my ball. The wind was so rough that Rosetta had to hold on to both bags of clubs to keep them from crashing to the ground while I swung. Three shots later, I got my ball close to where hers had landed on her first try.

"This whole me-golfing thing is so lame," I said.

Rosetta touched my arm. Loose strands from her pony-tail were flying all around her face. "You have to remember that I've been playing since I was three years old. Think of this as a competition with yourself to get better, not to try to beat me."

While I was nodding, lightning flashed across the sky. It wasn't long before thunder started rumbling. "Um, that isn't good," I said.

"Why must you conspire against me?" Rosetta asked the sky, shaking her fist. Then she said to me, "Let's try using the power of our brains to hold off the rain for another couple of hours."

"Think that'll work?"

"We'll see."

And then—*right* then—it started coming down. Boy, did it ever. This was not your typical Washington rain that drizzles on and off all day; it was a full-on, tropical-rain-forest-style downpour. It was as if God had pulled the plug on a lake in heaven and was funneling it onto Rich Bitch Hill Country Club.

Within seconds, our clothes and hair were soaked. The wind was picking up, making the evergreen branches slam together and the air whistle through. Rosetta pulled me under a tree, but it only blocked us a little because the rain was blowing sideways, too. "I guess we didn't have to wait long to get the answer to that brain power question," she said. "What's our new plan?"

I held her close. Kissed her again. Being stuck in wet clothes and shitty weather is not one of my favorite things, but I wasn't minding this.

Smiling, Rosetta turned her face away. "Seth, we need to focus here."

I *was* focusing. Just not on what she wanted, I guess. "How about if we head to your place now?" I gestured across the way. "If we cut through, we'll get there pretty fast, right?"

I'd never been inside her house, but she'd pointed it out to me once. It wasn't the absolute hugest or fanciest around these parts, but it was pretty damn close.

"We *could* do that," she said, biting her lip. "I don't think you'll like it much, though. My aunt and uncle are home, and they won't give us even one second of peace. They'll probably try to make us stay in the family room and play Scrabble with them."

"That's out, then," I said, quickly. "I'm no good at that game."

Rosetta laughed, and I'm sure she knew that I just wanted to be alone with her.

Another surge of wind rolled through, trees bent over, and there was a loud *crack!* A huge branch—longer and thicker than an entire Christmas tree—crashed about ten feet away in the spot where Rosetta and I had been standing before the rain came.

We stared at each other. Her eyes were wide open with shock, and I'm sure mine were as well.

"Holy shit," I said.

"No joke," she said.

Rosetta handed the guy in the pro shop the bag of clubs she'd borrowed for me. "Just so you know," she said all casual, "a huge widow-maker just fell in the middle of fairway one."

That might have made zero sense to me if I hadn't seen it myself—and if Rosetta hadn't told me that when tree limbs fall like that they can spear right through a person and kill them instantly.

I wasn't going to worry about what could have happened, though. Really, I was more interested in trying to figure out where Rosetta and I could go to change out of our soaked clothes and keep dry for a while. She had a bunch of friends who lived nearby, of course, but the idea of hanging around any of them sounded as bad—or worse—than being stuck with her aunt, uncle, and a pile of board games. My place was our best bet, really. Jared and the guys were all out of town, and Mom would be heading to Good Times for her shift soon. The problem, of course, was Rosetta's car phobia. The Valley is a long walk from the golf course.

Rosetta came over to me after finishing up her conversation about our near-death experience. Together, we stood dripping on the carpet next to a rack of men's jackets as we stared out the window at the rain pelting down on my sad-looking car. "Any ideas yet?" she asked.

And that's when I got one. A good one. The *best* one.

"Yeah, I'll tell you in a minute," I said, trying to sound calm even though my heart was already beating faster at the thought that I might be able to make this happen today. "First, let's put your bag in my car so we don't have to worry about it."

Rosetta followed me back into the storm and waited as I dealt with the bag and stuck it in the trunk. Then I took a deep breath, walked around to the passenger side, and opened the door. "I know this is earlier than we'd talked about, but I think you're ready," I said.

"Ready for what?"

But I could tell by the way she'd started chewing on her lip and shaking her head that she knew.

"This is a serious situation here," I said. "We're completely soaked, the trees are trying to kill us, and any second we could get struck by lightning. So we should get out of here. I'll take you to my place. We'll get dried off. Change our clothes. Figure out what to do with the rest of our afternoon. Sound good?"

"Seth, no," she said, shaking her head harder now. "I'm not prepared to do this. I mean, not at *all*. I'm supposed to have seven days left. Remember?"

My excitement was fading already, but I had to follow through. I'd known it wouldn't be easy ever since that day at the coffee shop when she'd first told me she had this phobia, but now I had to do my best to convince her. "Rosetta, just try. That's all I'm asking."

"I don't think I can—"

"See, you're setting yourself up to fail. Don't do that.

Maybe it will help you to try to think the same way you did when you convinced yourself to go bungee jumping that time?"

"That was *different*."

I pretended like I hadn't heard her. "Ready?"

She was hanging back, shivering and wringing her hands. She didn't look like she was ready, or like she was capable of getting there on her own. I helped her out by putting my hand on her back and scooting her closer. The seat and floor inside were getting soaked already, but I didn't care about the car. This was going to be so worth it.

"You can do this," I said. "I know you can."

Rosetta moved with me, her body tense like she was about to bolt at any second. I wasn't going to let that happen, though. If I could just think of the right thing to say, I could calm her down. I would help her do this. I had to.

"You're going to be fine. I promise," I said.

Rosetta was staring at the car. She reached out, touched the edge of the open door, and then jerked her hand back like she was afraid of getting sucked in.

"Seth, I can't," she said between quick, uneven breaths.

Should I back off? Try to come up with a new plan?

We were so close here. *She* was so close. It would take only a few quick movements for her to go from standing next to the car to sitting inside it. This was not the time to give up on her. If she just ducked her head, stepped in, sat down . . .

"Try thinking about how great you're going to feel when this part is over," I said. "Like free-falling or whatever, right?"

She was standing frozen now, chewing her lip like crazy. Her eyes were wide and unblinking. I wished I knew more about how this whole overcoming-your-fears thing was supposed to work. Was I doing it right? Was this helping her at all? She looked so scared.

"You don't have to be afraid," I said, wiping streams of water from my face with one hand and rubbing her back with the other. "I'll drive carefully. I'll be the safest driver you've ever seen."

That must have made something click because finally Rosetta started moving.

Just . . . not *toward* the car.

Instead, she pulled away from me and stepped backward. "I'm sorry," she said, bending to grip the tops of her knees as she panted like she'd just finished a marathon. "I can't do it. I *can't*."

Then she took off running.

5:14 P.M.

Through the sheets of falling water, I could just make out Rosetta as she sprinted to the grass, stopped suddenly, and sank to her knees. She was crying. Because of me. Because I'd been so sure that I could make her get in the car even though she'd said she wasn't ready. Because I'd fooled myself into thinking *I* could somehow cure her of a clinical disorder.

Still standing where she'd left me, all I wanted to do was punch something. Repeatedly. My own face, maybe. I mean, what was my *problem*? But instead of dwelling, I closed up the car and ran through the rain after her. The closer I got, the more my insides felt like they were being squeezed.

I'd fucked up. Completely. And I didn't know how to fix it.

She was sitting all scrunched so that her knees were pulled up, hiding her face.

"I'm such an asshole," I said, lowering myself onto the grass next to her.

She didn't respond with words. She just sobbed onto her pants.

When I'd seen her crying in the stairwell, I'd been clueless about what she would want or need from me. Unlike then, this time it was my fault she was crying. I had little doubt that what she wanted was for me to stay back and keep my hands off her. Part of why I'd pressured her at the car was because I'd wanted so badly to get her alone. I knew it and was pissed at myself. She probably knew it and was pissed at me too.

"I shouldn't have done that back there," I said. "I know it didn't help you. I only made things worse, and I'm sorry. I'm a jerk. A dick. A complete asshole dickhead *loser*—"

"Stop," she said quietly, still not looking up.

I stopped.

And then we sat there in the wind and the rain, soaked and shivering beside each other. I tightened my jaw to keep my teeth from clanging together like hers. This had been such a bad, bad idea. All of it. I should have taken her up on the Scrabble when I'd had the chance.

After a few minutes, Rosetta stopped crying. She raised her head, looked at me, and then looked away, dabbing at her nose with her sleeve.

I said, "I really am sorry."

She said, "It isn't your fault."

I didn't believe her. I didn't believe that *she* believed herself either. But she was giving off a vibe like she didn't want to talk about it anymore, so I decided to let it go. For now.

"We need to get you out of this rain, but I'm kind of out of ideas here," I said. "Do you want me to walk you back to your house?"

She shook her head. "I'd rather walk to yours. I mean, if you don't mind."

Unexpected, but it was exactly the thing I'd needed her to say. I stood and helped her to her feet. "I don't mind."

5:57 P.M.

By the time we were in sight of the faded Riverside Trailer Park sign, Rosetta and I were as soaked as two people could get. My jacket felt like it weighed a hundred pounds, my pants were chafing against my legs, and my socks and shoes were completely waterlogged. But even with the wet clothes, I was burning up. Long, treacherous walks can have that effect on a person, I guess.

"Here we are," I said, pointing at the wreck I call home. Mom's Honda and Kendall's MINI Cooper were parked in the driveway. "Home sweet dump."

Rosetta grabbed my hand and gave it a squeeze, but she didn't say anything. This was more embarrassing than I'd thought it would be. I couldn't stop wondering what she was thinking. Up where she lived, everything was nice and perfect. Down here, everything was tacky and broken.

She waited on the steps that led to the covered porch while I went to the door. I couldn't see into the living room—we hadn't bothering opening that set of curtains for weeks—but I could make out noises from the TV. After flinging the door open, I stood in the doorway and yelled, "Mom! Can I get some towels out here?"

Her voice rang out from what sounded like her bedroom: "Is that you, Seth?"

"Yeah!"

I didn't know who else she had calling her "Mom" these days with Jared being out of town.

About two seconds later, Kendall came through the kitchen. Her hair had been dyed black with blue on the ends sometime in the less-than-twenty-four hours since I'd seen her. With her purple top and short black skirt she had kind of a comic-book chick-villain look going on. "Anita, it *is* him," she called over her shoulder. Then she said, "What happened to you?"

"Rain."

Mom came out with curlers in her hair, dressed in a skirt for work but with her shirt still unbuttoned. Peeking out the kitchen window, she said, "Baby, I didn't hear the fan belt-slash-muffler that usually announces your arrival, and I don't see your car out front. Based on that and the looks of you right now, I'm thinking you broke down or wrecked somewhere." She put her hands together as if she were praying. "Tell me I'm wrong."

"You're wrong."

"Really?"

I nodded. "The car's fine. We just . . . felt like walking."

At the mention of "we," Mom and Kendall glanced at each other, puzzled, and then leaned to look past me at Rosetta. "Towels," Mom said, running off. "You need towels!"

Kendall raised her eyebrows, and then headed to the kitchen like she was pissed about something.

A minute later—with the important buttons done up now—Mom came back, handed me the towels, introduced herself to Rosetta, and then closed the door on us so we wouldn't let all the heat out as we took off some of our wet stuff.

"Is Kendall here to see *you*?" Rosetta asked, holding the base of her very messy-looking ponytail with one hand and sliding off her hair tie with the other.

I pulled my shoes and socks off and dropped them out of the way. "No. She used to live next door. She hangs out with my mom all the time."

Rosetta leaned her head over the rickety railing and started ringing her hair out. "Oh. I didn't realize that."

There hadn't been much chance for Rosetta and me to talk after we'd left the golf course. Our adventure trekking down the Hill, with all the nonstop pummeling rain and violent wind, had kept us busy. But I'd been thinking the whole time, and we definitely had more important stuff than Kendall and my mom to discuss. I wasn't sure I had the guts to go there, though.

"I'm wondering about something," I said, shrugging out of my jacket. "It's about your parents. About what happened to them. If you don't want to talk about it, you don't have to. I don't want to push you. And I don't ever want to make you cry again. So maybe I *shouldn't* ask."

She was watching me. Curious. "You can ask. It's okay."

I let out a loud breath. "So. I've been thinking. Your parents. They were killed in a car accident?"

She nodded.

"And you were with them at the time?"

She nodded again.

"And that's why you don't ride in cars."

That one wasn't a question, but Rosetta answered anyway. "That's exactly why." She pulled off her jacket and set it next to where I'd put mine on the railing. "We were T-boned on the passenger side. And nobody around here really knows this part, but I was the one driving my dad's car at the time."

Whoa.

Ever since the dance, when I'd found out *both* Rosetta's parents had died right before she moved here, I'd been thinking it must have been from an accident of some sort. A car wreck had seemed most likely because of Rosetta's phobia. But it had never occurred to me that she'd ever learned to drive, much less that she had been behind the wheel at the time of the crash.

Rosetta went on. "The other driver was drunk and didn't have a seatbelt on. I was the only one in either vehicle who lived. The cars were mangled and there was glass and blood everywhere. I mean, *every*where. It wasn't until the paramedics got me out that I realized very little of that blood was mine."

The only time I've ever seen a dead person was when I found Isaac. He'd been lying there on the lawn, looking pretty much like he was asleep. But Rosetta. She'd been trapped in a car with her parents. Her dead and bloody parents. I couldn't even imagine what that must have been like.

Even though I figured it would mean next to nothing, I said those same useless words I was always saying to her: "I'm sorry. I'm *so* sorry."

Rosetta had tears in her eyes as she threw herself against me. I held her tightly. Kept her upright. But she didn't break down. I guess maybe she was too exhausted by now. "I'm not much fun to be around, am I?" she asked, her face partially buried in my neck. "I mean, it probably isn't every day that you get stuck listening to someone talk about how she killed her parents."

I shook my head. "Rosetta, don't even say that. You didn't kill anyone."

"Maybe not. But if I'd been a more experienced or observant driver, maybe I could have avoided the collision. Or if I'd been driving faster. Or slower. Or turned down a different road. There are thousands of things I could have done differently. Any one of them could have prevented it."

I pulled back a little and looked into her eyes. "You said I couldn't have guessed what was going to happen to Isaac that night. That's just as true, if not more, for what happened to you."

"That's what my former shrink was always trying to drill into my head, but I never believed it." She looked away. "Did it help when I said it to you? Did you stop holding yourself responsible?"

I thought about it for a second. And, actually, no, I *hadn't* stopped. I didn't want to admit that to her, though, so I just said, "The thing is, all you did was get in a car and drive like millions of people do every day. You couldn't have known anything like that would happen. It was *not* your fault."

She nodded. "On an intellectual level, I get that. And yet here I am, making us both miserable. I've been thinking, maybe I should see if trying a new therapist might help me.

Does that sound like a good idea?" She smiled the tiniest of smiles. "Or do you think I'm just plain crazy here?"

I pushed her wet, tangled hair off her forehead. "I don't think you're any kind of crazy."

6:13 P.M.

"I'm not sure why you're bothering with this," Kendall said. "Rosetta already noticed the mess on her way in."

Rosetta and I had come inside now, and she was taking Mom's suggestion and getting warmed up in the shower while Mom finished putting on makeup in her bedroom. This had all been going on only about five minutes, but so far I'd already changed clothes, thrown the dirty ones into the washer, kicked all the crap under my bed, and taken an armload of dirty dishes from the living room to the kitchen sink. Now I was putting the scattered mail on the table in a pile.

"I'm bothering because if it's cleaner when she comes out, she might think what she saw before was her imagination," I said.

"Hmm. Interesting theory." Kendall picked up Mom's fuzzy pink blanket, folded it, and set it on the back of the couch. "So, it's pretty weird how you two felt like going for a walk in the middle of a hurricane, huh?"

"Not really. Rosetta has that 'no riding in cars' deal going on, remember?"

"Oh, right." Kendall smacked her forehead. "Her environmental pledge thing!"

The way she'd said it, I couldn't tell if she'd honestly forgotten or if she was just being a bitch. Either way, I was too drained to get into it with her. "How are things with your dumbass secret boyfriend? You kick him to the curb for good yet?"

"That's my plan," she said. "Assuming, of course, that I can get ahold of him and convince him to meet me in a secret place to have the secret discussion where I end our secret relationship."

"Right. Like you do." I stepped around her to grab Mom's sweater off the chair in the corner. "So will that talk be happening before or after you have your last secret hookup?"

She punched my arm. But she was smiling, so I could tell she wasn't really pissed.

Mom came out of her room. "I'm off to make my millions. Kendall, you want to run and scootch your car over so I can pull out?"

"Actually, I'm leaving too," Kendall said. "There's no way I'm hanging around here while Seth's trying to get laid."

Mom fake screamed and covered her ears. "Okay, you absolutely can*not* say things like that about my baby boy!"

"I'm sorry," Kendall said, patting the top of my head. "It's just that wittle Seff is gwowing up so *fast*!"

I gave her my best "eat shit" look. I wasn't sure what the

hell she was trying to do, but this was not a conversation I ever wanted to be having in front of my mother.

Mom cleared her throat. "Enough of that. Let's get a move on, girl. I'm already running late."

They both grabbed their purses and headed out the door. But before closing it Mom came back inside, her forehead lined with worry. She kissed my cheek and glanced in the direction of the bathroom. "You be good."

"Mom—"

"I'm dead serious here, Seth. *Promise* me."

I sighed.

8:01 P.M.

Rosetta's phone chimed. She grabbed it from the coffee table. "All right," she said, looking at the screen. "Vicki's text says she'll cover for me if necessary. But only if I tell her what I'm *really* up to tonight."

"You might want to hold off on that," I said. "You know how Vicki feels about me."

Rosetta pressed a few more buttons and held the phone to her ear. After a few seconds she said, "Aunt Coco, it's me . . . Yeah. Everything's fine. I'm just calling to let you know I'm staying over at Vicki's tonight." She kind of rolled her eyes at me about telling the lie while she listened to whatever her aunt was saying on the other end. "We're just watching movies and stuff here. I'll come home in the morning, okay? . . . Yeah. . . . Okay. . . . Bye."

With the call ended and her mission accomplished, Rosetta smiled at me. I let out the breath I hadn't realized I was holding. It was official now. Rosetta was staying *here* tonight. All night.

I knew that when Mom got home, she was going to be as upset as Rosetta's aunt would have been if Rosetta had told the truth, but really, there hadn't been any other option. The rain had let up somewhat, but it was very wet and dark outside now. Walking back up the Hill wasn't only a hassle at this point; it was dangerous, too. Or, at least, that's what Rosetta and I had been telling each other for over an hour now.

"I hate lying to her," Rosetta said. "But it isn't like I had much choice, right?"

"Right."

My heart had started beating like crazy, and I wanted to get up and sit on the couch with her. To just be *close* to her. Instead, I stayed where I was on the reclining chair, held on to the Magic 8 Ball, and pretended to be engrossed in the crappy reality show on the TV. Following Mom's order to "be good" sucked. I wasn't sure how much longer I'd be able to pull it off.

The oven timer went off in the kitchen, so we both jumped up and headed over.

"What do you think?" Rosetta asked as she pulled the pan from the oven and set it on the stovetop.

I had no clue what I was looking for. All I knew was that fudge brownies and Rosetta's shampoo—or *my* shampoo, I guess it was—smelled amazing together. "Didn't the box say to stick a toothpick in it?" I asked.

"Ooh! That's right!"

Surprisingly, Rosetta was about as a bad a cook as I was. For dinner I'd managed to make cheese sandwiches in the toaster oven without burning anything, but she'd let the Ramen boil over. She did save the day later, though, by noticing that I'd misread the glass measuring cup; she stopped me just in time before I poured a full cup more vegetable oil into the brownie batter than the directions called for.

After we finished the toothpick test, I watched Rosetta bend to put the pan back in the oven. She was wearing one of my T-shirts and black sweats. I'd never had any idea how *hot* those clothes could look.

"We should have waited five years to meet," Rosetta said as she set the timer for two more minutes.

I leaned against the counter. Close enough to keep checking her out. Far enough away not to touch her. "Why do you say that?"

"Just think about it. If we were five years older, there wouldn't be any reason for me to lie about where I am right now. We wouldn't have to check in with anyone. Ever. And in five years you'll probably be some big rock star, and if things go well, I'll be done being crazy and off doing whatever it is I'm going to do with my life. Attending college or, I don't know, playing professional golf maybe."

"Then how would we meet in the first place?"

She tapped her fingernails on the counter as she considered. "Maybe I'd be in a tournament somewhere and your band would be playing in that same town. We'd see each other at, say, a restaurant. You'd recognize me from having watched the golf channel during a fit of insomnia, and I'd recognize you from MTV and probably every magazine out there. And we'd somehow strike up a conversation and then start hanging out all the time and it would be really, really cool."

"I think I hate that idea," I said.

Rosetta's mouth fell open. "Why?"

"Because. I wouldn't want to have to wait five years to meet you. I like knowing you now."

She pushed her hair over her shoulder and smiled at me in that way she had. My heart just about seized in my chest. And then the timer went off again, so I hurried to deal with the brownies and jab another toothpick in. "They're done," I said.

"Perfect!" Rosetta picked up Isaac's Magic 8 Ball, which I'd set on the counter. "I love these things. All the answers to life's mysteries are in the palm of my hand. Now, I'd like to test the accuracy of this device, if you don't mind. Do rectangles have four sides? Oh, look! It says, 'Yes—definitely.' So far so good. How about something more challenging? Tell me, Magic Eight Ball, am I wearing underwear right now?"

Guh. It had not occurred to me to wonder about that. But

now that she'd brought it up, I wasn't sure how I'd ever be able to *stop* wondering.

This time she smiled at the 8 ball's answer but didn't read it aloud. "This thing is sure good at what it does. And now for the most important question of all: Is Seth McCoy ever going to kiss me again?"

My heart rate kicked it up about a hundred notches. Rosetta wanted me to kiss her. I wanted to kiss Rosetta. We should just *be* kissing. Yes.

"Isn't that just so typical?" Rosetta said as she glanced at the answer this time.

I stepped forward. "What does it say?"

She turned her wrist so I could see the white lettering through the blue liquid: *Ask again later*.

"What's the definition of 'later'?" she asked, biting her lip. "Do you think it would be okay if I ask again right now?"

But before she got the chance, I was leaning in and touching my lips to hers.

9:15 p.m.

An hour later, we were still kissing. We'd kissed all over the kitchen. We'd kissed on the reclining chair. We'd kissed on the couch. We'd fallen *off* the couch and kissed on the floor. And now we were kissing on my bed.

It felt like we were never going to stop. I didn't ever want to stop.

She'd taken off her shirt. She'd taken off *my* shirt.

My lips were on her face, mouth, neck, breasts.

Her fingers were on my hair, face, chest, back.

I took off her pants, then mine.

Her skin was soft, smooth, warm. She smelled so good, tasted so good, felt so good.

I was touching her. Everywhere.

And her hands were all over me.

This was really happening. Or it was about to happen.

"Do you have . . . ?" she asked.

"I think so."

I forced myself to pull away from her, pushed back the blanket. Walking to the dresser, I felt self-conscious and made sure not to check if she was watching me. I mean, it was dark and all, but the lights next door were coming through the curtains somewhat, so we could still *see* each other.

I dug through my sock drawer, ripped open the box that had shown up at some point courtesy of the Condom Fairy, reached in, and grabbed one. A whole chain of five or six others came flapping out with it. Jesus *Christ*. Who needs that many at once?

I got back under the covers, dealt with one condom, hoped I seemed calm about the fact that I was about to have sex with Rosetta.

We lay there facing each other. She really did have the most beautiful face I'd ever seen: very light freckles on her nose, a small scar—from her car accident, maybe?—near one of her eyebrows, a fallen eyelash on her cheekbone.

"You okay?" I asked.

She touched my face, smiled. "Yes. If you are."

Oh, I *was*.

We went back to kissing. Very slowly at first, then even more urgently than before. Her breathing was quick, sexy. She whispered, "Just let me know what I'm supposed to do, okay?"

I knew she was a virgin from what she'd said on the bleachers. She didn't know anything about me, though. Her guess that I had all the moves down, and that I was experienced enough to make this decent for both of us was obviously not even close to being the truth.

If a tree falls and no one is around to hear, does it make any sound?

Probably.

If a guy's had sex but doesn't remember it, can he fake that he knows how?

Probably *not*.

"Rosetta," I said. "I don't know exactly what to do either."

She smiled in that same surprised way she had at Pete's party when she'd misunderstood about the drinking thing. For a second, I wondered if it would be better to go that route again, to let her believe whatever she wanted. But, no. I couldn't. I wasn't going to be that guy. "What I'm saying is, I've been with a girl before. It's just . . . I don't remem—"

"You don't have to tell me this," she interrupted.

"I just thought—"

She pressed her hand over my mouth, smiling. "No, really, Seth. I'm *begging* you not to tell me."

Was I an idiot or what? "Sorry."

"It's okay." She kissed my nose, ran her fingers through my hair. "I think we can probably figure out together how to, um, *do* this, don't you?"

"Yeah, I do."

And then . . . we did.

SUNDAY, **OCTOBER 17**

1:17 A.M.

Hours later. Rosetta had been asleep since around eleven o'clock, but I was wide awake. It felt strange—in a cool way—lying with her next to me. I'd let her have the good side of the bed so she wouldn't have to put up with this goddamn poky mattress spring. But my brain just wouldn't turn off.

I couldn't take it anymore. Careful not to wake her, I climbed out of bed. In the dark, I threw some clothes over the boxers I'd put on when Rosetta had gotten redressed a few hours before. And then I headed to the kitchen.

Minutes later, I was at the table with the 8 ball, a glass of milk, and the entire pan of brownies—which were tasty but kind of dry—feeling even more wired now that I was up. I couldn't stop thinking about what had happened, about how it was almost like I'd lost my virginity for the second time. And the coolest part was that the way I was feeling after sex with Rosetta was nothing like waking up hungover next to Kendall. It was a relief not to have to wonder what had happened this time. It felt *good* to remember.

My door creaked open down the hall, and then Rosetta came over, squinting in the bright light. "You disappeared," she said, sitting at the table next to me.

She didn't sound accusing or anything; it was more like she was concerned.

"Insomnia," I said, handing her a brownie. "And I have a feeling there's no pro golf on TV to help me get past it."

Rosetta smiled as she took a bite, but she didn't quite look at me. She'd been shy like this ever since everything happened earlier. Which, in a way, I understood, since I was feeling a little exposed myself. I hoped she wasn't regretting it. I knew I wasn't.

"I'm thinking those two extra minutes in the oven might have been about two too many," she said softly.

"Stupid toothpick test."

Rosetta pushed her hair behind her ears. "I have to say, when I woke up this morning—or yesterday morning, I guess it is now—I had no idea I'd be doing this."

"Eating dessert in my kitchen?"

"Doing *any*thing in your kitchen."

She blushed and looked away again, but it seemed like a good sign that she was talking about it.

"I didn't expect this either," I said. "It happened kind of fast, huh?"

"Kind of," she said, biting her lip. "Of course, I've had a crush on you pretty much since you gave me that rose on Valentine's Day, so maybe it was kind of *not* fast from my point of view."

I stared at her, speechless at that shockingly awesome announcement.

She went on. "You know, I was sort of in hiding for most of Pete's party, but then when I heard that you were there and that you'd gone outside alone, I decided to make my big move and actually speak to you." She smiled; still shy, but she held my gaze. "And I'm glad, Seth. About everything, I mean. About tonight and that it was with you."

Now it was my turn to get embarrassed. It was weird how we couldn't talk about it without one of us turning red. "Me too. And I'm especially glad that you're glad."

Rosetta got up from her chair and sat sideways across my lap. She wrapped her arms around my neck as I put my hands on her waist to hold her steady. "I wonder," she said, "how long it will be before it sinks in that, after seventeen years, I'm no longer in the 'never had sex' group of people."

"You're seventeen?" I asked.

"You're not?"

"Sixteen. For a few more months."

"Wow! I've always assumed that you're older than me.

Now all of a sudden I'm feeling like a sexual predator or something."

I rolled my eyes. "Oh, please. You have, what, a few months on me?"

"When's your birthday?"

"February twenty-eighth."

"Mine's August twenty-eighth. Which means we're exactly . . . six months apart. Six whole months."

"Six months is nothing," I said.

"It's three-and-a-half years of a dog's life!"

"A dog's life?" I burst out laughing. "Where do you come up with this stuff?"

She laughed too. "Actually, that seven-year myth is the old-school, lazy way to figure out dog years compared with human years. But it's so much simpler than having to consider the dog's size and breed. I mean, who has all those charts memorized, anyway, right?"

She was being nerdy just for the sake of nerdiness. I could play along with it. Maybe. "You know," I said, "my age is about sixteen years and seven and a half months right now. Sometimes in math, you're supposed to round decimals of point five or higher up to the next whole number. So, if we do that, I'm seventeen. Which means that you and I are the same age."

"*That* sure is a relief," Rosetta said.

I kissed her cheek. "If you say so. But maybe I like older women."

WEDNESDAY, **OCTOBER 20**

6:44 P.M.

Three days later. Brody stopped midsong to yell at Xander for the third time. "Will you cut out the fancy stick-twirling and try playing the song the *right* way?"

"Sorry," Xander said as he bent to pick up the drumstick he'd just dropped. "I'm working on improving my stage presence."

I closed my eyes. Looking cool and playing with energy so the crowd gets into the music was one of the things Jared used to bug me about when I'd first started playing with the Real McCoys. I'd made an offhand comment about it to these guys last week. Now Xander was obsessing and I was wishing like hell that I'd kept my mouth shut.

"Do me a favor and knock it off," Brody said to Xander.

"Our show is in three days, and I don't want us to look like a bunch of screwups."

Brody acting like a typical asshole front man—like my brother—was getting hard to take. My own stress about playing this gig was through the roof, and Brody's attitude all week was not helping.

Xander and Taku exchanged grimaces behind his back. I was over it. Leaning my bass against the wall, I said, "No one's feeling this right now. Let's wrap it up for the night."

"I agree," Taku said. "We're trying to force it, and, if anything, our playing is going to get worse."

"Whatever." Brody ripped his guitar off over his head, dropped it on its stand, and stomped over and threw himself on the couch. Putting his elbows on his knees, he leaned forward and covered his face with both hands.

Taku, Xander, and I stared at each other.

Xander came out from behind his drums. "Brode, what's going on with you?"

Brody shook his head, but didn't speak.

"Um, dude, you're kind of freaking us out," Taku said.

"You should tell us what's up," Xander said. "We'll help you."

Brody looked up at him. "I'm not telling you anything if you're going to try to use your sympathy tricks on me."

"Empathy," I said.

"What?"

"Empathy," said Xander. "It's like sympathy except

instead of just acknowledging someone's feelings, you feel what they're feeling too."

Taku coughed into the shoulder of his black T-shirt. That one sounded like a hiding-a-laugh cough, but it was hard to tell.

Brody shook his head. "I don't know if I can do this, you guys."

"Do what?" Taku asked, taking a seat on the arm of the couch.

"Play live gigs. Play *this* gig. It isn't what I'm about. I like doing our thing here in the basement and messing around with recording and stuff, but that's all I want to do."

Xander grabbed his energy drink off the table and leaned against the wall, frowning. "Being in the basement and recording is all fine and good, but if we ever want this to turn into something more, we're going to have to play live. I mean, it isn't an option not to."

"I'm not sure I want to turn it into something more," Brody said. "This was supposed to be fun, and now it isn't. When it stops being fun, maybe it's time for me to stop."

"I don't get it," Taku said. "Why is this not fun? Isn't sharing your music with people kind of the whole point of creating it?"

Brody shrugged. "I don't know. The thought of playing onstage stresses me out. I mean, I still get nervous playing in front of Seth, and he's only *one* new person."

I didn't have to try hard to muster up some empathy for

this one. Brody was standoffish for a good reason; he was suffering from stage fright.

Xander pushed his hair out of his eyes and looked at Brody. "It sounds like you're over-thinking it. Like maybe you're focusing on the wrong thing. Seth, you tell him. Playing music onstage is always going to be nerve-racking, but it's a rush, too."

I didn't answer; I was still trying to process Brody's confession and work out how it might affect this coming weekend, as well as the band in general.

"It *was* cool, right, Seth?" Taku prompted. "You felt good about your shows, like they were worth getting nervous over?"

"I don't know." I knew I wasn't helping their cause, but with Rosetta's and my deal being officially off since her panic attack at my car—we both thought it would be better to let her work with her new therapist instead of pushing her to meet a deadline—I was A-okay with this live gig not happening. "Maybe we should cancel the gig," I said, trying to sound as casual as possible. "I mean, there was never a reason for us to rush into this in the first place."

"There's a reason to do it *now*, though," Xander said. "We have a performance scheduled at a real, live venue. We don't want to be flaky amateurs and cancel with three days' notice!"

"It's a thirty-minute set at a dive in Kenburn," I said. "Believe me, they aren't going to hold it against us. We were tacked onto the bill at the last minute, and they can pull us off just as easily."

Taku shook his head fiercely. "Look, I know you have connections and all, but Xander and I have been playing music together since we were twelve, and for us, it's kind of a big deal. We want to do it."

"It isn't up to *only* you and Xander, though," I said.

Things were getting tense here in the dungeon. Xander and Taku seemed shocked that I wasn't taking their side. And Brody seemed plain miserable. Feeling like shit over letting everyone down was something I could relate to all too well. I have to say, it was a relief that Brody was the one bailing instead of me.

"Stage fright is a serious thing," I said. "Lots of performers have it. Elvis Presley did, Kurt Cobain. Jim Morrison too, I think. It's rough. So, you know, maybe we shouldn't be putting pressure on Brody to do something he isn't ready to do."

"All right," Taku said, shrugging. "But all those guys you just mentioned? They had stage fright and still made music their careers. They figured out ways to deal with it."

I was about to tell him it was more than likely that those ways had been along the lines of what mine and Isaac's used to be, but the door opened and Rosetta walked in. Unexpected but awesome.

"Sorry to interrupt," she said. "I just wanted to pop in to say good night." She gave a quick wave. "So . . . good night!"

Now that I'd seen her, I hated for her to just leave. "I'm on my way out too," I said to her. "Can you hang on a quick second?"

"I'll wait outside."

After she'd gone, I turned back to the guys. "How about if I ask the eight ball? Magic Eight Ball, should we cancel the show?"

My bad-luck charm came through in a big way: *Signs point to yes.*

I turned it so they could see. "That settles it, right? So I'll see you all later. Brody, don't feel bad. This isn't our only chance or anything. If you decide in a few months that you want to play live, I know I can set it up. Let's just keep rehearsing and writing new songs, and see what happens, okay?"

Xander and Taku were kind of shaking their heads, but Brody smiled for what might have been the first time since Xander had booked the gig. "Thanks a lot, Seth."

6:56 P.M.

Rosetta was standing in the front yard when I came out. "What was all that about down there?" she asked as I jogged over. "Everyone looked extremely on edge."

I'd only seen her for those few short seconds in the doorway, but now I had a better look at her sequiny top and skirt. She looked amazing. Lifting her off her feet, I breathed in her flowery shampoo. "All *that* was about the fact that Brody just called off our gig," I said, spinning her around a couple times before setting her down again.

"Brody did *what*?"

"It's crazy, huh?" I couldn't hide how stoked I was. "He told us he's afraid of performing and doesn't want to do it. Xander and Taku were pissed, but *I* supported his decision one hundred percent."

"Did you happen to mention that you have that same affliction?"

"Nah. I didn't want to steal his thunder."

She laughed. "Well, for your sake, I'm glad it worked out. But now I'm sad because I don't get to wear my 'I'm With the Bass Player' T-shirt to your show!"

"You don't really have that shirt," I said, half hoping she *did*.

Leaning close, she grinned up at me. "Okay, maybe I don't. But what if I get one that says 'Seth Rocks!'? Would that be embarrassing for you?"

"A little, yeah. I'd still think it was awesome, though." I kissed her forehead. "So why are you all dressed up, anyway?"

"Oh, I'm meeting my aunt and uncle at the club. Our dinner reservation is in"—she glanced at her watch—"less than five minutes, actually. I have to hurry."

I walked the several blocks there with her, keeping my arm around her the whole time and wishing like hell she'd bail on this dinner thing and hang out with me instead. Of course, that would bring us back to our usual issue of *where* to hang out. Having a girlfriend who wouldn't ride in cars had a serious downside at times.

The biggest building at the country club—which they called the clubhouse—was all lit up when we got there, and a few cars were rolling around the circular drive for the dressed-up people coming and going. Rosetta and I stopped outside the main entry doors, and from there I could spot all the chandeliers and fancy furniture in the lobby.

"I wish you could come in," she said. "But, you know, there's the whole jacket-and-slacks thing going on tonight. I'm going to talk to my aunt and uncle about inviting you to dinner soon, though, since they want to meet you. Is that okay?"

From the few things I'd heard from Rosetta about her aunt and uncle, I had a feeling they weren't going to be my biggest fans. But I nodded. She was worth it.

"I have to get in there now. Looks like they might have already been seated," Rosetta said, sliding her arms around my neck and kissing me gently. "I miss you already."

"I miss you too."

This whole "missing" exchange was kind of weird, I guess, since we were pressed against each other at that exact moment. But I got the feeling that what we both meant by it was something much . . . bigger.

7:36 P.M.

I'd been waiting at the signal by the grocery store for what felt like forever when, under the streetlights, I spotted some tall dude with a backpack and a guitar case who was jaywalking and holding things up at the other end of the intersection. With his dark hair and slightly slouching shoulders, he looked like Daniel. Then he turned. Definitely Daniel.

I would have honked the horn, but it had been broken since long before Jared bought the car. So when it was my turn at the light, I rolled my window down and yelled his name. Then I pulled off to the shoulder and waited while he busted back across traffic to get to me.

He shoved his stuff onto the backseat and climbed in up front. "How's it going, Dick?"

"What the hell happened to you being on tour?"

"It's a boring story," he said. "Let's just say it involved me, cops, guns, and a meth lab."

I stared at him. "What the *fuck*?"

"Nah, I'm kidding. It was about me, a couch, some skanky chick, and her jealous boyfriend."

I shook my head and pulled back onto the road. "Do I want to know how that combination led to you wandering the streets a thousand miles from where you're supposed to be?"

"*I* don't even want to know about it, but I can tell you anyway," he said, reclining the seat a little. "After our set in San Fran on Tuesday night, I was in the green room while the Rat Rodders were onstage. This chick started coming on to me. She was hot, so I went for it, right? Next thing I know, Owen's coming in, causing a scene. Turns out she's his girl-friend."

"You screwed Owen's girlfriend?"

"Well, I didn't *know* she was his girlfriend."

"Isn't she the blonde with the huge rack who always wears plastic cherries in her hair?"

"Yeah, I guess."

I glanced over. Daniel was somehow managing to keep a straight face while trying to bullshit me, and I didn't feel like letting him get way with it. "How could you not know who she was? She goes to all their shows around here. Plus, you were traveling with them, right?"

"Okay, fine. I had an idea of who she might be," he said, sighing. "Anyway, Owen went crazy and said he was throwing us off the tour. After a bunch of back-and-forth, Jared got him to let them stay on if I left. Then they sent me home on a Greyhound bus, those bastards."

"They're finishing the tour with Jared as the only guitarist? I bet he's pissed about that."

Daniel nodded. "Him and that Craig were all up in my shit. And Mikey! Mikey was all, 'Daniel, why can't you ever just keep your pecker in your pants?' He kept bringing up that Isaac and Kendall thing from a year ago, like it had anything to do with what was going on. It was unbelievable."

I pulled into my driveway and turned off the engine. To me, the unbelievable part of all this was that Daniel wanted to blame everyone else and couldn't see how he was the one at fault here. "You do kind of have a habit of getting with other guys' girlfriends," I said.

He gave me a hard look. "I've been stuck on a bus for

over twenty hours. You really don't want to start in on me right now."

"Well, I can see why they get pissed when you—"

"Think about it," he interrupted. "How is it *my* problem if some chick with a boyfriend hooks up with me? Is it supposed to be my job to keep everyone else's relationships happy?"

"I guess not. But Isaac was your friend."

"No, Dick. Isaac was *your* friend. I just happened to be in a band with him. Besides, he treated Kendall like shit."

I stared at him, not knowing what to say to that.

Without another word, he jumped out of the car and lit up a smoke. The porch light and the shadows were falling on his face under my carport in such a way that he appeared to have a matching set of bruises under his eyes, and you'd have thought his life depended on that cigarette with how long and deep his drags were. He looked like hell, actually, and even though getting kicked off the tour was his own fault, I felt kind of sorry for him.

THURSDAY, **OCTOBER 21**

7:36 A.M.

The next morning. The very second Taku and I stepped out of the tutoring lab, Xander came over wearing a huge grin. Somehow, I knew I wasn't going to love whatever he was about to say.

"We're back on!" he said, walking with us. "After you guys left last night, I was able to convince Brody to play the gig."

Now Taku had a matching grin, but I was pissed. Since leaving rehearsal, I'd been calm and relieved. I'd even gotten a full night of sleep. Xander's announcement put me right back in that stressed state I'd been in.

I stopped at the drinking fountain, held down the button, and brought my lips to the icy-cold water. Then I started gulping. And gulping. And gulping.

Xander and Taku kept their conversation going while waiting for me. "How'd you manage to change Brody's mind?" Taku asked.

"We talked for a while," Xander said. "I was there for hours. That thing Seth said about Elvis and Kurt Cobain helped a lot, actually. You know, since those guys had stage fright and went on to become megastars. Then we got online and did some reading up on the subject. There's so much information out there. Tons of theories and strategies. We learned that one of the guys in the Dave Matthews Band wore sunglasses for every gig to keep his stage fright under control."

"And that worked, huh?" Taku asked.

"Sure did," Xander said. "I told Brody he can try whatever he wants. Sunglasses might help. Or, if he wants to play with his back to the crowd, that could work too. I know we've been talking about cool stage presence and connecting with the crowd, but it seems more important right now for Brody to just get up there and do it than to worry about that. Don't you guys agree?"

I glanced up to see Taku nodding. "Yeah, totally," he said.

I went back to drinking instead of adding to the discussion. My stomach was getting that too-full-of-liquid feeling, but I couldn't stop.

"One of the things I read last night, in particular, made a lot of sense to me," Xander said. "Stage fright doesn't exist."

That gave me the push to step away from the drinking

fountain. Shaking my head, I spoke for the first time since he'd shown up. "I'm sure anyone who has it can set you straight in a big hurry."

"Well, the fear is real, of course," Xander said. "But the article said people aren't afraid of actual stages. They're afraid of other people. They're afraid of being judged. So I think if Brody can try to understand that, he'll be less nervous about performing."

I wasn't convinced. "How would understanding that help?"

Xander answered, "Because if he can isolate what he's worrying about, he might be able to figure out how to deal. Right now he's obsessing over how he doesn't think he can play *onstage*. That isn't what it's about, though."

"Right," Taku said. "It seems like he's worried that people will think he isn't good enough or that he doesn't deserve to be up there. He just needs to figure out how to work past that."

They were talking like it was so easy. Like following the advice of some stupid article could change everything.

I was about to argue some more, but someone tapped my arm. I turned, and Rosetta was standing there, glaring as if someone had just tried to run her over in a crosswalk or something. I did a double take—yup, that was definitely anger there—and then my mind started racing to work out what that look could be about.

"Hey, are you okay?" I asked, putting my hand on her shoulder.

She jerked back. Her voice was sharp as she said, "Can I talk to you for a minute?"

Xander and Taku were watching us, looking only about half as confused as I was feeling.

"Um, yeah," I said to Rosetta. "Of course."

Without a word to the guys, I followed her, my stomach sloshing the whole way.

She seemed to be making it a point to keep several feet between us, and my heart was hammering like crazy. Seeing her was always—without fail—the best part of my day, and things had been so awesome with us when I'd left her at the country club last night. So this, whatever it was, made no sense.

Stopping near the announcement board at the less-crowded end of the hall, Rosetta turned to face me, looking even more pissed than she had twenty seconds before.

"What's wrong?" I asked.

"I honestly trusted you," she said, crossing her arms over her chest. "With everything. My friends have been warning me about you from the very start, but I refused to listen. They were right, though, weren't they?"

"What are you talking about?"

"I'm talking about you and Kendall." Rosetta's voice was quiet, but with her flashing eyes and tight lips, she looked anything but calm. "I'm talking about how you told *her* every single thing about my parents, the accident, my phobia, and my shrink."

"What?" I practically yelled. About ten heads turned my way, so I lowered my voice. "That's ridiculous." And it was. The most ridiculous thing I'd ever heard. "I never said any of those things to her. Where'd you hear that I did?"

She bit her lip and looked at the floor. "Mostly from Carr after dinner last night. But a couple of other people filled me in on the rest of it."

Great. Just great.

"You can't be serious with this," I said. "Even if I'd talked to Kendall—which I *haven't*—she wouldn't have said anything to Carr of all people. Don't you think it's possible that your busybody aunt was spreading that stuff around and Carr's blaming it on me?"

"That did occur to me." Her mouth was still turned down, but already she was looking and sounding less fierce. "I just don't see what he would get out of lying about it. Besides, doesn't it seem like an awfully strange coincidence that right after I told you, everything got out?"

It stung that she thought Carr wouldn't lie to her, but that *I* would. "I'm telling you. I didn't tell Kendall. I didn't tell anyone."

She raised her eyebrows. "Well, you also once said that Kendall was your enemy, and that you came to homecoming with her because you wanted to see *me*."

"I *did* come to see you," I insisted. "And I didn't say she was my enemy. I said she was my nonenemy."

"Whatever that even *means*," Rosetta said, tossing her

hair over her shoulder in frustration. "You know, I didn't want to believe it when people were saying that you couldn't keep your hands off each other at the dance, but I can't keep ignoring it if it's still going on."

"Nothing is going on."

"I've had to hear from everyone how she was all over you at the bowling alley, and then you disappeared together." Her voice was cracking now like she was struggling to keep it together. "I need you to tell me what this is, okay? The truth. Are you playing me because she's the one you want, or vice versa? Or are you playing both of us?"

This was exactly the thing I'd been worried about with Kendall—that the wrong people would get the wrong idea and it would get back to Rosetta.

"It's none of those. Kendall was hanging around me to try to make some other guy jealous. But I am totally into *you*, Rosetta. You're the only one I want to be with. I swear."

Then we stood there staring at each other for several long seconds. Rosetta wasn't looking angry now as much as hurt. I could tell she wanted to believe me as much as I needed for her to.

"Okay," she said. "You're telling me there's nothing between you and Kendall. Not now, not ever?"

It was the "ever" part that threw me, of course. I hesitated, trying to work out the best way to tell the truth without hurting her more.

"So there is something," she said flatly.

"No! I mean, not really." I couldn't think about it anymore; I had to blurt it out and try to make her understand. "I got drunk one night at the end of summer, and, well, it just sort of happened, I guess. But it was a one-time thing and—"

"Wait." She put up her hand. "Are you saying you slept together?"

With my heart pounding so hard I could feel it in my ears, I nodded.

And just like that, tears were spilling down Rosetta's cheeks. "I flat-out asked you about her! All you would say was that she wasn't your girlfriend. You told me she hangs around your house because she's friends with your *mother*. How stupid was I to believe that?"

It's crazy when the truth sounds like lies. I took a few deep breaths to try to force back my panic. "Everything I told you about Kendall is true. And I tried to tell you the rest of it, too, but you asked me not to. All I can say now is that it happened before I knew you, and I was so wasted I don't remember it anyway. The Kendall thing was a huge mistake, and it doesn't mean anything to me."

I waited, hoping I'd said it the right way. Hoping Rosetta understood that no one had ever mattered to me the way she did.

"That's great," she said, wiping her eyes. "'The Kendall thing.' So I guess being with me was the 'the Rosetta thing'?"

She hadn't gotten it.

Rosetta rushed to get away, and, not knowing what else
to do, I let her go.

7:45 A.M.

I was on a hunt. For Kendall. For Carr. For *anyone* who could
explain what the hell was going on.

"Is everything all right?" Xander asked, walking fast to
catch up with me.

I had the headache from hell, and my stomach was
about to explode. Really, I wanted to tell Xander to back off,
but instead I just said, "No. Nothing is all right."

I spotted Kendall coming out of the girls' bathroom and
went after her. Xander came along.

"Kendall, I need to ask you something," I said.

She stopped short. "Go for it. But just so you know, I'm
not having my best week ever."

"Yeah, neither am I. Rosetta's pissed. She said you told
Carr a bunch of shit about her that came from me. Obviously, I didn't tell you anything, so can you maybe clue me
in on what this is about?"

Kendall made an irritated growling sound in her throat.
"That asshole is so dead."

I don't know if it's possible for *hair* to be aggressive, but
that's how Kendall's black-and-blue strands looked, swinging behind her as she stomped away.

Xander gave a low whistle. "Yikes. Yesterday, Carr was

telling some of the guys in Spanish class that Kendall's been following him, and he's going to the police with a bunch of evidence or something."

I would be the first to admit that Kendall would make an excellent stalker if she wanted to be one, but I didn't believe this shit. What was Carr's deal with her, anyway?

"He is such a liar."

"Oh yeah, I know," Xander said quickly. "I don't think anyone was taking him seriously or anything. After seeing her now, though, I'm thinking he's just given himself a good reason to worry."

Just then Kendall's voice rang out from down the hall. "This is going to happen one of two ways. We can go outside. Which, for the record, is my preference. Or we can have it out in front of everyone here. It's your choice."

I didn't want to stand there staring like the other thirty or so people leaning in to watch. But I needed to know what was going on so I headed that way. Kendall was outside the cafeteria with her hands on her hips, glaring at Carr. I hadn't quite caught his answer, but her reply was loud and clear: "Then right here it will be."

Carr smirked at his friends and then at her. "Really, Kendall," he said, raising his voice. "I'm flattered by all this attention, but I'm not interested in you. And, to be honest, it's getting kind of awkward having to say so all the time."

For a second, Kendall looked shocked, but she recovered

quickly. "As you well know, that is hilarious on many levels," she said, flashing one of her fake smiles. "*I'm* kind of flattered that these past few months have meant so much to you that you're bothering with this smear campaign. But if you don't stop spreading lies about me, I'll make sure you regret it. Are we clear?"

I don't know about Carr, but I was getting clear on something. I'd been wrong about Pete Zimmer all this time.

"I have plenty of evidence of the stuff you've been up to," Carr said, performing for the crowd. "Text messages. Voice mails. E-mails. I'll go to the police with all of it if you don't stop this harassment."

As if it wasn't bad enough that Carr had been calling Kendall a slut behind her back while he'd been hooking up with her. Now that she'd decided to end things with him, he was trying to get back at her and make himself look like some kind of victim. He'd also made it a point to ruin things between me and Rosetta in the process. Un-fucking-believable.

"Give me a break, Goodwin," I said, stepping forward. "Kendall has evidence like that against you too. And she has the good stuff. You know, videos and pictures and DNA samples."

Carr looked back and forth between us, frowning. "No, she doesn't."

Kendall didn't say anything, but she kept her expression bland enough that, for all I could guess, she really *did* have that shit. The girl could roll with anything you threw at her.

I shrugged. "If you don't get off her case, you might get to find out the hard way that she does. Maybe she'll wait until someday in the far-off future when you're trying to run for governor or whatever to make it really hurt. Or, hell, she might hang on to this stuff to keep you in line for the rest of your life."

Carr wasn't even trying to look cool or composed anymore. He was too busy freaking about what kind of videos and DNA Kendall might have, I guess. I didn't even want to imagine what he was imagining.

Behind Carr, Vicki was watching me. I had a feeling she'd be running off to tell Rosetta about this the first chance she got. Which *sucked*. But I couldn't just leave Kendall now. I had to hope that after Rosetta found out the whole story about Carr and Kendall, she'd see that she should have believed me all along.

I gave Kendall a nudge. "It's about time to head to class."

She hesitated, but I poked her again, so she started walking. I turned to follow. But before I'd made it three steps, there were hands on my shoulders and I was being flung sideways into a row of lockers. My arm and head crashed against the metal. I stumbled but managed to stay upright. When I spun around, Carr was standing his ground—surprisingly—and watching me with that *smirk*.

"Come on, Seth," Kendall said. "Let's just leave."

For about half a second, I considered it. Walking away, I mean.

But then I thought about how Carr was a guy who used girls and then told lies about them. He was a guy who would shove you into a swimming pool or against the lockers when your back was turned. A guy who'd screw things up between you and the coolest girl you'd ever known just because he could. When it all came down to it, Carr Goodwin was a waste of space who severely needed to get beaten down.

So, after about three seconds of considering all that, there was no way I could walk away.

Instead, I lunged right at that fucker.

7:49 A.M.

My senses were overloading.

I heard my own hard breathing, people yelling, Kendall shrieking.

I tasted blood.

I felt an ache in my jaw, throbbing under my eye, adrenaline pumping all through my body, the floor under my back, Carr's fist in my water-filled gut.

I smelled floor detergent, Carr's deodorant.

I saw fluorescent lights, Carr getting pulled off me by Xander and Pete, and lots of shocked faces looking down.

It was over already.

After years in the making, my big fight with Carr

Goodwin had wrapped up in thirty seconds, give or take. And the wrong one of us had been left lying on the floor.

4:48 P.M.

The drizzling was starting again, but I didn't get up from the boulder by the river I'd been on for almost an hour. Instead, I took another swallow of the Southern Comfort I'd swiped from home, and winced at the pain in my ribs as I raised and lowered the bottle.

The ass-kicking Carr delivered that morning had given me a bunch of bruises and an immediate five-day suspension from school. Maybe I should have been glad that the vice principal considered Carr the instigator and gave him *six* days, but it was hard to give a shit. I'd lost the fight without managing to get in even one decent punch. Worse, I'd lost Rosetta because she trusted Carr more than me.

Right then, a girl's voice rang out over the roar of the river. "A ha! I knew I'd find you here. Of course, your car over at the park gave it away."

I turned my head toward Kendall, who was making her way down the bank. She wore a long-sleeve T-shirt and baggy exercise pants. I hadn't even known she owned clothing that covered her legs.

She was watching me the whole time she jumped across the rocks. Then, after she'd settled on mine, she said, "Seth, your *eye*. Oh my God. That looks awful!"

At that moment, I had a dark red ring around my eye spanning from my eyebrow to my cheekbone—a nasty shiner in the making. "Yeah, well, it's only going to get worse."

She reached one of her gummy-bear-scented hands out as if she was going to touch it, but stopped inches short and set her hand on her lap instead. Then she kind of scooted her butt around like she was trying to get comfortable.

"This has been a horrible day," she said. "I've been feeling so guilty."

"It isn't your fault, so you can quit with the guilt."

She chewed one of her fingernails. "Rosetta was pretty upset over that stuff she thinks you said about her, huh?"

I nodded. "I called her a little while ago, after she should have been out of school. She wouldn't pick up."

"I am *so* sorry. I never meant for you to get mixed up in any of this. You know that, right?"

"Like I said, I'm not blaming you. Carr lied to Rosetta about me. And he lied to everyone about you. That shit is all on him."

"I know. But Carr wouldn't have said anything to her if it hadn't been for me. And if he hadn't said it, she wouldn't have gotten upset with you, and then you wouldn't have been trying to brawl with him. Which means that you wouldn't have been suspended from school, and you wouldn't be out here drowning your sorrows and looking like a freak right now!"

I couldn't help smiling at the way Kendall was so hysterical on account of me. "You don't think I look kind of badass?"

Kendall glanced away, not speaking or smiling back—which was fine with me, really—so we sat there with only the sound of the wind and the river filling the air.

I took a few hard swigs and held the bottle out for her.

"There's something I have to tell you," she said, waving it away. "It's the reason I'm here, actually. The thing is, I don't *want* to tell you at all, but I know you're going to find out soon enough. I think it will be better if you hear it from me. I'm scared of how you're going to react, though. I like being your nonenemy, and I don't want you to start hating me."

A knot was forming in my stomach as I studied Kendall's profile. She was gazing at the water, looking like she might start crying at any second.

And then I got the feeling that I knew exactly what she'd come here to say.

I was having a hard time breathing, but I managed to sound only *half*-crazed as I asked, "You're pregnant, aren't you?"

Kendall jerked her head up. "Seth, no. This is about Rosetta."

"Rosetta's pregnant?"

"No! Nobody's pregnant that I know of."

I was relieved, but then, with Kendall still making that face and not explaining, I started getting worked up all over again. "What then? What *about* Rosetta?"

"Oh, Jeez." Kendall shifted on the rock and tucked her

legs up pretzel-style. "I don't want to do this right now if you're going to be all belligerent."

"You'd *better* do it right now. You can't start a conversation like this and not follow through with it."

She sighed. "Remember how I told you that I was going to call things off with my so-called secret boyfriend who you now know was Carr?"

I nodded.

"Well, we had the talk the other day. And Carr didn't take it well. He started saying all this insulting shit to me, and then I snapped. He thinks Rosetta's an amazing, perfect girl, so I told him that she was probably screwing you at that exact moment. And I also let him know that she's been lying about her save-the-environment thing to cover up her car phobia."

I stared at her. "How the hell do you even know that?"

She started chewing on her nails again. "Well, because I was in the living room while you two were drying off on your porch. I heard everything you were saying."

I wanted to hold on to the hope that she was joking, but I knew she wasn't. "Jesus fucking Christ!" I yelled. "I can't believe you did that to her. And to *me*."

"I'm sorry! I was just tired of Carr acting like I'm not good enough for him but that Rosetta is. I swear, I had no idea he was going to tell her what I said. And it never even occurred to me that he'd drag you into it and twist everything around like he did."

I didn't care about Carr and didn't want to waste any more time talking about him, but there was no way I could let what Kendall did go ignored. I turned so my back was to her and my feet were dangling a few feet over the water. "Rosetta's had some shitty things happen to her, and you made it worse. I'm the one person she told that stuff to, and now she thinks I'm some untrustworthy jerk. On top of that, people keep telling her stuff about you and me, and it doesn't make me sound too cool when I have to say, 'No, I don't have anything going on with Kendall, but, yeah, now that you mention it, we *did* hook up at the end of summer.'"

"Oh, God," Kendall moaned from behind me. "Please tell me that you didn't actually say that to her."

"I had to. She wanted answers, so I gave her the whole truth. Believe me I didn't want to tell her."

Kendall was silent for a few seconds, but then in a small voice, she said, "The thing is, it didn't happen."

"What didn't happen?"

"You and me hooking up."

I whirled my head around. "What are you talking about?"

She was hugging her chest and watching the water again. "You were sloppy drunk that night and no one in your band wanted to deal with you. So I drove you home. And . . . that's all."

"What do you mean 'that's *all*'? We were in bed together half-naked the next morning!"

She nodded. "Yes, but only because after you puked in my car, I dragged you inside, where you puked all over me and then on yourself. I stripped us both down and threw everything in the wash. I stayed to take care of you, but nothing happened between us like that. You were passed out cold as soon as I got you to bed."

I couldn't believe this. I mean, she had enough details to make it sound like the truth, but it made no *sense*. "Then what was all that 'lover' bullshit about? And why the hell would you have wanted to fool me into thinking something happened in the first place?"

"At first, I was teasing you," she said, looking into my eyes. "I'd been up all night making sure you didn't die or anything, and then you were a total prick and wouldn't even let me explain. I was going to tell you everything after you apologized. Which never did happen. And then I was going to do it when we were in your car before the dance, but you changed the subject in a big hurry. You seemed relieved that I hadn't known you were a virgin, so I thought maybe it would be better for your confidence if I just let it go."

I was having an impossible time wrapping my head around this. I'd stressed about whether Kendall was knocked up, felt guilty over getting with Isaac's girl, and hurt Rosetta by confessing it to her. It was all for nothing.

Kendall and I *never even had sex*.

"Look, I don't blame you for being upset," Kendall said,

looking all pouty. "I've made a lot of mistakes, and I'm really, really sor—"

"Shut up. Shut the fuck *up*."

"Seth—"

"No," I said, shaking my head. "Don't talk to me. I can't trust a word that comes out of your mouth. I mean, do you even get how screwed up it is that you did this to me? *Do* you?"

Her response was to start crying. I wasn't having any of it.

For more than six weeks, she'd known the truth but hadn't bothered clueing me in. Because she was waiting for an apology that I hadn't even known I owed her. Because she thought keeping me in the dark would be better for my *confidence*? It sucked. Plain and simple. And no matter how I looked at it, everything that had gone wrong with Rosetta led back to Kendall in some way.

I finished the last of the Southern Comfort in one, two, three, four, five, six, seven, eight big gulps, threw the bottle as hard as I could, missed the tree I'd been aiming for, and watched it land in a mess of tall weeds. Not getting to hear the shatter of glass was more frustrating than I could have expected.

5:01 P.M.

Getting away from Kendall was never easy, but right now it was impossible. She'd followed me—off the boulder, up the bank, and down the path—while I stumbled my way to the parking lot and did my best to ignore her.

At the Mustang, I pulled my keys from my pocket and gave my head a hard shake. Big mistake, that shake thing. It made me dizzier.

"What do you think you're doing?" Kendall asked.

My plan was to get my jacket from the backseat. Then maybe I'd return to the river for a while. Or walk to Daniel's. Or home. Either way, I didn't need to explain myself. Not to *her*.

"I'm done with you," I said, without looking in her direction. "So why don't you get in your little Rich Bitch car and get the fuck out of my life."

"Let me just drive you home."

"No."

I reached to give the lock a try, but then Kendall was next to me, twisting my arm and ripping the keys out of my hand.

"Ow!" I yelled. "God!"

I tried to snag them back, but her fingers wouldn't budge. Before long, we were struggling and it was turning into a *thing* where she was slapping at me and I was grabbing at her. "Quit. Being. An idiot," she said, banging her elbow into my side.

A strobe-light effect was happening in my brain, and everything kept switching between fast and slow and dark and bright. I had to get Kendall *off* me.

I gave her a shove. She fell backward and landed on her ass. My keys hit the cement next to her.

It was what I'd wanted. Except, it really *wasn't*.

I stared down at her and she stared right back. Her cheeks were still streaked with tears and makeup. Her eyes were open wide. Her mouth too. That expression. She'd never looked at me like that before. *No one* had ever looked at me like that. It was a combination of shock and anger and fear. Like I was someone to be afraid of. My stomach started feeling . . . not so great. "Shit," I said, looking away. "I'm sorry. I didn't mean to do that."

"You didn't *mean* to?" she asked, jumping to her feet and full-on slamming me against my car. "I can't believe you! I cannot *believe* what a fucking asshole you are!" She paced in front of me while she kept on shouting. "Yeah, you had a fight with your girlfriend. You got beat up by Carr and were suspended from school. All that stuff *sucks*. But why doesn't it ever occur to you to deal with your problems instead of getting trashed? Why can't you let people *help* you instead of just pushing everyone away? Instead of pushing them to the *ground*, you dick!"

I flinched at that, but shot back, "Who's going to help? *You're* the one who screwed up the only good thing I had going."

Kendall swiped her hand across the fresh tears sliding down her cheeks. "You have more than *one good thing* in your life, Seth McCoy. But for some reason, you'd rather keep punishing yourself instead of seeing any of it. Well, guess what? I'm not going to let you drag me down with you. I refuse to stand here and watch you turn into Isaac."

With that, she picked up my keys from the ground, ran to her car, and tore off.

5:20 P.M.

My walk home wasn't long—only a couple of blocks—but with each step, I became less and less sure I could make it.

Spinning.

So much spinning.

The rocks, the grass, the blackberry bushes, the trailers, the mailboxes.

Faster and faster and faster and faster and faster.

The driveway. Finally. My shoes scraped across gravel. Slipped out from under me. I landed hard on my hands and knees. Stood up. Shuffled toward the front steps. Tripped over the garden hose and onto the lawn. Crawled to the rosebush where Isaac died. And puked.

11:27 P.M.

Six hours later, I was in bed doing that hazy in-between-awake-and-asleep thing where every time I'd open my eyes, I'd see that a whole hour had passed instead of the five minutes it had felt like.

It made no difference, though. Asleep. Awake. Everything was shit.

My body ached from the fight with Carr, and I was exhausted from puking so much. My head was a bass drum in a never-ending sound check: *Boom. Boom. Boom. Boom. Boom.*

Even worse, anger, disgust, and frustration were burning through me like acid. When I thought about how Kendall had fooled me with her "nonenemy" crap and then stabbed me in the back, I hated her. When I thought about our argument and me pushing her down, I hated myself.

My bedroom door creaked open and light spilled in from the hall. Lying on my side, I squinted at Mom as she came in and stood over me.

"How are you feeling?" she asked.

"Not great."

The words came out kind of croaky.

Mom shook her head and sat on the bed next to me. "Oh, *Seth.*"

I figured she was talking about my black eye. I pulled the covers over my face so she wouldn't have to look at it anymore. Bonus, I spared her my puke breath at the same time.

"We need to discuss this," she said.

I didn't want to discuss it. Not with her. Not with anyone. Not ever.

"I'm not good at this sort of thing," Mom said. "I had Jared almost nineteen years ago, but I still don't know what I'm doing. I'm a *terrible* mother."

I'd never heard her say anything like that and it kind of freaked me out. "Mom, stop it," I said from under the blanket.

"Well, seriously! I found out more yesterday from your guidance counselor than I ever do from you. She had a lot of good things to say too. Like that you haven't been skipping at all this year, you're passing math, and you're getting an A in Speech."

It was sort of embarrassing that Ms. Naylor had been talking me up—especially since Mom had come to school in the first place only to sign me out for my suspension. "It's Interpersonal Communications, not Speech," I said. "Anyway, the class is a joke. I'm sure everyone's getting an A in there."

She sighed. "Your brother tells me what's happening with him, even when it's about things I maybe wouldn't *want* to know. But you. You're always keeping things all bottled up. I shouldn't let you get away with it, should I?"

I didn't say anything, so after about thirty seconds, she slid the blanket off my head. "Baby, tell me. Why did you do this to yourself?"

She didn't sound pissed. Just tired.

I didn't answer her question because I didn't know the answer. I was thinking that maybe I'd done it because it would have hurt too much not to. But the booze hadn't made things better. I was still suspended, Carr had still come out ahead, and I still didn't have Rosetta. Basically, I was a loser all around. A loser who'd spent an hour throwing up in my front yard until Mom found me there and dragged my ass inside.

"Your guidance counselor thinks that what happened to Isaac has affected you more than you're willing to let on," Mom said. "Is that what this is about? Is it why you were fighting at school? And getting fall-down drunk?"

The way she was fidgeting and bouncing her legs, I could tell she was having a hard time asking these questions. Not as hard a time as I was having trying to answer, though.

I rolled onto my back and stared at the ceiling. Jared had helped me stick glow-in-the-dark stars up there when we were kids, and over the years, all but three had fallen off. "Things just suck sometimes, okay?" I said.

"Okay?" Mom prompted.

"Rosetta's pissed at me. And I was suspended. And Isaac. Definitely Isaac. And I just . . . I don't know how to make any of it *not* suck."

"Well, you're not doing yourself any favors with the alcohol binging. You need to find a better way to escape. What about using your music? You have that gig coming up with your new band in a couple of days to get ready for."

"That isn't going to *help*," I said, sitting up and meeting her gaze. "I don't even want to play that show. I'm stressed as hell about it."

"Baby, you *are* gonna play it," she insisted. "And you're going to be amazing too."

I shook my head. "Mom—"

"You just focus the next two days on getting yourself ready to perform. Put all your energy, every single thought and feeling you're having, into those songs. And then, when you're onstage, you can just let it all out."

Like Xander and Taku, she was talking like it was easy. I'd never once thought of a live performance as something I could use to distract myself from other things. But I didn't want to get into it with her, so I just said, "All right, I'll try."

Mom raked her fingers over her hair. "I know this has been a hard few months for you. There was never a dull moment with Isaac, and after he was gone, it got so quiet around here. You and Kendall turned into zombies."

Kendall. Just being reminded of her made me want to never leave my room again.

Mom went on. "It was hard for me to see you go through that. I kept wishing there was some way I could make it easier for you."

"Why should it have been easy?" I asked. "Isaac *died*, Mom. And a week later, no one even seemed to care. Jared wanted to get back to band rehearsals. Daniel wanted me to drive him around and party with him all the time. It was like everyone thought I should just hurry up and get over it."

She shook her head. "Nobody thought that, I promise you. You just didn't want to talk about it, so we were all trying to make a new kind of normal for ourselves. And for you, too. *Especially* for you. Isaac was your best friend. The only reason he was in our lives was because he was in yours."

"And Kendall's," I said, practically choking on her name.

"Okay. Kendall's, too. But not one of us would have put up with Isaac just for her."

Mom was partway smiling, but I knew she meant it. And she was right; sometimes Isaac *was* the type of person who had to be "put up with." He did tons of stupid shit.

God. Like me. Pushing Kendall in that parking lot.

"Oh, speaking of Kendall," Mom said. "She stopped by here looking for you after school. I thought you were at the car wash, so I sent her there."

I wanted to pretend like nothing had happened, like I hadn't even seen Kendall. But Mom was going to find out the truth no matter what; she needed to hear it from me.

"She found me at the river, actually."

"Oh, good," Mom said. "Is that how you got home without your car?"

"No." I couldn't bring myself to look at her, so I studied my comforter instead. "Actually, we sort of . . . got into it. Arguing and everything. I, um, pushed her on the ground and she drove off and took my keys with her. I ended up walking home after that."

Silence.

I waited. Only to hear . . .

More silence.

Finally I glanced up. Mom had tears in her eyes.

Shit.

On top of everything, now I was making my mom cry. "Mom, I'm *sorry*! I feel like a complete—"

"*What* is that girl's problem?" she interrupted. "I can't believe she'd leave you like that!"

I stared at her. I'd just told her I'd roughed up a girl, and she was blaming *her* for it?

"Tomorrow," Mom said, sniffing. "Tomorrow I'm going to have a little chat with Miss Kendall about this."

I shook my head. "I was being a jerk. She *should* have left me."

"But after Isaac, I would have thought she would make sure to look out for you! You weren't in any shape to get yourself home. You could have fallen in the river and drowned. Or been hit by a car."

One of those things could have happened to me, maybe. But it wasn't Kendall who had made me chug all that Southern Comfort. Or refuse a ride. Or shove her on the ground. Those were things I did. Choices *I* made.

"After Isaac," I said, "I think Kendall's done taking care of drunk assholes and getting pushed around and puked on."

Mom opened her mouth like she was maybe going to keep arguing, but this time I interrupted *her*. "If something had happened to me, it would have been my fault. Not Kendall's. Okay, Mom?"

Slowly, she nodded. Then she leaned in and pulled me into a tight hug.

I was pretty sure she understood.

And now, finally, I did too.

FRIDAY, **OCTOBER 22**

10:52 P.M.

There were less than twenty-four hours until the Good Times gig, and all I wanted was sleep. Actually, "wanted" is the wrong word. I *needed* it. Instead, I was channel-surfing on the couch, all wound up with nerves, nerves, nerves.

Xander had come up with a strategy to distract Brody from his stage fright, and I'd listened in and stolen it for myself. It mostly involved breathing slowly, imagining over and over again playing a successful show, and keeping busy on the day of until heading down for sound check. I wasn't so sure this corny New Age shit was going to work, though. Which meant I couldn't stop thinking about it. Maybe if Xander had come up with a plan for how Brody could keep himself distracted from worrying about the plan, *then* I'd be getting some sleep here.

The phone on the end table rang. I grabbed it in a big hurry, hoping, hoping, hoping it was Rosetta finally returning one of my calls. "Hello?"

There was a bunch of laughter coming from the other end. "Is this Seth McCoy?" asked some ditzy-sounding chick.

Damn it.

"Who's this?" I asked, suspicious.

A pause. More laughing. Loud voices.

"Look, Seth," she said over the noise. "Daniel's at Eric Kingman's and he wants you to get over here."

I groaned. Daniel had wasted no time hooking up a delivery for a party on the Hill. This time whatever he'd taken was small enough to fit in his jacket pocket, so he hadn't needed a ride from me. Which had been perfect as far I was concerned; I was in no mood for a party.

"So are you coming?" the girl asked.

"No. Tell Daniel I'm sleeping."

Without bothering to cover the receiver, she yelled. "He says he isn't coming! He's trying to sleep!"

A few seconds later, Daniel was on the line. "Listen, Dick. You need to get over here. I'm serious."

He sounded cagey, and my heart beat faster. "Why? What's wrong?"

"Nothing's wrong. Just get in the car and drive your ass to Eric's."

Now I was getting pissed. "Daniel, if you need me to pick you up, just say so. You don't have to try to freak me out."

"I don't need a ride. What I need is for you to hurry because there's someone here who wants to see you."

Daniel had to be talking about Rosetta. Who else on the Hill would want to see me?

I had more questions, but before I could ask, there was a *click* and silence. I set the phone down and went to my room to throw some jeans on, planning what I would do when I saw Rosetta.

I didn't entirely blame her for not returning my messages over the past two days; she needed time to cool off and think things over, I figured. But maybe seeing me in person would speed things along. Maybe she'd be willing to hear me out. I knew the truth about Kendall and Carr and the truth about Kendall and me. If I told Rosetta, she'd have to see that I deserved another chance.

11:12 P.M.

When I walked in the front door at Eric's, the party was in full swing with all the major ingredients in place: a bunch of kids, a bunch of noise, and a bunch of beer.

Usually, I wouldn't be too worried over crashing a Rich Bitch Hill party, but tonight was different. It was the first time I'd ever shown up by myself. It was also the first time I'd been suspended for fighting with one of their own. Finding Rosetta was my number one priority, but avoiding getting my ass kicked was high up there too.

It was anyone's guess which—if either—I'd be able to pull off.

I headed to the kitchen first out of habit, I guess. About ten kids drinking from red plastic cups were leaning against the counters. They stopped talking midconversation to stare at me. And then they didn't start talking again.

Yeah, *this* was going to go well.

Rosetta wasn't with them, so I rushed on. In the dining room, Brittany, Tara, and some other chicks were hanging out, and they all turned to watch me too, probably just checking out the damage from my fight with Carr. The stares were making me self-conscious, but I figured it couldn't hurt to ask for help. "I'm looking for Rosetta Vaughn," I said in a loud voice. "Anyone know where she is?"

They all shook their heads, so I kept moving. Brittany came after me, yelling over the music. "I don't think I've ever seen a black eye that's so . . . *black* before."

"Yeah," I said. "That's about the only way to describe it, huh?"

From where we were standing, I could see into the living room or whatever it is that rich people call the room that has fancy furniture and no TV. No sign of Rosetta in there, either, but it was packed with people—including Eric and a bunch of football players—so I didn't have the best view.

While I was trying to work up the guts to stroll over there, Brittany started talking again. "I just wanted you to know, the way you stuck up for Kendall the other day was really cool. You were, like, her hero."

My stomach twisted up and I stared at the floor. Of all the things Brittany could have said to me, that was probably the worst.

She went on. "And you were the only one calling Carr out on his crap, so you get lots of credit for that, too. He is a total sleaze as far as I'm concerned. I'm *glad* he lost his ASB position."

"What? Why did he lose his position?"

"*Because*," Brittany said, smirking, "starting a fight in front of the entire student body and having a suspension on your record is against the rules for our trusty school politicians. They're supposed to be model students, you know."

"Oh." I pretended to consider for a few seconds. "Does this mean I've blown my chances at becoming president next year?"

Laughing, she smacked my arm. "Right, Seth," she said, turning to go back to her friends. "I'm sure you were *completely* eligible before this happened."

On my own again, I took a deep breath. Just that short talk with Brittany had drained me, but I had to do this. I maneuvered my way to where Pete Zimmer was kind of lounging on the back of a couch, cracking up while his pals told some loud story and reenacted a football play or something. I leaned around him to see if Rosetta was one of the girls on the couch. She wasn't.

Pete was watching me. All I wanted at that moment was to get out of there, but I met his gaze. "Ouch," he said, gesturing at his face while nodding toward mine.

Then a hand clamped down on my shoulder.

I jumped.

"McCoy, where'd you learn to fight?" Garrison asked, staring down at me. "My grandma could have landed a more solid punch than you."

I waited—my whole body tense and unmoving—wondering if he was going to give a quick demonstration for everyone. But actually . . . he was smiling like he was only messing around, not like he was trying to start something with me.

"No kidding," I said, relaxing somewhat. "I bet your *great*-grandma could have done it better."

Everyone laughed. With me? *At* me? Honestly, I didn't care.

"It's the thought that counts, anyway," Garrison said. "I've wanted to take Carr out for years, but I've never had a good enough excuse."

My mind was blown that Carr wasn't as friendly with these guys as I'd always thought, and that Brittany ranked Kendall higher than Carr. I didn't know what to say, so I changed the subject to the one and only thing I cared about right then. "Have any of you noticed Rosetta around tonight?"

Pete shook his head. "I've seen her at exactly two parties in my life, and this isn't one of them."

There was still a chance she was hiding out, but it was

a long shot. If I'd stopped to think about it before, I'd have realized it had *always* been a long shot. Rosetta hated parties full of pod people.

"You're in Brody's band, right?" Pete said to me. "Aren't you guys playing in the Valley tomorrow night?"

Like I wanted to talk about that right now. "Yeah. But, hey. What about Daniel? Have you happened to see him?"

"Behind you," said Eric.

I turned.

"Glad you could make it, Dick," Daniel said, grinning. "Now, if I'm not mistaken, you've got some unfinished business to attend to. How about if we go and get started on that?"

11:20 P.M.

"I should have called sooner," Daniel muttered. "It's probably too late now."

"*What's* too late?" I asked.

For the past five minutes, I'd been following Daniel through the main level at Eric's house while he tried to find whomever it was that he'd called me here to see, but he still wasn't telling me anything. Now we were in the second floor hallway—the last area we had left to scope out—where every single door was closed. I was getting so irritated I wanted to throw him against one of them.

Daniel didn't answer my question. He just opened the first door, stuck his head in for a few seconds, and then ducked out, shutting it again. "Nope. Not in there."

"How could you tell with the lights off?"

"Oh, I could tell. Trust me."

I shook my head. This was kind of sick. "How would you like it if someone busted in on *you* at a party?"

"Are you kidding? Happens to me all the time. I get over it." He moved to the next door and twisted the knob. This time, before he had a chance to look, some guy inside was yelling, "Hey! This room's in use!"

"Sorry, dude." Daniel slammed the door, laughing.

I wasn't finding it funny at all. By now I was sure we weren't looking for Rosetta, and the whole thing—me coming to this party—was a huge letdown. I'd gotten my hopes up that Rosetta and I could fix things tonight, but doubt was taking over and I was realizing she might really be done with me.

"You know what?" I said. "This is ridiculous. If you don't tell me what the point of this is, I'm out of here."

"Oh, *fine*," Daniel said. "Carr Goodwin was going around earlier, blaming you for his suspension and everything else, and it was pissing me off. I was going to take him down, but from what I've heard about your fight with him, you need a shot at redeeming yourself. So, *you're* going to do it. As soon as we find him."

God. Could Daniel *be* a bigger dumbass?

"You had me come here so Carr can kick my ass again?" I asked.

"No. That's not how it's going to happen. I've got your

back, okay? We're not going to let him get away with it."

"What are you saying?" I asked, crossing my arms over my chest. "You and me fighting him two against one is going to change things?"

"Probably not. But it'll make *me* feel better," Daniel said, grinning. "And you too, right?"

The thought of Carr ending up with bruised ribs and a black eye like I had did improve my mood, no doubt about it, but I couldn't go along with this plan. It just wasn't worth it.

But before I could say so, Daniel was pushing the third door open. "Jackpot!" he said, reaching in to flip the light switch. "Well, sort of."

11:22 P.M.

From the doorway of Eric's parents' room, I spotted Carr right away. He was passed out on the floor next to the huge bed.

Daniel and I stared down at him. Looked at each other. And burst out laughing.

It wasn't funny. Not really. But at the same time, it kind of *was*. After the effort Daniel had put into making this happen, Carr couldn't fight. Or move. Or do anything except lie there on his back, snoring with his mouth hanging open.

Lucky for me, I guess.

"That's one way to get out of a beating," Daniel said, shaking his head. "What a bastard. You should take a leak on him or something."

"No way."

He reached for his belt buckle. "I'll do it, then."

"Daniel, no."

I shoved Daniel into the hall, where we started cracking up again even harder than before. It felt good—all the laughing—except for the fact that it also hurt.

"No one's going to take a leak on anyone," I said, when I was able to speak again about a minute later. "Well, no one except Carr. All over himself."

Daniel leaned against the wall to finish catching his breath. "You know. For being named Dick, you don't do nearly enough dicklike things."

"Maybe because my name's Seth?" I suggested.

"Maybe." He started for the stairs. "This party blows. I'm getting out of here. You?"

"Definitely."

But when I reached the first step, I changed my mind. I wasn't ready to leave quite yet.

I headed back to the bedroom and glanced at Carr one more time.

Then, using my foot, I rolled him onto his side.

All right. Now I was ready.

11:49 P.M.

In my imagination, stopping by Rosetta's house after Daniel and I split up paid off hugely. Rosetta was staring out a second floor window when I drove up. She ran out to see me. We sat in her front yard and used all our IC skills. It was as cold as hell, but it was okay because after we'd finished with the apologizing and forgiving, we held each other close and kissed all over the place and it was *mind-blowing*.

In real life, though, none of it was going down like that. I was driving past super-slowly for the fourth time, and Rosetta still wasn't looking out any window. She wasn't coming outside. Her house was all curtained up and dark, and, most likely, she was in there fast asleep.

This drive-by routine wasn't going to lead to anything good, so I left Rosetta's block and took a few turns to get to the main road leading down the Hill. That's when an all-too-familiar blue MINI Cooper caught my eye. Kendall's car. Parked in front of Kendall's house.

I thought about that thing Brittany had said about me being Kendall's hero. And about the fact that I *wasn't*.

I needed to get home. I needed sleep. Much more than that, though, I needed to talk to Kendall. When she saw me at her door, she'd probably scream some more, maybe even throw things, but it needed to happen. It was the only way I'd be able to look at myself straight again.

I flipped a U-ey, parked in her driveway, and headed up the walkway. There were lights on in the house, which meant someone was awake.

About half a minute after I knocked, Kendall opened the

door. She didn't say anything at first, just stood there in her tank top and pink pajama pants, staring at me. "Right," she said. "You want your keys."

It wasn't that big a deal; I was using a spare set. "Actually, no—"

But she closed the door before I could finish.

Letting out a loud breath, I leaned against the handrail, waiting. Was she going to come back with them or was she really not going to talk to me tonight?

A minute later, there was a noise above me: Kendall had opened a window. After a second, something dropped from it and hit the ground next to me with a clang. My keys.

At least she hadn't thrown them *at* me.

I snagged the keys and knocked on the door again. This time when Kendall opened up, she immediately crossed her arms over her chest.

"So, thanks," I said. "That isn't really why I'm here, though. I was kind of hoping to talk to you about what happened the other day. You know, in the parking lot?"

"I'd rather we didn't."

"Look, Kendall, I'm really sor—"

"Don't," she said, putting up her hand. "We're not doing this. I screwed you over. You got back at me. We're even and that's the end of it."

"We're *not* even, okay? And one thing I've been figuring out is that there are times when talking through crap is the only way to resolve it. So . . . I think we should."

Kendall pressed her lips together and narrowed her eyes like she'd never heard anything as annoying as me trying to use IC stuff. It was probably true, but I kept talking anyway. "You don't have to forgive me. I'm not even sure if I want to forgive you. But I want you to know that *I* know I fucked up big-time. I shouldn't have pushed you down like that. I was out of line and I'm sorry. That isn't me and I don't want it to be."

She waited a few seconds before softly saying, "Understood." Then she flipped her black-and-blue hair over her shoulder and said in her regular voice, "I'm freezing. You should come in."

I stepped inside and followed her as she walked in a stiff, hobbling way back to the home-theater room. At first, I wondered if she'd busted up her feet or something, but then I noticed sparkly gold separators wedged between her pink painted toes.

We each took a seat on the largest of the poufy dark leather couches facing the huge TV. I'd been here a few times to watch movies and hang out. That had always been with Isaac, too, though.

Kendall aimed the remote to turn down the *Gilmore Girls* rerun on the screen. Then she grabbed a bottle of clear nail polish from her plastic toolbox-looking makeup holder and set one of her feet on the coffee table. "Did you really drive all the way up here in the middle of the night just to talk to me?" she asked.

"Well, that's why I drove 'here' to your house. But I'm 'here' on the Hill because Daniel tricked me into it. He had a plan to kick Carr's ass, but Carr was passed out by the time I got there."

"Figures," she said, rolling her eyes.

I didn't know if she meant me, Daniel, or Carr. Probably all three.

She twisted open her nail polish, leaned way forward, and started in on another paint layer on her toes. The fumes started stinking up the place, covering up the vanillay smell of the room. I wasn't too stoked about sitting around and watching Kendall give herself a pedicure, but I didn't want to leave yet; things didn't feel finished.

"I looked for Rosetta at Eric's party tonight," I said. "She wasn't there. What was she like at school?"

"I don't know. Why? Haven't you two made up yet?"

"She hasn't called me back."

Still not looking at me, Kendall brought up her other foot to get started on it. "She thinks you had sex with me, so she won't even talk to you? Talk about insecure."

Now it was my turn to roll my eyes. "She isn't talking to me because she thinks I lied to her. Big difference."

I kind of expected that she might apologize again—it *was* her fault, after all—but she just said, "What are you going to do about it?"

"I don't know. I'm definitely not going to drive slowly past her house all night."

"Good call. Girls don't like being stalked. Except, I guess Rosetta isn't what anyone would call normal, so maybe *she* does."

A flash of irritation shot through me. If I let this conversation go any further, I'd probably get pissed off all over again. "So why weren't *you* at Eric's?" I asked.

Replacing the brush, she set her bottle on the table and put both her feet back on the floor. "Because I'm too busy moping around here and feeling humiliated, obviously."

"Well, you don't have to be. Seems to me that everybody hates Carr and is taking your side in what happened."

"That makes it worse," she said, sighing. "Like, the whole world already knew the truth and I just was being stupid. It's Isaac all over again, except this time I *really* should have known better."

I sat up a little straighter. "Well, *I* didn't know. About Isaac, I mean. After all the stuff you've been telling me, I've only just figured out that you were right."

"I was right about what, exactly?" she asked, tilting her head.

"That Isaac was reckless. And an ass a lot of the time. He pulled a lot of shit that I blamed you for."

She shrugged. "I'm sure he left out all the parts that were his fault."

"Yeah. And if he was always doing that, how good of friends could we actually have been, you know?"

All this time, I'd assumed she'd be glad if I started seeing things her way, but instead she frowned and threw a

MINDI SCOTT

300

small pillow at me. As I caught it, she snapped, "You were *best* friends, Seth. He was on your side and you were on his. That's how it should have been."

"It doesn't make the stuff he did okay."

"Of course it doesn't! But don't start thinking you were stupid or wrong to care about him. You weren't. *We* weren't. No person is all good or all bad, Isaac included. He was really sweet most often and a really, *really* big asshole the rest of the time."

I held the pillow against my chest and slouched deep into the cushions, not sure why I'd missed seeing that for so long.

Kendall went on. "Isn't it weird that I ever went out with Isaac? Back when you first started hanging out, I couldn't stand him. But I still clearly remember the first time I ever noticed he was cute. It was in seventh grade when he beat up that high school kid at the arcade who tried to steal your money. Do you remember?"

I nodded. Isaac had gotten himself—and all the rest of us—banned from the place for six months after that. It wasn't one of *my* best Isaac memories ever.

"And then," Kendall said, "I went to your first gig after you and Isaac joined Jared's band freshman year. Oh my God, the way Isaac played guitar! So hot. Afterward, some guy tried to start a fight with you and Mikey in the parking lot, and Isaac just walked up and decked him. Right at that very second, I was completely in love."

Another not-the-best Isaac memory. "It really turned you on when he hit people, huh?"

At that she burst out laughing. "I think what I liked was that he was fearless. And when he wasn't screwing everything up, he was loyal. He would have punched anyone in the face for you, Seth. No questions asked."

Kendall was right about all of it. Isaac: fearless, loyal, impulsive, reckless. Not all good things, not all bad. Just . . . Isaac.

"He'd have done that for you, too," I said. "Taken down anyone who messed with you."

"You think so?"

"I know so."

"Hmm," she said. "I guess that makes us the only two members of the People Isaac Would Have Punched Everyone Else in the Face For club?"

I wrinkled my nose, and Kendall and I exchanged small smiles.

"Doesn't have much of a ring to it, does it?" she asked.

"Not so much," I said.

SATURDAY, **OCTOBER 23**

2:07 P.M.

Whenever it wasn't raining, Saturdays were crazy at the car wash. Today was no exception; vehicles had been lined up all the way to the street for five hours straight. Say what you will about Kenburn, but we do like us some clean cars.

Lyle came up to me while I was handling one of the pre-wash hoses. "It's your turn for a break," he said, holding out a soda.

I shook my head. After being up most of the night, I was trying to work through my exhaustion, afraid that stopping would mean not being able to start again. Lyle wasn't having it, though. "Seth, drink the Coke. And I don't want to see you back here for at least fifteen minutes."

"Fine."

I handed my job off to him and I went around back. Leaning against the building, I guzzled my second Coke of the day and waited for another temporary lifting of the cloudiness in my head. I had exactly one goal: stay awake long enough to get through my shift and the gig. After that I was going to crash.

As I was tossing the empty bottle in the bin, a red Miata came rolling around the corner. And, to my surprise, Mrs. Dalloway was behind the wheel. I'd never stopped to think about what she drove, but if I had, I probably would have pictured some regular old sedan or minivan. This was kind of impressive. I mean, a Miata isn't the end-all of cool or anything, but it's more styling than I would have expected of her.

After she'd pulled up next to one of the vacuums and got out to punch the payment code into the machine, I yelled, "Hey, Mrs. D.!"

She glanced around all confused, and then, spotting me, smiled in her crinkly nosed way. "Hi there, Dick! So good to see you." I was sure she was going to make a comment about the black eye, but instead she said, "I've been told that you won't be back in class until next Thursday?"

I nodded. "Yeah, Thursday."

"We're all going to miss you," she said. "In a class as small as yours, it makes a huge difference when one person is gone."

I knew she wasn't speaking for everyone with the

missing-me stuff, but I couldn't help wondering whether Rosetta missed me. Because, God, I missed *her*. The way she bit her lip when she was nervous, the flowery scent of her hair, her pretty laugh, the off-the-wall stuff she said. I missed holding her. And kissing her. And just being with her.

Right then I mentally changed my plan for the rest of my day: get through my shift, play the gig, find Rosetta, and get her to listen to my side of things.

Mrs. D. yanked on the vacuum hose to get ready to go to town on her interior. It wasn't hard to use, but she was making it *look* hard. I still had a few minutes before I needed to head back to work, so I went over. "Here, let me give you a hand with that."

She hesitated. "No, it's fine."

"No, really. I work here. It's part of my job to keep customers from busting up the equipment."

Laughing way louder than my comment deserved, she handed it over. While I started the vacuum, she spoke up so I could hear her over the engine. "So tonight's the big night for your band, right?"

"How'd you know about that?"

"Alex was talking about it in class. Yesterday he asked us all to attend, saying that if you have a big crowd, the place will be more likely to have you back. And he was also collecting ideas from us to help with your lead singer's stage fright."

I shook my head, but I couldn't help smiling. Typical Xander.

"Did he get any good ideas?" I asked.

"Honestly, I'm not sure. Managing stage fright is so individual, and each person has to try different strategies until they find something that works for them. It took a long time, but I'm in a good place with mine."

I glanced up. "You have stage fright?"

"Yes. Well, I'm not a performer, but I do have a terrible fear of public speaking. I'm fine with one-on-one, but put me in front of a group and I'm an absolute mess."

"But you're a teacher! That's what you do all day."

She laughed. "I know. It sounds silly, doesn't it?"

"Kind of, yeah. What tip did you offer up?"

"Proper breathing is key. You want to make sure you're taking breaths from deep in your abdomen. If you do it wrong and breathe from your chest instead, you can hyperventilate and make it much worse for yourself." She put one hand on her chest and the other on her belly. "See? You can check to see if you're doing it correctly by which of your hands rises and falls as you breathe. You want to make sure it's the lower one."

"Okay," I said, imagining how stupid I'd look onstage with my hands pressed on my body like that. "Anything else?"

"Well, the other thing I find consistently helpful is scanning the room for someone with a friendly face and focusing on them until I'm calm. I'm sure it worries the heck out of *them*, but after a few seconds, I'm usually ready to get started. And that's it!"

Breathing right and focusing on a friendly face? That's *all* it took for her?

I popped the trunk and ran the vacuum through the whole area in about twenty seconds flat. Easy enough.

"Looks like you're all set here," I said, hanging up the hose. "Your car's clean inside and out."

"I appreciate the help, Dick."

"No problem. But, you know, outside of your class most people call me Seth."

She smiled. "Actually, I *did* know that, Seth McCoy."

Of course she did.

8:45 P.M.

Daniel took a seat next to me on the hood of the Mustang and pulled out his special flask. "How are you guys holding up?" he asked, opening the built-in side holder for smokes.

"I feel good," Brody said from my other side.

"I feel like shit," I said.

Laughing, Daniel lit up. The bulb above Good Times's back door was burned out and the nearest streetlight was way out front, so his orange-tipped joint was the brightest source of light around. He took a hit and then held it out for me.

I shook my head. Honestly, I kind of did want to get stoned with him. But the last thing I needed was weed-induced paranoia added to my queasiness and jitters.

Scratching at the 8 Ball had finished sound check around eight—which was before most people had started showing up—and Brody and I had been hiding near the Dumpsters ever since. Taku and Xander kept coming out every few minutes to make sure Brody hadn't run away, but, oddly, Brody was the calmest of us all. At least all this stage fright research was helping *someone* out.

After a few more tokes, Daniel put out the joint and snapped the "secret" compartment shut again. "By the way," he said to me, "Eckman's looking for you, so I'd better go let her know you're out here."

"Right," I said. "Or you could *not* do that."

Not that it mattered much to me one way or the other, but I kind of wanted to stress out in peace.

"I'll think about it," Daniel said. "It's hard to resist that girl's incredible charm, though. And by 'charm,' I mean 'rack,' of course."

Brody snorted.

Daniel pushed himself off the car. "Dick, you look like you're either dead or on your way there," he said, pressing his flask into my hand. "You've stressed out like this before every show you've ever played, and you know what? You always get it together and kick ass. I'll see you in there."

He disappeared through the back door.

"Is that true?" Brody asked. "You're always tense like this before gigs?"

I nodded. "And Daniel knows that *this*"—I held up the flask—"is how I used to cope with my stage fright."

"So the truth comes out," Brody said, smiling. "And here I'd thought you were being so cool about my lame freak-out because you were practicing that fake empathy stuff from your class."

"No way. My empathy was real."

Brody nodded toward the flask. "Let me check that out."

As I was handing it over, the back door flew open again. Even in the dark, it was easy to recognize the chick heading toward Brody and me.

"Looks like Daniel really *can't* resist Kendall's 'charm.'" Brody said, standing. "Be right back. I'm going to grab something out of my car."

As he was walking away, Kendall came up to me. "You'll never guess who called me a bitch today," she said, placing her hands on my knees.

I shouldn't have been surprised by her huge smile or by the fact that she was acting, well, the annoying way she'd been acting toward me for years. And yet here I was, surprised.

"I have no clue," I said, sliding her hands off and scooting farther back on the car. "Who?"

"Rosetta Vaughn."

Oh, the nausea. Having Kendall spring this on me on top of my headache, nerves, and queasiness was too much.

"What did you do to her?"

Kendall settled beside me on the car. "Nothing *bad*. I just told her everything about Carr and me. About the true reason I asked you to homecoming. About what I said to Carr about her. And what didn't happen with you and me that I'd let you believe *did* happen. She knows all of it now."

I waited for her to go on, but she sat there, obviously enjoying keeping me in suspense.

"So, what did she *say*?" I prompted.

"Oh, right." Kendall waved her hand like it was no big deal. "Well, she was somewhat shocked to find out about Carr. She said I was a bitch for not telling you the truth about your virginity sooner. And then I said *she* was a bitch for not taking your calls."

"Great."

"Oh, don't you worry," Kendall said, patting my leg. "It's all good now. We had it out and we're fine. But the best part—the part that matters to you—is that she feels horrible, she misses you like crazy, and she hopes you'll give her another chance."

"She said all that?"

"Well, no. But I could tell she was thinking it. You should go see her tonight. After you're done here, I mean."

I let out my breath, and relief flowed through me, starting at my stomach and sort of branching out in all directions from there. It honestly couldn't have worked out much better for me. Unless . . .

"What if you're wrong?" I asked, tensing again.

Kendall looked into my eyes. "I'm *not* wrong."

Another big exhale. Kendall had done some screwed-up shit lately. We both had. But she'd come through for me on this, and now I had another reason to look forward to the gig being over. I was going to find Rosetta, who—if Kendall had it right—missed me like crazy.

Taku came busting out the back door. "Where's Brody?" he called to me, looking around all panicked.

"He's at his car. He'll be back in a second."

Taku puffed on his inhaler. It was the first time I'd seen him use it without Brody reminding him. "We're on in five or fewer," he said, running past me.

"All right," I said, somehow managing to sound cool and casual when I was feeling anything but.

I stood and Kendall did the same.

"I just noticed, you seem sober," she said, as we walked toward the back door. "Is it true?"

"It's true." I held up one of my shaking hands so she could witness my jitters for herself.

"This is so *totally* the opposite of how you were for your last show."

"Don't I know it," I said, sighing.

She reached for the door to go in, but I touched her arm. "Hey, Kendall. Thanks. You know, for everything."

She smiled. "You're welcome. You know, for everything."

Then she disappeared inside, and someone poked my back. I turned to face Brody and Taku.

"I read about this," Brody said, holding out a chunk of bubble gum for me. "Concentrate on chewing when we get onstage. Slow and methodical. It's supposed to help with the nerves."

"Seriously?" I asked. "Gum is the answer?"

Brody shrugged. "It's no worse than Xander's ideas, right?"

On cue, Xander came outside. "Are you guys ready? Because we're on!"

I pulled out the Magic 8 Ball. "Don't you want to ask if we're going to play a decent set?"

"Nah," he said, smiling. "I think we all know the outlook is good."

Taku went in after him and held the door open for Brody and me, but I needed another second or two . . . or million.

My heart was skipping beats as I shoved the 8 ball back in my pocket. Then I peeled the paper wrapper off the red gum rectangle, popped it into my mouth, and started chewing.

Brody pulled Daniel's flask out of his back pocket. "Oh, hey. You want this?"

"What for?" I pointed at my mouth. "I already have magical, nerve-calming watermelon Bubble Yum."

He set the flask on the ground against the wall. "Okay,

then. I think it's time for us to go play the successful gig I've been visualizing nonstop for the past few days."

I followed him inside.

9:01 P.M.

Dive-bar-quality stage lights were shining in my eyes, electronic equipment sounds were humming in my ears, and the weight of my bass was pulling so hard that I was going to be dragged through the stage floor any second now.

I hadn't looked at the rest of the band.

I hadn't looked at the crowd.

They were out there, though. All of them. Staring at me. I knew it. I could feel it.

They were watching the dude with the scary black eye. The dude who could hardly keep his instrument from slipping out of his trembling hands. The dude who was *choking* even though the set hadn't even started.

I chomped on watermelon gum like my life depended on it.

I took the deepest abdomen breaths I could manage.

I tried to run through every piece of stage fright advice I'd ever heard.

Except . . . my mind was 100 percent blank.

I had nothing.

Nothing.

I needed something.

Something, something, something!

Shit, shit, fuck, fuck. Christ, damn, hell.

And then it came to me. A friendly face. I needed to find one. Fast.

I glanced up.

Front and center: Vicki, Pete, Eric, Garrison.

Not too bad.

Farther back: Brittany, Tara, Lorraine, a few other chicks from IC class.

Getting better.

Way back: Mom and Kendall.

Good.

Next to them: Daniel trying to look down Kendall's top.

Pathetic.

Then I noticed *her*.

Near the middle and off to the side, staring up with an expression of friendliness, excitement, and, above all, hope.

Rosetta.

She was here. To see me.

Amazing.

She smiled. Shy.

Then she pointed at her T-shirt. Written across the front in thick marker were the words SETH ROCKS.

I couldn't help it; I laughed.

She laughed too.

And somehow, that's the moment I knew I would live

through this. I was going to perform these songs. I was going to kick ass. For her.

And for me.

My heartbeat slowed. Not much, but enough. And now I could breathe again too.

I held Rosetta's gaze. Behind me, Xander hit his sticks together to count off the first song. "One! Two! Three! Four!"

And then . . . I started to play.

ABOUT THE AUTHOR

MINDI SCOTT lives near Seattle, Washington, with her drummer husband in a house with a non-soundproof basement. *Freefall* is her first novel. Visit her online at mindiscott.com.

NEED
A DISTRACTION?
READ ON THE EDGE WITH SIMON PULSE.

YOU HAVE BEEN CHOSEN.
YOUR INITIATION STARTS NOW.

THE RECRUIT

AND LOOK FOR YOUR NEXT MISSION:

THE DEALER

FROM SIMON PULSE I PUBLISHED BY SIMON & SCHUSTER

a novel by Jason Myers

LIVE ON THE EDGE.

exit here.

THE MISSION

JASON MYERS

a novel by the author of EXIT HERE

JASON MYERS

FROM SIMON PULSE
PUBLISHED BY SIMON & SCHUSTER